MC'MERCS

MC'MERCS

CRYPTID ASSASSIN™ BOOK FIVE

MICHAEL ANDERLE

LMBPN

DISRUPTIVE IMAGINATION

LMBPN Publishing
PMB 196, 2540 South Maryland Pkwy
Las Vegas, NV 89109

First US edition, April, 2020
eBook ISBN: 978-1-64202-856-0
Print ISBN: 978-1-64202-857-7

THE MC'MERCS TEAM

Thanks to our Beta Readers

Jeff Eaton, John Ashmore, and Kelly O'Donnell

Thanks to the JIT Readers

Jeff Eaton
Diane L. Smith
Peter Manis
Jeff Goode
Deb Mader
John Ashmore

If we've missed anyone, please let us know!

Editor
Skyhunter Editing Team

CHAPTER ONE

There were few things worse than staring at a letter that would be sent to the family and loved ones of the dearly departed.

It was like looking into the eyes of the person who had passed away and they asked her how she would deliver the news. Would she be cold and professional or warm and compassionate? Phrased differently, would she be someone who helped or hindered the healing process?

The experience was odd. Niki was only required to check the letter the agency had already written to make sure all the details contained therein were accurate and revealed no classified data. Once that was done, all she had to do was sign her name and send it off to be delivered.

It wasn't something she would ever enjoy or get used to, but it was a part of the life that she had chosen for herself. Of course, it was also one of the reasons why she had issues with it.

One of their cryptid hunts hadn't gone the way she'd hoped it would. While that was fairly standard when it came to these missions, as long as the monster was dead and wouldn't come back, her superiors called it a win.

In the meantime, she was left with the unenviable task of looking at the harsh and even painful reality that two of the four hunters she had sent in hadn't returned alive.

And the worst part was, it didn't need to happen. She sighed and signed the paperwork as well as the letters to be sent to the next of kin. With slow, deliberate movements, she slipped each of them into the relevant manila envelopes, sealed them, and placed them in her outbox. At least, she reasoned, she didn't have to deliver them in person.

The phone on her desk rang almost immediately and caught the attention of the agent seated at the desk across from her.

"Agent Banks?" a man's voice said on the other side of the line. "This is Andrews from ground control on the last hunt. I want to make sure you've received the last mission reports we sent before we close up shop here."

"Yeah, I got them."

Niki realized that her tone was a little sharper than was necessary when he was quiet for a few seconds. Ordinarily, she kept a tight rein on her emotions and while she could be scathing, it was almost always directed at the responsible party. It wasn't like her to snap at others like this, and it frustrated her even more that she hadn't seen it coming.

"You know we did all we could, right?" he said after a long moment.

She sighed and rubbed her temples with her free hand. "Yes, I know, and I don't blame you guys."

He acknowledged that with a grunt that might have

been acceptance of her unspoken apology. For some weird reason, his lack of verbal response pushed her to provide an explanation—like she wanted someone to understand the nagging frustration within that she couldn't fully understand yet.

"It's only that it was a little unnecessary and it pisses me right the fuck off," she said quickly before she could think it through. "My suggestion was to call in the Cryptid Assassin—you know, the guy who gets the job done on his own most of the time. But since the assholes in the offices upstairs can't bear to see their budgets mucked around with, they call in the dumbasses fresh off the boat from the Zoo, put them in aging, decrepit suits of armor, and send them into unknown territory. Seriously, can you imagine that kind of disrespect? They spent years putting their lives on the line in that fucking jungle and are killed on their first mission on what should be safer home territory."

"Well, yeah—"

"And that's not the worst part," she continued. The floodgates were open, apparently, and for better or worse—probably worse because she simply knew she'd regret it—the resentment demanded a voice. "No, the worst part is that on top of that shit salad, we'll have to pay fatality benefits to their next of kin that will end up costing us twice as much!"

"That's the worst part?"

"Well, no, but it's mixed in there with all the other straws that broke the camel's back. I'm not as upset at the payouts as I am at the truth that we shouldn't be in a position where we have to pay them at all. People died unnecessarily and the fatality benefits are a reminder of that."

She sighed and tapped her pen on the desktop in an agitated rhythm. "Anyway, yes, I got your report, thank you. Everything's tied up this side. And Andrews—thanks for doing what you could. And…uh, for listening to me vent. Hopefully, this will be the one and only time." He chuckled and she grimaced when she imagined the stories that would circulate around this conversation. "I'll be in contact when we have another operation."

She slammed the receiver down—another rare indulgence. Dammit, she needed to get a handle on whatever this was. Still, if there was one good thing about the older models they still had in their offices, it was how satisfying it felt to thunk one down and vent a little frustration. They were sturdy enough to take the punishment.

The agent seated across from her stared in silence, a confused expression on his face. His reaction was an uncomfortable reminder that she was acting out of character and needed to pull herself together.

"What?" she snapped and shook her head. "You know I'm right."

He coughed.

"What are you—sick?" she asked. "Get yourself—"

Niki stopped when she realized he had used the cough to cover the fact that he pointed at something behind her.

Someone, rather, she decided since inanimate furniture was unlikely to creep up on her.

She turned her swivel chair and her gaze settled on a tall, slightly rotund man with a receding hairline who stood in silence and simply regarded her with a raised eyebrow.

"Oh shi— Sir!" she said and winced inwardly at her

crappy luck. He would choose the one time she gave in and spewed her honest opinion to make an appearance. "I…uh, didn't see you there."

"Here's the part where you apologize for what you said." His tone carried a rumble of disapproval.

For a moment, she considered it, torn between common sense and the voice of obstinacy within. Finally, she shook her head. "I don't think I will. I meant every word of it. You guys fucked up."

He smirked in response. "Well, in that case, I need to speak to you in my office at your earliest convenience."

Niki knew she would regret asking but couldn't help herself. "What about, sir?"

"About interesting intel that came in from Italy. Your earliest convenience, Banks."

Which meant right fucking now. She tried to show no emotion as her superior walked toward his office.

"Shit," she muttered as she tidied her desk calmly.

"It was nice knowing you." Her colleague chuckled.

"Yeah, I'm a real fucking delight." She muttered under her breath as she pushed from her seat. "Wait until I'm buried before you steal shit from my desk, Evans."

"Will do."

Elisa's phone rang yet again. Why did it always ring when she was about to place her lunch order?

She pulled the device out of her purse and grimaced at the office number on the display. With a sigh, she pressed the answer button.

"Yes?"

"Very cordial," a young woman said.

"I'm on my lunch break, Karen. What the hell is it this time?"

"He wants to see you but didn't say why, only that it was urgent. He wants you in the office as soon as possible or he'll find someone else to take the job."

She snorted. "Yeah, right. Like he would trust anyone else with something this important in our little operation."

"Don't be like that, El. You know we're trying to get ourselves taken seriously in this business, and you also know that if you don't respond, he'll groom someone else to take your place. I suggest you get back here as quickly as possible."

"Fine." She sighed. "I'm a little way away, though, so I think it'll be about half an hour before I get back."

"I'll let him know."

Elisa hung up and slid her phone into her purse as one of the workers at the restaurant moved to the counter with her order.

"Lunch order for Elisa?" the waitress called, almost like she didn't know who had ordered the food.

"Can I get it to go, please?"

"Sure."

Traffic was hellish during the lunch hour, which gave her time to eat on the way to the office. It wasn't a pleasant meal since it had to be interrupted every few minutes to drive her car through the Chicago traffic to the building where she worked.

Twenty minutes later, she pulled into the parking lot reserved for employees of the Crypto-Inquirer. The name had always felt a little too on the nose for her taste, especially if they wanted to be considered as more than merely a tabloid by the journalism community.

Maybe Cas would rethink it and rebrand their little venture before too long. She tossed the used takeout plate into the nearest garbage can and stepped into the elevator.

Over the years, she'd honed a particular ability almost to an art form and it had come in handy in the fast-paced life she had elected to live. People always expected her to look her best no matter when or where she was, and there were small tricks that enabled that—like a portable makeup kit in her purse as well as a comb and scrunchies for her hair.

It was quick work to comb her dark hair back, bind it, and touch her makeup up during the time it took the elevator to reach her floor. It wasn't the kind of thing most people tended to think of, but they always forgot how much a long drive could ruin someone's look.

The doors opened as she straightened her skirt, and she stepped into the hallway. The sound of telephones ringing and people talking at an elevated tone struck her like a wall. They were still a small operation, but after it had been bought out, the Inquirer had surged under the new management style. There had been a flurry of new hires, which brought their numbers up to almost forty.

They would need to get bigger offices before too long.

"El, you took your time," the short, red-haired secretary called as she emerged from behind her desk which was piled high with paperwork. "Cas is climbing the fucking walls waiting for you."

"Well, that's what he gets for calling me during my

lunch break," Elisa replied. She'd expected the line and had practiced her rejoinder on the drive. "Do you know anything about what he wants from me?"

"You'll have to find out when you talk to him. Good luck!"

"Yeah, yeah," she muttered and didn't bother to knock on the door before she pushed into her boss' office. The lean man with short blond hair was on the phone and motioned for her to take a seat in front of his smallish desk.

The office smelled of the cigarettes he liked to sneak when he had the time. It was adorable how he thought no one knew simply because he got all the smoke into the vent next to his chair and drowned the place in air fresheners when he'd finished.

He finally finished his call, hung up, and narrowed his eyes at her. "You know I could have given this job to someone else? Where the hell do you go to get lunch that it takes you half an hour to get back?"

"Well, for starters, it was mostly the traffic, which I usually avoid when I come back after my break since the lunch rush hour is over by then. And secondly, it's a little Greek place halfway to Schaumburg."

"Why can't you go to a place nearby? Almost everyone goes to Pisano's."

"I don't like deep-dish pizza," Elisa responded. "Hell, I don't like Chicago's hot dogs either. New York style is the worst and should simply be called tomato paste on toast. Oh, and I also think proper tacos should be made with flour tortillas instead of corn. Sue me."

"I think you managed to piss off most of the damn

country, including but not limited to most of Chicago, half the pizza-lovers in the country, and every red-blooded resident of New York, Miss Fallaci. Oh, not to mention virtually anyone who eats food in Mexico too."

"I'm opinionated. You know that. It's what makes me such a good reporter, not to mention the best one you have on staff at the moment. So why don't you go ahead and tell me what you called me for during my lunch break and get on with it?"

Cas laughed. They danced around like this fairly often, but like he knew she was the best reporter he had on staff, she knew he was far and away the best and most talented manager she would ever have at this level.

"Well, Elisa, let's get down to business. I'm sure you and the rest of the country know that a casino armored truck was held up at gunpoint by someone wearing mech suits of armor that are currently only in use in the Zoo. While there are enough people in the world who want to know about the Zoo monsters making their way through our country, there's a much larger audience out there. They want to know about the kind of people who would be able to stage a casino robbery while using tech that should be exclusive to the military."

"Yeah, I hear they're already trying to get the filming rights for a movie, touting it as the new *Ocean's 11* or something like that. Or was it a mix of James Bond and *Ocean's 11*? People have tried to give the heist genre that high-tech kind of boost. It's all well and good until you realize that the Las Vegas police department did precisely jack shit to find whoever that did it."

"Yes, well, according to contacts I have in that very

same Las Vegas police department, there might be a reason for that. As the story goes—according to those contacts—the people involved in the robbery have significant connections, both in the underworld of the city and also the local offices of the FBI. The kind of connections that would be able to kill any serious investigation into that kind of robbery. No one was killed and the casinos were all thoroughly insured. The only people who want to have a look at the guy are the insurance companies and surprisingly, they appear to lack the pull he has."

"Do you think it was an inside job? The mob still has any number of ties to the Vegas casinos, and if they wanted to get their hands on a neat little payout, they could have robbed their own armored vehicle, laundered the money, and taken the insurance payout."

"Well, that's a very interesting take on the topic—one I'm sure our readers would like to hear about once you have the right amount of proof to back it up. The last thing we need while we struggle for legitimacy is a libel lawsuit on our hands."

"Consider it done." Elisa pushed quickly from her seat. "As soon as I can find tickets to Vegas."

"I've already emailed your tickets to your account. I managed to upgrade you to business class so it should be a comfortable enough flight. I expect you to make good use of that time."

"I'll be nice and rested from the moment I touch down."

"That's not really what I was talking about."

"Oh, well, whatever you think I should be doing. When does the flight leave?"

"Take off from O'Hare is in three hours. Have fun in Vegas, Elisa, but not too much fun."

"Will do, boss. I'll call you when I get there."

Her mind had already begun to consider the possibilities as she hurried away. The distraction allowed her to look past any irritation she might have felt at the fact that Cas had dragged her butt into the office for something he could simply have said over the phone.

Of course, she was used to that—it was simply that he insisted on job discussions face-to-face for some weird reason—and her irritation was usually swept away by whatever assignment he doled out.

CHAPTER TWO

Niki took a deep breath and readied herself for what was to come. It wasn't likely to be a very pleasant conversation. Evans probably didn't know what it was about so at least she was spared his comments, but very little intel came from Italy that was related to her.

Of course, what did was unlikely to be good.

She paused at the closed door, tapped it lightly, and hoped there would be no answer.

It was, of course, a futile hope. "Come in."

With her expression schooled into calm and business-like, she pushed the door open.

Her superior was seated behind his desk. He wore a pair of reading glasses and studied a mission report, and he gestured for her to sit across the desk from him.

"Special Agent Banks, thanks for speaking to me."

That sounds too formal to be good. Fuck. Like I had any choice in the matter—could he really be this pissed about me shouting my mouth off? Or maybe the problem is Italy, which is way worse.

"No problem, sir," she said cautiously and resisted the urge to shift in her chair.

He looked at her from over the rims of his glasses. "Anyway, to business?"

Niki nodded and he closed the folder he had been reading and slid it across his desk to her. "I have a feeling you don't need to read what's inside to know what's written there."

"What would give you that feeling, sir?" They had a relaxed work relationship, but her survival instincts told her now wasn't the time for jokes, even though a few sprang readily to mind.

"The fact that your name features prominently. The *Polizia di Stato* had a couple of complaints about your actions during the liaison you had with their office."

"Complaints? We killed all the monsters, which they were completely incapable of dealing with on their own. The mission, in their own words, was an unmitigated success. They were glowing in their report. I should know. I received a copy of it myself."

"Yes, I'm sure they were. But a more thorough investigation produced troubling news—and before you say anything, I've done a little research of my own so I'm well aware of what the two reports contain and have verified certain facts for myself. These are the kind of facts that should never be associated with the FBI, especially when it can potentially become an international incident. The second investigation was sparked by the death of a whole group of people in a nearby villa—which included the owner, who happened to be someone of significant stature and something of a local celebrity."

"I remember that. Our man on the ground—"

"McFadden, right? Taylor McFadden was the man you had on the ground?"

"Given that he's our best asset and it was our first international cooperative effort, I thought we should put our best foot forward, as it were. Anyway, McFadden reported that the beasts had already attacked that villa by the time he got there. He said—"

"That it was the reason he was able to kill so many of them so quickly. They were distracted by the feeding frenzy. I'm sorry to interrupt you so often but like I said, I have read the reports. I also have a good idea of when I'm being fed bullshit. I've written these kinds of reports dozens of times. I've been Special Agent in Charge of my own task forces and I know when people work to cover their asses."

"I—"

He held a hand up. "I'm not finished. Sending McFadden was clearly a mistake since—as I'm sure you're not aware—the man who owned the villa and was killed in the attack is a member of *La Cosa Nostra*, the same family your man has dealt with in the past."

"Be that as it may, that Jason Momoa wannabe is still one of our best assets. Hell, he did more for this country when he was almost dead than those asshats on Capitol Hill do over their entire lifetimes."

Dammit. That was not clever. When will I learn to keep my fucking mouth shut—or at least find a better way to say things?

Fortunately, her boss chose to ignore her outburst.

"I don't disagree." The man pulled his glasses off and placed them on the table. "Whether what happened in Italy was fully intentional or not doesn't matter. Something needs to be done to show that we're very, very sorry about what happened. We have taken pains to cultivate our government friends in Italy, so this has to be official to send the right message. In simple terms, you will be fired."

Niki clenched her fists on the arms of her chair and tried not to let her anger show. She had known all along that these were the possible repercussions for her actions and had made her decision in the full knowledge that she could ultimately be fired. It still didn't make it any easier to hear, though.

"I know that's probably difficult for you to hear. I also know that what you did was possibly in the best interest of your operation and task force."

"Sure," she responded and barely managed to not clench her teeth. "I still have no idea why I'm being fired but I do understand that sometimes, office politics get in the way of keeping our country safe as the bureau is supposed to do."

"Right, you don't know about anything that happened. Exactly like I don't know about people who are thoroughly impressed by your actions and would be interested in your continued service for your country in a less politically-impeded capacity. I also don't know anything about them wanting to contact you in the next forty-eight hours about that job opportunity."

Niki narrowed her eyes at the man and leaned forward. "Wait, am I being fired?"

"Sure. But a more accurate description would be released for other duties."

How about I release my four-inch heels inside your ass? Thankfully, she managed to refrain from saying that aloud by reminding herself that the outcome had always been anticipated if not expected.

"For now, you're reassigned, pending a desk job," he said when she made no effort to respond.

"If you do that, I can guarantee I'll tender my resignation."

"You can simply remain in place for the next forty-eight hours. I'm sure—"

"I'll be in exactly the right place for someone to arrest me?" She raised an eyebrow at the man.

"It sounds like you have a guilty conscience," he replied.

"Maybe, but a more accurate description would be a cynical attitude."

He laughed and leaned back in his seat. "Very good, Agent Banks. That's the kind of attitude that'll serve you very well in the future. For now, though, I need you to clean your desk out and turn your badge and service weapon in to the quartermaster's office on the fifth floor."

Niki stood quickly. She could, of course, go the HR route and drag the dismissal out indefinitely. There were protocols in place for this kind of situation, even when international politics were involved. Unfortunately, that kind of complicated and drawn-out situation didn't appeal to her—and she suspected her superior was counting on that. Aside from the fact that she'd effectively be in limbo for however long it took, she didn't want anything to affect the task force she'd worked so hard to create.

More to the point, she'd prefer to not have too many questions asked over and above what had already been uncovered. That would shift considerable attention to Taylor and his team, which included Vickie. She could deal with what came her way, but there was no way she'd hang her cousin out to dry for a second strike that would end with her in the Zoo.

While she had no idea what his veiled references to other job opportunities might involve, her boss had basically told her she'd been fired in order to be hired elsewhere. Maybe all wasn't lost, although she would damn well look long and hard at whatever said opportunity might be. With a sigh, she straightened and looked him in the eye.

"Well, I guess that's it, then. Do you happen to know who'll take my position?"

"I can confirm that Agent Ramirez from the Dallas office will be relocated to take over thanks to his experience in aiding your task force in his area."

She nodded, impressed despite her resentment. "Ramirez is a solid choice. Not as good as me, but still."

"I know. I recommended him myself. Have a good day, Banks."

With nothing left to say, she stepped out of the office. Her hands shook and her fingers hurt from being held in tight fists for so long, and she dragged in a long slow breath. The hallway was empty, thank goodness, and it gave her an opportunity to restore her usual calm and focused attitude. She'd already betrayed herself once too many times and whatever emotional bug had crawled up her ass, it was time to be rid of it. She wouldn't give anyone the satisfaction of another emotional reaction. Her last action with the bureau would be a successful personal mission of professionalism with her head held high and her dignity intact.

The control over herself was maintained as she entered the building elevator and when she stepped into the quartermaster HQ. There wasn't much to see except for a tempered glass window in the wall with a small opening at the bottom. She filled out the requisite paperwork and turned her service weapon and her badge over to the man on the other side.

Nothing was said about the process, which didn't mean much. Agents who were suspended pending internal affairs investigations—as was likely happening in her case—were required to remove all ties to any investigative work they might have.

Niki noted her hands shaking a little as she placed the required items on the counter and pushed them through the small opening. She turned quickly and headed to the elevator again. The garage was her next destination, and she maintained her control during her walk toward her SUV.

Only once she was inside and the door was closed did she finally allow herself some reprieve.

She hammered her fists on the steering wheel of the car and the vehicle shuddered.

"Fuck!" she shouted as loudly as she could. No one was in the garage at this time of day and even if they were, they wouldn't hear the racket.

After a few repeats, her throat was a little sore and so were her hands when she finally relaxed against the car seat, but she did feel a little better. Her career was all but finished, and all because she couldn't resist giving McFadden a helping hand in his little vendetta.

It still felt like the right choice, despite the repercussions. Even so, she wished she could take it out on Taylor as much as possible and let him know what her helping him had cost. A part of her wanted to make him feel guilty about it but her habitual honesty challenged that head-on. She had made the decision herself and insisted she tag along. He had given her the opportunity to back out, so no one was more responsible for her current situation than she was.

Given that, it was also unlikely that he'd feel even slightly guilty and she had to acknowledge that his pragmatic attitude would be justified.

Niki pulled her phone out of her jacket pocket and found her sister's number quickly. She needed someone to talk to about this whole situation, and Jennie was the only name that sprang to mind. Worries about problems with national security secrets didn't quite apply in this case as the woman probably already knew about everything that was happening anyway.

It was a good thing that she was on their side. The kind of damage the girl could do if she ever chose to was the stuff of nightmares.

Not Niki's nightmares necessarily, but definitely someone's. Most corporate security directors and advisors, if she had to guess.

Her sister answered the phone almost immediately. "Hey, big sis."

"Do I need to tell you about what happened or have you already broken a few federal laws finding out about it already?"

"The laws were broken a long time ago. I merely like to keep myself apprised of what's happening with my family, so when any new paperwork with your name on it pops up, I get an alert. It's probably not a very efficient use for the software I designed to get it done, but I don't have any other purpose for it and better in my hands than the wrong hands."

"Your hands are the wrong hands. Just not the worst hands."

There was a moment of silence between the two sisters. Niki stared ahead into space, not seeing anything, but still wanted to talk to her sister. Hearing Jennie calmed her somewhat.

"I'm sorry, Niki," the woman said softly. "I know I make jokes about your work with the FBI but I know you cared about it and it meant a lot to you. And sure, you were making the world a better, safer place for all of us, but that's a lesser concern—to my mind at least."

"Thanks, sis. And yeah, it sucks all kinds of balls to see everything I've worked for over the course of my career turn to shit over one action."

"I know that. And the fact that you did what you did to protect me and Vickie...don't think any of that is lost on me."

Niki chuckled. "You don't fuck with my family and get away with it. Not while I'm still breathing. So no, I don't regret doing what I did, I knew the consequences very well when I made my decision, and I'd do it again. It still sucks, though."

"Well, I hope you know that I won't stand idly by and let you retire with no pension. I'm sure I could get you a job with my firm if you want it. They're always looking for former law enforcement to head security at their various installations."

"I actually have a few leads on the job front myself."

Jennie paused, likely trying to research the statement. "Have you been contacted by headhunters already?"

"Something like that. Is this line secure?"

Another voice connected. "I've already secured the line, Agent Banks," Desk said.

"It's not agent anymore. I don't think, anyway. My supervisor told me to stick around for the next forty-eight hours like he thought I would be contacted by someone about continuing in my line of work. His exact words were a 'less politically-impeded capacity' when describing the possibility. Given that you've not seen any orders for my arrest yet, I'll guess he wasn't lying and there might be something to what he said."

Jennie didn't answer immediately, and she knew that to mean her sister was probably typing on her computer, digging in the vast number of databases she had on hand to find what she wanted.

It was a little terrifying to think that almost any information in the government was accessible to the woman.

"I don't pick up anything right away," Desk asserted after a few minutes. She'd forgotten the damn AI for a moment, who would no doubt mirror the actions of the hacker she'd been based on. "I'll do a little research and get back to you."

Niki shook her head. "Don't worry about it. I don't want any more trouble to go into what happened."

"It's no trouble," the AI assured her. "It's what you do for family, after all."

Desk disconnected from the line, and Niki couldn't help but make a face. "Do you think she might be getting a little too personal? Desk knows she's not real, right?"

"She's been programmed with a large part of my psyche," Jennie explained. "That's why she's so protective of you."

"And I guess that's where the infatuation with Taylor comes from, right?"

"I was hoping you wouldn't notice."

Niki snorted. "Yeah, right."

Vickie looked up from her screen and frowned as the alert from her phone was brought up on the screen to her left.

"Hey, Bungees, are we expecting any new deliveries today?"

The man stepped away from the suit he was working on and removed the safety glasses he wore while Tanya paused her work with the soldering gun. The protective eyewear was unnecessary, but Taylor insisted on it anyway. It had simply become a habit they all accepted without complaint.

"What?" he responded. "Isn't it your job to keep track of when and where we're supposed to pick up new deliveries?"

"Well, yeah, but there's no delivery scheduled for today," she told him. "And yet a delivery truck is pulling into our back yard for some fucking reason."

"Front yard, technically," Taylor commented as he came

down from his room while he still pulled his shirt on. "And yes, we do have a delivery today."

"But there's nothing on the schedule," Vickie insisted. "And I should know since I compiled the damn thing."

"Oh, this isn't a business delivery. At least, not for McFadden's Mechs."

"God, that name sucks," the hacker protested.

"I know, but it's better than nothing," he agreed. "Anyway, we have something to look at. If neither of you is too busy—which, as your boss, I can say that you're not—come have a look."

Taylor, Bobby, Vickie, and Tanya walked out into the blazing Las Vegas sunlight as the truck beeped and backed up to a different section of the building.

"Of course, you all know I'm working on regaining the muscle mass I lost while lazing around in the hospital," Taylor said as he slid a pair of sunglasses on. "And I wondered if the best way to go about it was to simply go to someone else's gym and pay them a monthly fee, or whether I could purchase the equipment on my own and charge other people to use it."

Bobby stared as the delivery team began to carry the items into a separate area, one that wasn't connected to the shop. "Wait, so you went out and decided to build your own gym? I thought you were only spitballing with that idea."

"Well, I was," his boss admitted. "But then I thought about it and realized that having the kind of stuff we need in our area would be a great way for us to stay in shape and maybe even make some money off it."

"Have you thought about what we'll need to do with

our security system if we have to account for a horde of chicks in yoga pants who wander in at all times of the day to sip their healthy smoothies and talk about their alkaline levels?" Vickie asked, her arms folded across her chest.

"That...is an excellent point," he agreed. "And I have thought about it. But since we don't have the mob on our backs anymore, we might not need as much."

"We'll still need some," Bobby reminded him. "We don't work on fakes made in China out here, after all."

Taylor shrugged. "Right, so I haven't worked out all the kinks, but we have time for that later. It's not like I've advertised an opening date. For the moment, we can use them ourselves. We all need to keep ourselves in tiptop shape, none more so than me, and I can't think of a better way to use some of the eighty thousand feet that aren't currently occupied in this strip mall. So, what do you think —the unused thirty thousand feet here or the fifty thousand over on the end?"

The truck loaders finished their work quickly, which meant they wouldn't build any of the equipment. As lunch break time was approaching, Taylor's crew chose to start building them once they had ordered food at his expense.

Vickie was less than pleased about the situation and wiped her forehead as she worked on one of the elliptical machines. "Seriously, how obtuse do you have to be to make IKEA instructions seem like NASA documents?"

"How the hell do you know what NASA documents look like?" Bobby asked and took a bite from the pizza that had been delivered.

She paused and regarded him with an impatient

expression. "Don't worry about it. The point is that these instructions are completely obtuse. Fucking hell."

"Even if the instructions are difficult to understand, the machines themselves are intuitive," Taylor said, finished one of the squat machines, and patted it and the weights to be sure. "Basic engineering gives you a good idea of what's supposed to be where to emphasize exercise and safety."

"Well, tell me that again when I have an engineering degree," the hacker grumbled as she twisted some of the screws in. "After all, I don't get all up in your business about not cleaning the spam from your email."

"Okay, if you don't want to work in here, we could— wait a second, how do you know about the state of my email?"

She raised an eyebrow at him. "Come on, man. The fact that you think any part of your life is even remotely private at this point is adorable. Be happy that I have your best interests at heart and assimilate that into your life already."

"Whatever," he mumbled. "Anyway, if you don't want to work on this, you can head to the shop or maybe to school. This lunch was supposed to thank you guys for helping me here, but if you're not into it—"

"Ugh, don't be like that," she whined, straightened. and stretched her hands. It appeared she was finished with the elliptical. "You know I'm in this for the long haul but get used to the fact that I'll bitch and complain about it the whole way."

"Oh. Well, I appreciate that. Besides, you could probably put all this equipment to work to good effect. For instance, making your boobs larger or smaller."

Vickie narrowed her eyes pensively. "Okay, I get how I

can make them smaller—it's only subcutaneous adipose tissue—but how the hell would exercise help to make them larger?"

"Not make them bigger in real terms—I'm fairly sure the only way to get that is through surgery—but make them look bigger," Taylor explained. "Exercising properly can firm and tone the chest muscles behind your breasts and help improve your posture, which will help with the..."

"The presentation, yeah, I got it," she finished for him as his voice trailed off. "Fair enough, I might look into it. Not that I have any complaints about the gals in question but there's always room for improvement. By the way, has anyone ever told you that you might have an unhealthy fixation on the size of a woman's chest area?"

Tanya, who had been quiet for most of the conversation, barked a laugh.

Taylor, on the other hand, showed no sign of being bothered in the slightest. "Fixation? Yes. Unhealthy? No. When you think about it, the whole fixation coming from when we're babies and seeing them as a source of food is probably bullshit since straight women and gay men don't have it, but there's an evolutionary idea behind the attraction. It's an indicator of the woman's health and provides other markers that would show she's a healthy mate. The need to mate solely for reproduction might be gone but that kind of instinctive check to see if the mate is healthy will still be there for a long while. It's a similar reason as to why men have evolved larger penises than average in the animal kingdom. Compared to their size, anyway."

"Some men," Vickie retorted.

"I've never heard any complaints."

"You have to understand," Tanya said while she helped to put the weights in place on one of the shoulder exercising machines. "There are certain things a woman can take advantage of when it comes to her natural gifts. Having a guy stare at your chest means they won't watch your face or your hands. That can be amazingly useful. You have to use the gifts mother nature has given you."

Taylor pointed at the woman. "She has a point, you know."

"I don't think that's right." The hacker scowled as she began to help him with one of the treadmills. "Fair enough, if you have it, flaunt it, but intentionally using your natural gifts as an advantage—"

"Much like you do with your natural talents for software engineering?" Tanya interrupted.

"That's not the same thing. You have to work to be good at something like that. Using a guy's natural attraction doesn't feel right."

The other woman raised an eyebrow. "Well, the lion is naturally attracted to eating the gazelle. Does that make it wrong?"

"That's not the same thing and—you're fucking with me, aren't you?" Vickie scowled as the woman laughed again and returned to work with Bungees. "Well, ha-ha, you're very hilarious, and why the fuck are you taking Taylor's side in this?"

Tanya shrugged. "I'm not taking anyone's side in anything. I have a kid, and it seems like all children have a way of seeing the world when they're younger that makes us older folk want to slap knowledge and experience into them. Or, failing that, simply slap them."

The hacker shook her head. "So, what? Is my age a trigger for you or something?"

"No, only your ignorance," the other woman replied with a cheeky smirk and ducked to avoid the screwdriver thrown across the room at her. By now, the girl's propensity to throw things was anticipated and her aim was so bad, they were easily avoided.

Taylor grinned although he didn't add anything to the conversation. Vickie was much closer to him and less likely to miss if she decided to throw something at him, but she'd absorbed enough from his talks about safety to put no power behind her impromptu weapons. He hoped she'd simply outgrow the habit sooner rather than later.

Thankfully, the phone rang and the hacker retreated to the office but gave Tanya a one-fingered salute as she hurried out.

The woman laughed in response and offered her fist for Bobby to bump.

Bungees appeared less amused by their antics and rolled his eyes but still pressed his closed fist reluctantly to hers before the three of them returned to work.

CHAPTER THREE

It wasn't that she didn't feel safe in her own home anymore. Paranoia was a part of the business, of course, but Niki was suddenly more than aware of the fact that someone was probably out to get her—not necessarily to kill her but quite probably to arrest her or worse.

Even so, it was better to be alert and ahead of the problem. If it meant taking an extra-long time to have a coffee at the shop across the street from her apartment, so much the better.

Besides, the venue sold good coffee and was where she went to buy something each morning before she headed to work. Things had changed now that she didn't have anyone to work for, but the staff knew her well enough to let her remain in the little booth next to the window. She lingered, watched, and waited, while she hoped nothing would happen.

Damned if hoping would be the end of her, though. She leaned back in her seat and took another sip of the lukewarm coffee she'd ordered almost an hour before.

During the long stakeout—who had to stake their own home out anyway?—she had nibbled at most of the blueberry muffin and was likely the kind of patron these stores disapproved of, but she chose not to worry about that.

One thing at a time was more than enough.

Years of working with the government had taught her to notice their people from a mile away. It was mostly the subtle way they carried themselves and the icy demeanor of superiority they exercised whenever they were in contact with a member of the general populace.

There was also the fact that they drove into an area, pulled their big, black SUV onto the sidewalk, and exited with the knowledge that there would be no tickets in store for them.

Seriously, these guys needed to be much more subtle.

Niki tried to get a better view of the two men who exited the vehicle that had parked in front of her apartment building. They seemed in a rush and obviously already had the code to enter the building, which was suggestive of what they tried to do.

And it didn't look like they had plans to arrest her. At Desk's behest, she had left her phone on and streamed something inside her apartment, which meant anyone tracking it would think she was at home. Who the hell left their home without their phones these days?

She retrieved the burner she had picked up earlier that day and dialed the pre-programmed number. "Desk, are you there?"

"I am always here for you, Agent Banks."

"Well, that's a little unsettling. We'll move past that,

though, because I think I have plates I want you to run. I'm taking a picture of them now."

The camera on the burner wasn't quite as good as she preferred but it did the job, even through the thick-pane windows of the coffee shop.

"Those plates belong to the undercover fleet of the Department of Defense," the AI replied almost immediately after the picture was sent. "Did you manage to take any pictures of the driver?"

Niki scowled as she stood and pulled cash from her wallet to pay for her coffee. "No, I didn't. But I don't think I need you to look into who these guys are since they're probably only the foot soldiers. I have another favor I need to ask of you, though."

"I am all ears."

There was something about these press conferences that always got under Elisa's skin. The police commissioner was usually someone who had a history in public relations and therefore generally already knew what questions he or she would be called on to answer. Many of these would inevitably be hidden under the common shield of classified information.

There was rarely anything to be learned there that couldn't be acquired with the proper contacts anyway.

But someone needed to cover these boring briefings and occasionally, something could be gleaned when you looked in the right places.

She prided herself on knowing where to look, which

was why she was seated with about twenty other reporters. These were a mixture of the old-timers who looked forward to their retirement and the youngsters who wanted a story that would break open their careers.

The tall, older man in a police uniform walked slowly to the permanent podium across from them and positioned himself in front of the cameras and microphones. He cleared his throat once and studied his notes quickly before he began.

"Good afternoon, I'm Police Commissioner John Kelly. At approximately five-thirty AM this morning, our officers in charge of an investigation into the Sinaloa Cartel raided a house in Spring Valley and arrested thirteen members of the cartel, all of whom were armed with automatic and semi-automatic weapons. Over thirteen hundred pounds of cocaine were seized as well. It is a historic seizure for our department and one of the largest in our history. I will be taking questions."

One of the older veterans immediately raised his hand. "Were any of those arrested recent immigrants into our country?"

"All who were arrested were full American citizens. Next question?"

Elisa raised her hand. "Do you think those arrested had anything to do with the casino armored vehicle robbery that happened last month?"

The commissioner's eyebrows raised. He had clearly not expected that question. "There...there is no reason to suspect any connection between the two crimes. Next—"

She was not about to be dissuaded, however. "Does your department have any updates regarding the robbery?

Any new arrests or footage that might have been acquired?"

The official obviously had no intention to answer that and his face immediately assumed the bored expression he had worn earlier. "I am not at liberty to discuss any of our ongoing investigations. Next question?"

There weren't many asked thereafter. The operation had been a joint effort, coordinated by the FBI and the DEA, and both agencies had already issued their own press releases on the matter. The only reason why he had scheduled this particular press conference was because the commissioner was up for reelection in the coming months and he wanted as much good press as possible.

The conference finished in less than ten minutes and the reporters began to file toward the exits.

Elisa felt a hand on her arm and turned quickly to face one of the younger reporters. He was well-built with a physique that looked like he had once been an athlete, maybe in college, and a head of unruly bright blond hair.

"Hey, I'm Jason Harmon from the Las Vegas Journal," he said and proffered his hand. "Where are you from?"

She shook his hand firmly. "I'm Elisa Maria Fallaci with the Crypto-Inquirer. Like it says on my press pass."

"Oh, so you're here about the suits that were used in that robbery. Yeah, a number of people asked about that when it first happened and the cops weren't much help then either. Anyway, if you want real dirt on the matter, you want to dig into the casino that was robbed. They're not happy about it, but they've had a ton of people come over thanks to the press. There's nothing like having a robbery with futuristic tech to get those tourist dollars flowing in, right?"

"Right," Elisa replied. "If that's where the dirt is, why aren't you there?"

Harmon smirked. "It's not my beat. Honestly, not many people want to continue to dig into that since most of the government agencies are cracking down on giving the criminals any good press. But if you think you can get around it, the casino is the place to be. Believe me, the cops won't budge on their no-talk policy."

She nodded, shook the man's hand again, and took her card from her coat pocket. "I appreciate the tip, Harmon. I guess I owe you one. Let me know if I can return the favor sometime."

He nodded, took the card, and studied it briefly. "I might take you up on that."

"Try the buzzer again."

Jansen scowled at his partner. They had waited outside the apartment for about five minutes. Their intel had confirmed it as the location where Niki Banks lived but there was no peep from inside and no sign that anything was happening in there that might give them cause to break in.

Not that they were supposed to break in anyway. This woman was someone they were recruiting, not someone they had to bring in for questioning.

"I said—"

"I heard what you fucking said, Maxwell," Jansen

snapped, scratched his short black hair idly, and shook his head. "I think it's fairly damn obvious that no one's home."

Maxwell ran his fingers over the bristle that had begun to grow on his jawline. The man looked the part of a bruiser, and his partner knew he had been a boxer during his time with the Navy. He wasn't dull-witted by any means, but he was very methodical—the kind of person who would keep doing something even if it wasn't working simply because that was what he'd been ordered to.

He was orders-focused, not initiative-driven and wasn't the biggest creative thinker either. Which was probably why they had been teamed together.

"So, what? Do we wait for her to get home?" the larger man asked and looked around the hallway.

Jansen held himself back from losing his temper again and pressed the buzzer next to the front door one last time. "That probably won't help. We'll head back to the office and see if intel has gotten their collective heads out of their collective asses yet and if they can help us this time."

"The boss said not to come back without her."

"Yeah, do you want to knock on every door in this fucking town? Does wasting the taxpayers' dollars like that sound good to you?"

Maxwell's face scrunched before his lazy, relaxed expression took over again. "Fine. Let's head back."

Jansen didn't like it any better than his partner did, but they wouldn't achieve anything else today. They needed to return to the office and restart the process of finding Niki Banks. It made sense that she would lie low, but they needed her to know that they weren't there to talk about what happened at her old job but rather what would happen at the new one.

They reached the SUV and climbed inside. Maxwell took the driver's seat since it was his turn and Jansen sat in the passenger side and shifted to a comfortable position before he retrieved his phone. The sooner the guys in intel knew they needed to get back to work, the better.

Both men froze when a revolver's hammer cocked.

"Morning boys," a woman said from the back seat and pressed the pistol into the back of Jansen's head. "Do you guys want to tell me why you're rolling into my home at this time of day or do we need to do a little song and dance first?"

The gun was a snub-nosed .38 special—Smith & Wesson, by the looks of it—but his gaze was drawn to the woman's reflection in the rearview mirror. She wasn't too tall, her long black hair was tied in a ponytail, and she had Hispanic features and access to firearms.

If he had to hazard a guess, he would say they had found their target. Or that she'd found them, rather. But there were more important details to deal with first.

"Did you not lock the fucking door?" Maxwell asked as he too looked at the woman's reflection.

Jansen shook his head. "I thought you did. You were driving, remember?"

"It locks itself automatically, Tweedledee and Tweedledumbass," she pointed out and answered their question for them. "Exactly like it also unlocks itself automatically when approached with a phone that has the unlock code keyed into its RFID, which can be spoofed after a quick satellite connection. So, are we done asking stupid questions?"

Jansen couldn't help but stiffen a little in his seat as the barrel pressed into the back of his head with a little more insistence than before.

"Stupid questions are done. Unless...you have any you want to ask?"

"Yeah, I have one for you and it should be simple to answer," she stated. "What the fuck does the Department of Defense want with me?"

The two men exchanged a glance. They chose, almost telepathically, not to question the woman as to how she knew that they were DOD.

"We are a part of a newly formed operations branch," Jansen explained. He spoke slowly and clearly to ensure that nothing was left open to interpretation. "After the situation in Wyoming, the DOD wanted a task force ready to operate in situations that caused the spread of Zoo monsters inside the country's borders instead of reacting to their appearance. So far, the infrastructure is all in place. All we need is a qualified team and someone to lead the task force. You were tapped for the latter position, with the team being yours to select as you see fit. Unlike your work with the FBI, though, you would have access to almost unlimited funds—within reason, of course—and your performance would be judged on results instead of operation costs."

Niki raised her eyebrows. She hadn't expected something like this and he certainly understood that. Most people would want to bring her on in an analyst role, but the DOD was done reacting to problems once they were already dropping bodies.

"And how is it that you're in the know about this whole

thing?" she asked finally and still held the gun pressed to his head. "You're only the muscle behind this operation, it seems. I doubt your particular need to know would include the sales pitch. Don't you think your boss would rather do that himself?"

"He knew you probably wouldn't come in without real answers, which is why we were entrusted with some of them—but certainly not all. The kind that would hopefully interest you in the full pitch."

"So, was that it? Was that the full pitch?"

Jansen shook his head. "Nope. But you don't get the full pitch while you have a gun aimed at my head."

Niki thought about it for a few seconds before she lowered her weapon and de-cocked the hammer. "So, is this some kind of job interview?"

He relaxed visibly and took slow, deep breaths. "Didn't your former boss explain it to you?"

"He was a little vague—bordering on very."

"We can go somewhere to explain. How does a donut shop appeal to you?"

She tucked the pistol into an underarm holster. "If you had suggested a salad bar, I would have shot you. Let's move."

CHAPTER FOUR

Niki had already had coffee and had nursed it for most of the morning. Going to a donut place did seem like a good way to get a sugar high as well as spend time with the two bumbling henchmen, but there was such a thing as too much of a good thing. She'd settled for green chai to be served with the donuts, while the other two appeared more than happy with the coffee that was served.

"So," she began once everything had been delivered and they were on their own. "You guys were telling me about the operation you were starting and wanted me to head. Why do I have a bad feeling that I'll be the scapegoat should something go wrong? I'm Niki Banks, by the way, if we're pretending you two don't know my name."

"I'm Felix Jansen, and this is my partner, Tim Maxwell. We're former military, called in to work as your supervisory agents as well as bodyguards. We'll report to the people in charge in the DOD, which means we won't give you orders and you won't give us any."

She raised an eyebrow and took a slow sip of her chai.

"Okay, it sounds interesting. Do you know anything about how the operation started?"

"Enough to fill you in. I was a part of the original team. After working counterintelligence with the Navy, I was called in to help with the task force that tried to determine where these Zoo infestations were coming from. After almost two years of investigations, we've pinned down at least three locations that have been responsible for over two dozen of the infestations your FBI task force handled with...varying degrees of success. More success than the task forces used by the CIA and the NSA, though, so when the DOD decided they wanted their own team to proactively deal with possible future infestations, there was only one candidate for the job."

"Me, I guess. So, does that mean the DOD were the ones who leaked the Italy details to the FBI?"

"I wasn't briefed on that section of the operation but from a professional standpoint, I'd have to say yes."

Niki looked at the larger of the two men. "Your partner doesn't say much, does he?"

Maxwell shrugged. "I'm smart enough to understand that my conversational talents aren't why I was brought in on this operation."

She nodded slowly. "Fair enough."

"In the end, intelligence gathering was the original concept for this operation," Jansen continued. "We hoped to be able to transfer that intelligence to other branches and so focus our efforts, but that proved to be inefficient. Politics got in the way of getting the job done, so our superior determined that we would create a task force of our own. It will be similar to the kind you used to run but with better intelligence, better funding, and less politics. That was the message your boss was supposed to transfer to you when you were, quote, fired, unquote."

"Let me get this straight." Niki paused to take a bite from one of the donuts and gave herself a few seconds to gather her thoughts. "You want me to head an operational task force that would act on the intelligence gathered by the DOD against threats before they start to take lives. I would be able to build my team and operate at the discretion of you and Maxwell, who will report my every move to some person in the DOD who will supervise me."

"And once again, your mission is to make sure that lives aren't lost to these monster infestations. You won't need to worry about your financial backing. Leave that to us."

"And I can bring anyone into the team?"

"As long as they're qualified. You'll need to submit the candidates to your supervisor first, but you won't be forced to take anyone on who you don't feel is qualified. So yes, your man McFadden will be authorized. Your relationship with him—"

"Is purely platonic."

"Your purely platonic relationship with him notwithstanding, he is fully qualified to operate as a free-lancer for the Department of Defense. We've pre-cleared most of the operatives you've worked with in the past. There will be a list provided to you should you choose to use anyone on it."

Niki nodded slowly. "I guess there's only one thing left to do."

"Sign your paperwork?"

"Talk to your supervisor," she corrected him. "In person, this time."

There were worse things in the world than being on assignment in Vegas, Elisa decided, especially if one was comfortably settled in a Vegas hotel and casino. The prices for a room were low enough that she could justify them as corporate expenses, and so was most of the food. As long as she didn't spend any time gambling or submit any invoices with alcoholic beverages in them, she would be fine.

Of course, that only applied as long as she got the job done.

And there was a fair amount of it involved with this casino. There were many small inconsistencies in the paperwork she had looked into. It was all public record so she wouldn't do anything illegal—or at least, so far, she hadn't needed to.

Most of it was all openly available, and she spent her time reading through it at one of the best-priced coffee shops she'd ever been in.

Either these people were going gangbusters in the casino business, or they received sizeable amounts of illegal money on the side. She had seen the signs before. Many organized crime syndicates liked to run their money through small-time casinos, who could then charge much less for their services in the hotel and even used it as a way to attract as many guests as possible to make a show of how much money they made for the IRS.

Of course, the mob had been in Vegas since the city was first founded, which meant they didn't need to make do with small-time casinos. The larger, more established venues were much more effective and could run more money through them—legal money, which made the illegal money that much harder to trace.

She couldn't prove any of that, but with the proper financial paperwork, she could strongly imply it. Once the implication was made, she could get along with how they had used their foreign connections to buy armor suits from outside of the US to rob their own money and pocket the profits while still running the money through their business.

It was a laundering machine, as far as she was concerned, the kind the larger organized crime syndicates liked to have in their back pocket. If she had to hazard a guess, it was probably *La Cosa Nostra*, or maybe the *Camorra*. They had expanded their profit base over the past few years after their operations in Monaco and San Remo had gone the way of the dodo.

Without a doubt, she genuinely enjoyed this kind of work. Her major in college had been in journalism, but there had been a minor in business economics and she had enjoyed being an investigative reporter. Going up against the mob had always been something of a fantasy of hers, although she never really thought it would come to that in real life.

Of course, she was well aware of the dangers that came with the job. Sending any of this data to the office while she was still in Vegas was out of the question. She would brief Cas when she returned and would make sure the work was cleared with all the appropriate agencies before they published it, but damned if it wouldn't be a story for the ages.

People loved reading about the mob. Movies had made them something of a remnant of the Wild West of old, and while most of the stories about honor and family portrayed in the movies were bullshit, people still liked reading about it.

After a deep breath, she took a sip of the rich Italian roast coffee she'd ordered. There weren't that many people in the shop with her since the rush hour was usually in the morning. Mostly, it was people who avoided the mob at the breakfast buffet.

A small smirk touched her lips as the thought crossed her mind. Unlike many of her readers, she always did like a clever pun or even one that wasn't that clever. She tried to keep it out of her writing, of course, but she never let other people's opinions temper what she enjoyed herself.

She would need to be careful, but that didn't mean she would be overly cautious. Too many people let life pass them by while they hid away.

There was still considerable work to do. She would need to talk to someone who took the financial statements from the casinos. If there was something illegal about the numbers submitted to the IRS, these people would know about it. That was what they were paid for, after all.

Although who was paying them was up for interpretation. She would need to be extra careful and perhaps find someone who didn't do the paperwork for the casino but would know where to find it. The IRS always did like it when someone brought their attention to taxes that weren't paid.

They even paid whistleblowers a percentage of the money gained. Maybe next time, she could afford to come on her own dime and even gamble a little.

She pulled her phone out of her purse and searched her contacts for the name of someone she'd talked to about these kinds of matters before.

"Jan? Hi, it's El. You know the one. I have a favor to ask you and I need to do it in person. Maybe over dinner? Do you know any nice places in Vegas? Perfect, I'll see you there."

Elisa stood from her table and indicated to the barista to charge it to her room. She noted a man's gaze following her. An expensive haircut, expensive watch, and expensive suit all told her of someone who had expensive tastes. Yes, it was boringly repetitive, but expensive seemed the only word that applied in this situation.

Her kind of guy. She smiled when he realized she was staring in return and he smirked before he took a sip from his coffee.

Still smiling, she made sure he had something to stare at as she made her exit from the coffee shop. There were benefits to wearing a tight dress, after all, even if she was looking to display the business-casual look.

And maybe if she ran into him later, she could do a little gambling anyway and she wouldn't even need to charge it to her room.

She really did love her job.

CHAPTER FIVE

Niki had never been inside the Pentagon before. There were things that were simply never called for in someone's line of work, and even visiting it had never been on her bucket list. She knew what happened in there so there was no real need to play tourist.

Still, she did have some preconceived ideas and it didn't disappoint. The security was as impressive as she thought it would be. There were all the hoops she needed to jump through, starting with the car ride during which people checked her history like they hadn't done their research already.

They needed to be thorough, of course, but it was a pain in the ass to have questions thrown at her about every single detail even though they had the answers in front of them.

By the time she climbed out of the car they had sent to pick her, Jansen, and Maxwell up, she felt like she had been stripped bare and picked clean like carrion attacked by vultures.

At least they'd left the bones. She scowled at the entourage that waited for her outside, ready to resume picking at her to make sure there was no chance that she would betray anyone when she was inside.

"I'm sorry about the little song and dance, Agent Banks," a short man with a bald patch in his graying hair and a potbelly said as he removed a pair of sunglasses. "You understand that people in our position need to be thorough about your commitment to our country without question. It's not that we doubt you..."

"*Doveryai, no proveryai,*" Niki replied with a small smile. "Trust but verify, goes the old Russian proverb. That's not raising any red flags for me, is it? Using Russian proverbs like that."

"If that were true, Reagan would never have been allowed any knowledge of classified information, Agent Banks."

"It's not agent anymore. Or yet."

"I leave the ceremony to people who give a shit about it. Now, let's get this over with. I need to have a conversation with you and it's too fucking hot to have it outside." He strode into the building and left her to the mercy of the security teams, much to her silent indignation. The least he could have done was smoothed the way, but perhaps this was part of the gauntlet of measuring her commitment.

She couldn't help but agree that getting out of the heat was paramount. Metal detectors and a hundred different checks to make sure she wasn't a Russian spy provided her with her next challenge. Finally, an aide greeted her and guided her through the winding halls of the massive building until they reached a large office without a nameplate.

The door was open and the same man who had greeted her outside the building waited for her in the blessedly air-conditioned room. He toyed with what looked like a miniature of one of the older armor suit models and sat directly in front of a massive window that took up most of the back wall. The shades were drawn but even so, she doubted that an RPG could get through the glass.

"Agent Banks, I'm so glad to see you made the cut to walk these hallowed halls." He stood with a little effort, proffered his hand for her to shake, and gestured for her to take a seat. There were two comfortable chairs on the visitor's side of the desk and he joined her on the second one. "I'm sorry for not introducing myself outside but there are people who insist that my position here at the Department of Defense be kept at least slightly secret. I'm Rick Speare, liaison to the Joint Chiefs of Staff—the kind that makes sure they hit all the right notes."

"CIA?"

"That is not important right now. What is important is that you know we've followed your career with a great deal of interest. You're one of the best in the business."

"Which business might that be?"

"Operation direction. And while there's probably some kind of director's chair in your future, you'll show us how well you handle operations here inside the United States."

"I'm more of a field agent."

"I know, which is why we selected you for this partic-ular assignment. Keeping track of your operatives will see you in many different and exotic locations, and we would be remiss if we appointed a bean counter to the position. You have people who are loyal to you and who you trust to run these kinds of operations in secret. In turn, they need substantial funding to operate in that fashion."

"Fair enough."

"Now…can I offer you something to drink?"

"Are you asking so you have an excuse to dig into what I assume is an expensive bottle of bourbon in your bottom desk drawer?"

"It's actually scotch."

"Oh, well, in that case, I'll have a glass. Do you have ice here?"

Speare chuckled, stood, and moved behind his desk. He retrieved what looked like a damn good bottle of scotch and two crystal glasses and after another pause, a small container of ice from what sounded like a mini-fridge behind the desk as well.

With studied care, he dropped two cubes in each glass and poured three fingers of the auburn liquid. He handed her one before he settled into his seat.

"So, let's assume that you and I will meet every quarter or so to discuss your needs and overall performance and what we can do to improve it if needed. We're putting considerable trust in you, Agent Banks. Or should I say Special Agent in Charge Banks?"

"That sounds about right. Now, will we discuss the details of what exactly you and your…superiors, I guess, are trusting me to do while I work for the DOD?"

"I thought your former boss already covered that."

"Again, I can't overstate how vague he was when he

described it. The way he talked made it sound like someone would show up to arrest me or something."

"Which I guess explains the cold reception Jansen and Maxwell received."

"Yeah, sorry about that."

"Even so, I suppose your paranoia will be an advantage in your new role."

"Which is…"

"Oh, right. Well, I'm sure Jansen told you this operation used to be more for the gathering of intelligence than anything else. Of course, by the time our intelligence was filtered down the political pipeline, bodies were already dropping and we needed people like your team to step in. So, after a meeting and far too many pictures of dead bodies, the idea of a team directly attached to our intel was green-lit. Which…yes, we're aware that sometimes, the monsters you killed weren't exactly the kind that came from the Zoo and that's fine as long as tracks are covered."

"I have no idea what you're talking about."

"Of course. Anyway, if we go back to the beginning of our little operation, there are a literal shit-ton of companies, corporations, and conglomerates that are aching to get a piece of the action coming out of the Zoo these days. It's become the next billion-dollar unicorn that everyone wants to bleed dry. Of course, you of all people know that blood keeps coming. I don't know if you're old enough to remember the Internet boom from the early double-aughts and twenty-tens, but yeah, there's a company springing up every five minutes that promises a miracle age elixir based on what is yanked out of that fucking jungle."

Niki took a long sip from the scotch in her hand and

grunted softly in appreciation. "Right. Where did the name 'Zoo' come from? Is it a clever play on the sheer number of animals in there?"

"I think it originally came from the locals calling the place the Kudzu, which means something in one of the local languages but I can't remember what, exactly. Anyway, back on topic, those companies, corporations, and conglomerates are sometimes run by people with no morals, and others are run by people with no brains. Many times, the result is the same. It was our job to find out who the immoral sons of bitches were and contain them but now, we have to deal with the idiots too. Take, for example, your first problem child."

He stretched to the desk and retrieved a mission dossier which he handed it to her.

"Problem child?" Niki raised an eyebrow.

"It's a figure of speech. The issue has been contained but now, cleanup is needed since our local intelligence has revealed that problems might leak out. Anyway, this occurred Tuesday. Yeah, three days ago Tuesday."

"The day I was fired Tuesday."

"Right. Now, aren't you glad we started recruitment two weeks ago?"

"So, I was right in assuming you guys are the ones who got me fired."

Speare smirked, finished the last of his scotch, and poured himself another couple of fingers. "Technically, you were the one who headed to Italy and organized the death of one of the heads of *La Cosa Nostra*. Which, if we're honest, is probably the best decision you ever made for your resume. It's really why I sent the intel to your boss in the FBI."

"To get me fired?"

"To open opportunities for you with alternative agencies. Thankfully, we were perfectly placed to snatch you up before someone else did."

Niki shook her head and placed her glass on his desk. "Did anyone ever tell you that's more than a little cold-hearted?"

He leaned closer, took a coaster from the side of his desk, and placed it under her glass. "Sure. But the people who hired me are well aware that cuddling isn't exactly my strong suit, which is why the problems I'm called in to solve generally mean most people think of me as a bastard for the sake of the country. My headaches don't need a gentle, loving touch—simply put, they don't have a heart."

"What if I happen to have a heart?"

The man coughed on his scotch and after a few seconds of recovery, he began to laugh. He continued until his whole body shook and he needed to put his glass down to keep it from spilling. She grew annoyed by his amusement.

"I could have a heart, you gaping, prolapsed anus."

"Forgive me if I have doubts about that. You send your best out into the field with the full knowledge that they might die out there. It takes someone with something missing in the empathy department to send humans out to deal with monsters on a daily basis. Hell, you even manipulated your best man, McFadden, into sacrificing his life for the cause. Only blind, dumb luck had a helicopter drop and cover him enough to leave him alive. Barely alive, but still."

Niki had many ways to disprove him and she opened her mouth to explain precisely how wrong he was and in how many ways. As she did so, though, she realized that Speare really did think she was a cold-hearted bitch. He had read reports from people who had a similar mindset and came to the conclusion that she was the same cut of asshole that he was.

And who was she to correct him? He'd clearly done his research into her, right?

She sighed, leaned forward to pick the bottle up, and poured herself a little more. Her expression carefully inscrutable, she twirled the ice in the drink before she took another sip. "Well, there's nothing in the world like the feeling of getting the job done, no matter what."

"So, now that's out of the way, we can talk about the nitty-gritty. You'll find an operation like ours has...a slightly different approach to HR matters, so don't expect the usual documents and endless signatures. The most pressing order of business is that we need to go over the team you'll choose to send into an underground testing area."

"My first thought is McFadden and his squad."

"Really?"

"He is the best. They don't call him the Cryptid Assassin for nothing."

"I always thought that was a randomly assigned code name."

Niki shook her head. "You know that randomly assigned code names are all shitty. When you get something that cool, you have to earn it. And he has."

"I guess. He still holds the record for the most trips into the Zoo, you know."

"Yeah, he never ceases to remind me. As it turns out, he's kind of a gaping prolapsed anus in his own right."

Speare laughed again. "I guess that's why you and he get along so well."

"Get along is a strong term. Mutual tolerance is a little more accurate."

"Fair enough. We'll need paperwork to get them paid too. Do you happen to know his going rate at the moment?"

She shrugged. "An idea, but I'll need to contact him directly to get an exact number for him and his team."

"You'd best get on that. As I'm sure you're aware, time is of the essence in this particular situation."

The discussion was obviously over, and Niki rose when he did and followed the aide who had miraculously appeared. Her first instinct was to call Taylor immediately, but something held her back. Perhaps it was only her inherent mistrust—and the fact that she'd been so recently fired and scooped up by the DOD—but she felt it would be wiser to see how the next couple of hours played out.

She couldn't delay the call indefinitely, but she could use the next few hours to make sure this wasn't one of the too good to be true scenarios that inevitably resulted in a crash and burn scenario.

CHAPTER SIX

It was a little more complicated than simply bringing Taylor and his people on board to work for the DOD.

She didn't doubt that he would want to work for them, even though he probably had things against the people who ran it—him and Bobby. Still, given that they were looking at what was a blank check, within reason, she had a feeling he would go for it.

It had been a while since she'd called him in on a job. Ever since Italy, in fact. If Vickie was to be believed, the man was more than happy to remain at his business and keep doing that, but with memories of what he had been capable of in their missions together, she doubted he would leave it all behind if he could help it.

He was a little possessed—or was it obsessed? Either way, he had explained to her that he wouldn't rest easy with monsters hanging around so close to home.

No, she wasn't worried about Taylor. Even Bobby wouldn't be a problem. The man was more scared of the monsters in the Zoo than anyone else she knew, but he would go to the ends of the earth for Taylor if the ginger asshole asked him to. Tanya would be right behind him.

Her cousin would get nowhere near any of these operations, which was precisely where Niki wanted her.

But they needed someone to play the part of the man in the van—the technical support.

And, of course, Niki used the term "someone" very loosely in this situation.

"Who is this Desk you're asking to have transferred from the FBI?" Jansen asked and studied one of the papers she had pushed closer to him.

"Not who," she corrected him. "What. An experimental AI program I used as a handler for my operatives in the FBI. It was highly classified but very useful."

"We have our own experimental AIs you can use. There's no need to draw them from the FBI."

"Believe me when I tell you that you don't have any quite like this one. I was told I could assemble my own team."

"Within reason. The FBI will ask questions."

"It was part of my task force and it'll refuse to work with anyone else. Desk is vital to the operation."

Jansen took a deep breath. Niki could tell that he had begun to have second thoughts—or that those second thoughts had plagued him for a while and only began to show now. The DOD people had done their research on her. They wouldn't have given her the job if there hadn't been a thorough vetting process.

That said, she had the feeling the man opposite her had been one of the voices against bringing her on board. He did look competent and it seemed Maxwell had been brought in to keep him safe and alive. Although, they were both highly trained and the kind of men she would have liked to have on her task force if they weren't reporting on her to Speare. There was considerable work to be done, and she couldn't do it if they second-guessed her every choice.

"Sign the paperwork," Niki insisted and nudged it a little closer to him. "You said you would judge me on my results. That starts once I have the right team."

He sighed deeply to show exactly how unhappy he was with the decision before he scrawled his signature on the piece of paper and passed it to her. "I hope you know what you're doing."

"That's what this whole thing is about, right?"

Elisa knew she would find the trail. Corporations always needed to put in tons of it to make sure the IRS knew not to give them a hard time for sustaining the economy of the country.

She merely hadn't thought it would be so easy. Someone had been lazy or was paid off. It was one or the other and she couldn't tell which.

Of course, dirty government officials made a better story than incompetent government officials. She wouldn't push either story, even if she knew one was better than the other, but she always enjoyed waiting for the pieces to fall into place and show her exactly what happened in a way that would allow her to work through it all. They wouldn't do that by themselves, though.

It was one of the most gratifying parts of being an investigative journalist.

Unfortunately, she couldn't be that all the time. There was only so much she could do in a day before she felt a little burnt out. Her bosses would never tell her to take a break, a breather, and come back to it with a fresh mindset. They wanted her to put in as much work as possible.

She had learned to recognize when she needed a break and to take it at the right time. It was a part of keeping herself healthy. She put her laptop in the room safe and stepped out of her room, made sure to lock it, and headed to the elevators. Regretfully, she would probably hold off on visiting the tables and instead, simply go out for a drink. It would be good to have something to help her relax and unwind after most of the day spent hunched over a laptop.

A couple of hotel workers exited the elevator as it arrived, smiled politely at her, and walked in the direction she'd come from. They didn't carry anything to bring to the rooms and there was no housekeeping cart she could see. Maybe they were there to help someone who had been locked out of their room?

But since when did that take two people?

Elisa narrowed her eyes as a bad feeling crept into her gut. The elevator moved slowly toward the ground floor. She stepped out, cautiously avoided a crowd of drunken vacationers who surged toward the casino, and hurried out of the building to where she could call a taxi. There were apparently nice dance clubs in the area that she had thought were worth checking out.

She had been to Vegas before but it had been as part of

a bachelorette party, which hadn't allowed much time to take in the sights.

When she emerged on the street, she realized that the man she had noticed earlier in the coffee shop was waiting for a cab too. He turned to look at her and a small glimmer of recognition touched his eyes.

"Hi." She had never been too timid to make the first move. "From the coffee shop, right? I'm Elisa."

"Tiago," he replied with a chuckle and shook her hand. "There is a long wait for a cab tonight. I think there must be an event in town."

"Do you want to share one?" Elisa asked.

"You don't know where I'm going."

"Do I need to?"

He tilted his head and shook it gently. "I guess not. There's a party at my friend's penthouse. I'm not sure if I'm allowed a plus one, but we can always try?"

She smirked. "Sure, why not?"

Suddenly and too quickly for her alarm to register, a large, black SUV pulled up in front of them and he moved in closer. Something cold and round pressed against her ribs.

"Get in the car and don't make a sound," he whispered in her ear.

Elisa had always known it was best to resist in cases like this. Robbery was one thing, but when her life was in danger anyway, it was better to resist and make as much noise as possible.

Unfortunately, that knowledge didn't translate into action and before she could fully grasp what was happening, she was shoved into the back seat of the car. The man joined her and shut the door so the SUV could accelerate away from the casino as quickly as it had arrived.

"What do you want?" she asked and looked at each of the four men who were in the vehicle with her.

Aside from the man who had pushed her inside, they all appeared to be bruisers with over-developed loyalty and flexible morals like she'd seen in reports about mobsters brought to justice.

"You've asked too many of the wrong questions lately, Miss Fallaci," the man said with his revolver still pressed against her ribs. "It's time you got all the answers you've been looking for. Straight from the source too."

Niki looked up when the door to her office opened. Jansen and Maxwell stepped inside and shut the door behind them.

Calling it an office was something of an exaggeration. Even a workspace wasn't appropriate for the tiny conference room that no one had been using at the time. It would have to do until the official processes had completed and she was set up in a location she could make her own.

Then again, she would probably simply shunt around the country with very little time spent in DC. It was very likely she wouldn't even have her own office and if she did, she wouldn't spend many hours in it.

Maxwell took a seat across from her while Jansen moved to the screen on the far side of the room and connected his laptop to it.

"We have updates on the facility we've been monitoring.

There isn't much information about what's inside there, unfortunately. The corporation involved with the situation refuses to share details, citing trade secrets. Of course, people are fighting it on that front, but it's tied up in a messy legal battle in the DC Court of Appeals. That could take months and might end up costing lives until they finally decide to do the right thing."

"I guess that's what I'm in here for," Niki noted and picked up the file Maxwell passed over the table to her. The same information was displayed on Jansen's screen, but there was something about having the actual, physical paper in her hands that made her feel a little more grounded in reality.

"Indeed. You'll need to call your team in for this. Many people have tried to get into the files on the base, but the whole place is locked off the grid. All data files need to be accessed from inside."

"What kind of a base are we talking about?"

Jansen pressed a couple of buttons on his laptop and brought up pictures of the location in question. "It's an area that was set up in Southern Arizona, back when that was all the rage and the real estate value of the area was still low. Anyway, they've put in numerous additions, including dozens of underground levels where most of their testing is said to have been performed."

The fact that the base was set up in one of the more wooded areas of the state concerned her. The goop always flourished when there was a good source of biological material to grow from. "Said to have been?"

"Again, all the details are thoroughly tied up in legal disputes. We have seven different blueprints of the base's layout, and none of them match our radar scans of the facility."

"So, what exactly am I expected to do here?"

"You'll head into the building, clear it of all surviving test subjects, and collect all data from the local servers. That second part could be a little tricky since they may try to wipe the data before you reach it. It's imperative that the servers are secured but you'll have to do this at the same time as you make sure there are no escapees. Getting the information out quickly would avoid the politics that could get in the way."

"Right. What exactly happened there?"

He called up various reports. "Last Tuesday, there were calls to the security company that was supposed to prevent this kind of thing. Those we've seen were all labeled 'containment breach.' They stopped about fifteen minutes after they started and all surviving personnel were evacuated. Of the hundred and fifty who were inside, seventeen made it out. Those who did were immediately locked up until they signed punitive non-disclosure agreements that keep them from being able to make any official statements to the authorities. They were all given severance packages in the realm of millions and cut loose."

"Why are these people so desperate to keep what happened in that testing site a secret?"

"They have a large number of government contracts—almost exclusively, actually. I assume there are details about the breach that would compromise those contracts extensively."

Niki nodded slowly and leaned back in her seat. There were many interesting details to be read up on, but she had a feeling the most intriguing secrets would be found once they were inside.

"I guess it's time to assemble my team," she muttered softly.

"Indeed. Disposing of the monsters is, again, your highest priority."

"Right, alongside the data retrieval," she reminded him and smirked when he merely shrugged. "To dispose of them, you'll need to dispense some of that cash everyone keeps mentioning—flight tickets, transport arrangements, and weapons. Most of it should be sent to Vegas, I think, except for— Did you manage to acquire that software I requisitioned?"

"The FBI wasn't too happy about it, but yes. It's set up in our servers and is awaiting activation pending Speare's direct authorization. Depending on when that comes through, you might not have access to the AI for this mission."

"When, not if?"

"Based on assumptions of his trust in you, when."

Niki acknowledged that with a sharp nod.

"Let me know when you want transportation to Arizona."

Niki drew a deep breath. "As soon as possible. I want to be there to help to engage the setup before the rest of my team arrives."

Jansen disconnected his laptop from the screen and he and Maxwell moved to leave the room. "I'll email you the details as soon as I have them."

"Thanks."

She settled into her seat, watched them leave, and

rubbed her chin idly. It was good to be surrounded by competent operatives—the kind who knew full well what the stakes were with what they were dealing with.

But if nothing else, it showed how high the stakes were for her. This was make or break for her career. If she failed in this—and if Taylor failed her in this—there would be no takers for her particular set of skills. At least, not in the US government.

CHAPTER SEVEN

About fifteen minutes into the ride, they pulled a black bag over Elisa's head, although she wasn't sure why they bothered. She had been through a similar experience before and it didn't take too much brainpower to realize that they took four turns and returned to the casino where they'd started from. Maybe they didn't know she had been in this kind of situation before, which meant they hadn't done their research.

Or maybe they simply didn't care.

The car pulled into an underground garage. She assumed it was mostly empty from the sounds of the tires squealing and echoing off the walls around them.

The SUV halted, and heavy hands grasped her shoulders and hauled her out of the car. They walked through hallways and the men practically carried her for the latter section, which made her heels fall off.

It was too bad. She had picked them up during a sale and they looked exactly like Fiocchis but with small alterations. They were from a market near her apartment in Chicago that made a ton of money selling good rip-offs.

She could always pick up another pair, she told herself. Assuming she made it that far, of course.

Elisa didn't want to think of the possibility that she wouldn't make it out of there alive. It was difficult, but she didn't want to turn into a crying puddle of uselessness that would simply be left to die. The first step into despair was one she refused to take. She wouldn't allow anyone to force her into that.

The walking paused, the hands set her down, and a metallic door clicked open. She was pushed forward again and moved blindly with the bag still over her head as they stopped her and shoved her onto an uncomfortable metal chair.

She took long, deep breaths to steel herself for what she would have to go through next. They wouldn't stop her search and they had to know that. Someone would pick her laptop up and everything she had gathered would be out in the open.

Unless there were two hotel workers who had broken into her room and the safe and gotten their hands on her laptop. That would make things considerably more difficult to deal with.

She sighed softly, shifted awkwardly, and tried to find some way to make herself comfortable on the chair. If they already had what they wanted, why were they taking her through this? Did they really think she needed to be intimidated, at this point? Despite her resolution, she was afraid. Her hands shook, her heart pounded, and she needed to use the bathroom. She couldn't possibly be more terrified than she was now.

The bag was pulled off. The room she was in was mostly dark and only a couple of lamps here or there illuminated the black tiled walls. No, not tiles, she realized. Those were sound-proof squares. This was a room probably designed in the good old days when the mob had free reign of the city of Las Vegas and they beat card sharps and tried to make a solid living out of funneling money through their casinos.

That was a long time ago, though. She hadn't thought anyone would still think it was the good old days.

Three men were in the room but the younger, handsome man was missing. The bruisers had been in the car with her and all looked like they were more than comfortable with the lack of anything even remotely legal or moral in the situation.

"Do you expect me to talk?" she asked and a tear trickled unbidden down her cheek. She sniffed. "Do you want me to be scared? Because I'm fucking terrified."

"Well, that was the idea behind bringing you here," a voice said as the door opened slowly. The man who stepped in could not have been more different than the three who were inside already. He was dressed in a tailored suit that could easily have been the most expensive on the market and wore an impressive watch and an expensive haircut. He could have been a brother to the young man who had baited her into getting into that damned SUV.

"Who the fuck are you?"

"Names aren't really important at this stage." He

chuckled and sat on the table across from her. "I did want my friends here to give you a traditional Italian welcome to the city of Las Vegas, but I don't think we have the time for that. So, here's what will happen. I will ask you some questions and you will answer them."

"Do you think I'm scared of you?" Elisa could hear the tremble in her voice and the condescending smile that touched his lips said he'd heard it too.

"Me? No. I'm not the kind of guy to get his hands dirty —literally or metaphorically. But my friends, on the other hand...yeah, you've already admitted you're scared of them. And while we can safely remove all ideas of you ever leaving this room alive out of your mind, you will leave it far quicker, much less painfully, and in fewer pieces if you simply tell us what we want to know. Does that sound fair to you?"

It didn't, honestly—nothing was fucking fair about being kidnapped and threatened with death—but she could agree that the option he presented was preferable to the unspoken alternative. She wouldn't give him the pleasure of hearing her say that, though.

"Now," he continued, "you can tell me why you're sniffing around my hotel and casino. Let's start with who you are and who you work for."

Niki had a long to-do list before it was time to leave, and it would be the wrong kind of uncomfortable for everyone if she was tardy for her flight to her first mission as head of this DOD task force. A car waited for her in the underground garage, and she had to head to the airport soon. While her first instinct had been to contact Taylor immediately—the hour or two she'd allotted to finding assurances were up—she wanted to see what an on-site assessment revealed. If they needed anything over and above what she had already requisitioned, she could arrange for this to travel with the team and by her reckoning, they could still make it there within the forty-eight hours specified.

Time, however, was running out and she needed to get there so she could take control. As her first mission with the DOD, she definitely didn't want to fuck up.

Thank goodness she didn't need to go through the whole damn gauntlet of checks she'd endured on her first visit. She had a card she was required to swipe in front of the heavily fortified guardhouse with two burly guys who probably had a small arsenal tucked under their desk. From what she knew of their types, they were probably aching for something to do.

Although probably not along the lines of having to spring into action, she reasoned. Still, they needed to be ready for that kind of thing. She wondered what drills they ran to prepare and where they did them. There couldn't be many locations on Earth that mimicked the fucking Pentagon.

They asked her to hold up before she proceeded to her car. She couldn't tell what they expected her to do until two men walked out to join her.

"If you thought you would leave on your own, you were sorely mistaken," Jansen stated, flashed his badge to the guards, and walked through.

She rolled her eyes as she followed them to one of the

SUVs in the DOD fleet.

"So, did they buy three plane tickets?" she asked and slid into the back while Maxwell took the driver's seat and left the shotgun seat for his partner. "Or are you guys merely coming along in my luggage?"

Jansen shrugged and pulled his seat belt on. "Didn't you read the email?"

"I didn't get an email."

"Oh…well, read the email. That'll answer all your questions."

They drove out of the garage and past another level of security before they were on the open road.

"Well, if this doesn't remind me of old times," Niki noted and retrieved her phone. Sure enough, an email waited for her. "Now I only need a gun in hand and to hold it against Tweedledee's head over here, and it'll be exactly how we…met…"

Niki's voice trailed off as she read the message, then read it a second time. It wasn't a plane ticket like she'd expected but rather a confirmation of how her paperwork had been fully processed. The details were interesting enough, but as she studied what exactly would be at her disposal while at the head of the task force, her surprise continued to grow.

"Holy shit," she whispered.

"I know, right?" Jansen chuckled. "The salary isn't fair when you compare it to what our brothers in the FBI make. The DOD is about as good as you can get while still in the service of your country."

"Well, hell yes," she admitted. "But that wasn't what the holy shit was about. Is this all correct about the task force resources? The vehicle fleet, the transport...holy shit, do we actually have a plane?"

"Oh, yeah, that was a new addition. The DOD holds a whole fucking shitload of them in reserve for the use of specialized task forces. Like yours, now that I think about it. Anyway, you can thank the military defense budget, which the DOD gets a piece of. How do you like that spending of taxpayers' dollars?"

"Well, at least this cash will save American lives," she pointed out. "So, we'll fly to Arizona in our new personal plane, right?"

"I thought it would be a good idea to break the baby in," he replied. "Unless you have a better idea?"

She shook her head. Sometimes, it was wiser to not have any better ideas.

Taylor wasn't sure why it had taken so long for them to set the gym up. He honestly should have simply paid the extra few bucks and had the professionals assemble everything. Still, once they were done, there was a certain amount of satisfaction that came from looking at the fruits of their labors.

Next time, though, he would let the professionals handle it. Bobby, Tanya, and Vickie were better at their current jobs than they were at reading the instruction manuals. The damn things were harder to understand than they needed to be.

After a nice long workout, it was apparent that they had put everything together in the right way. His whole body was left with the pleasant kind of burning ache that came after a hard workout in the gym.

And he hadn't even gone to the gym, he reminded himself with a grin.

He took a little longer in the shower than he usually did and enjoyed the water spraying over his skin, after which he went through his early morning routine. The process was virtually automatic by now—trim his beard, comb his hair, brush his teeth, and finally, pull clothes on before he wandered down to the shop.

It no longer surprised him to see Vickie still in front of the computer. Bobby always came in and left at the same time every day, like clockwork, and he and Tanya had begun to come in and leave together more and more often. Not that he minded. It was nice to see the two of them hitting it off so well.

Of course, Vickie wasn't one to be governed by such a small thing as a schedule. She tried to be around during their business hours to deal with calls from the Zoo, mostly because that was where most of her paycheck came from.

But sometimes, she stayed all night and seemed to not care that she didn't get enough sleep. Well, it was her choice and he wouldn't be the one who told her she couldn't stay.

"Morning." Taylor grunted and rubbed the feeling into his sore muscles. "Will you head to campus tonight or do you plan to crash in your old room?"

"I thought that was Tanya's room," Vickie responded and didn't bother to look away from her screen.

"She's spent more time at Bobby's than here. I can't say I blame her on that score, though."

"Yeah, Bobby has a nice place. Besides, I think they're cute together."

"I wouldn't put it quite like that but sure, let's call it cute. Anyway, do we have anything on the docket for tomorrow?"

"You know, the usual putting together of weapons of mass destruction. Nothing we haven't done before. Oh, a message was left for you while you were working out. Someone called Rod wants you to call him about a developing situation."

"Someone called Rod? Do you not know who that is by now?"

"Of course I do. I wasn't aware of any reason why you would be on speaking terms with the asshole, though, so I wanted to see if you would try to cover it up."

"You're always trying to trap me, aren't you, Vickie?"

"I'm only looking out for you, Tay-Tay. I want to make sure you don't get into bed with the wrong people—metaphorically speaking. And I don't want to get involved in any way with your love life. I get the feeling that even talking about it will give me an STD."

"That's probably wise. Did Rod leave a number to call back on?"

"I already sent it to your phone."

"Thanks."

Taylor moved into the gym area and dialed the number he had been sent.

It rang a couple of times before the call was answered.

"Rod Marino's phone," said a pleasant, feminine voice.

"Yes, hi. I'm returning a call."

"Mr. McFadden, I presume?"

"That's what they call me."

"I was instructed to give you a message regarding a problem Mr. Marino thinks you might be able to handle for him."

"Nothing else about it?"

"Only a set of coordinates you should visit within the next couple of hours if you plan to at all. If not, you likely shouldn't get involved."

"Cryptic and vaguely threatening. Send me the coordinates via text and I'll see if I can help Mr. Marino with… whatever the fuck he's itching about."

"Of course, sir. What should I tell Mr. Marino about your plans for the evening?"

"Are you asking me out on a date?"

The woman paused for a moment, possibly to let him think about the comment. "I'll tell him you're currently undecided."

"You do that." Taylor couldn't help a small smirk as he hung up and tucked his phone into his pocket. He had planned to get an early night's sleep, but if he had to deal with the mob boss who couldn't mob boss right, it was probably best not to leave the man waiting.

"Fucking shit," he grumbled, walked into the shop, and grimaced when he realized Vickie was still there. "I'm heading out. Try to locate me if I'm not back or haven't called in the next couple of hours."

"Do you want me to mount a daring rescue?" she asked as he climbed into the four-by-four.

"Sure, but if we plan on that rescue working, you might want to call Bobby."

She pouted. "That is hurtful."

"And accurate. See you later, Vickie!"

CHAPTER EIGHT

He knew that heading out alone to meet the man who not that long ago had sent trained killers out to deal with him and his staff probably wasn't the best idea, but Taylor felt he could handle whatever was planned. The coordinates sent to his phone were for an area some ten miles outside of Vegas. From the Google maps image he could get of the location, it was as abandoned as a grave-yard site could be. If the man planned to kill him, he had made an intriguing enough suggestion about it.

Still, it was probably best not to go in there with only his dick in his hands. He drove the four-by-four in a small detour to the parking garage he still had a couple of months on. When he arrived, he drove in next to the van he had left there.

It wasn't far out of his way and he'd made the trip a couple of times in the past now that the investigations had wound down to nothing and the authorities seemed to have lost interest in him. He still took a slightly circuitous route and checked constantly to make sure he wasn't followed because he knew better than to simply assume they were in the clear. At the same time, he also needed to check on the suits and cash that had been stashed in the location to make sure nothing had happened that might need his intervention.

He pulled the lighter of the two armor suits out and put the pieces on quickly. It had been one of Bobby's more inspired moments to alter the suit based on ideas he'd received from a colleague. He was a fan of the leaner, lighter design, especially as it connected to what looked like a motorcycle helmet as an HUD.

It was bulkier than not wearing a suit at all but still small enough to allow him to drive in a larger car like Liz or his four-by-four without too much difficulty. He climbed into the driver's seat of his vehicle and took a moment to adjust to the added weight of the armor on his body. He could tell that the shocks took the brunt of the weight well enough, and once he was satisfied, he started the engine and headed out.

Taylor doubted that Marino trusted him at all, and the feeling was mutual. If it came to blows, he would have a small advantage with the suit that the man probably wouldn't expect.

Or even if he did, it would take a damn anti-tank rifle to get through it. With that kind of protection, he liked his chances—or at least the fact that those chances had been significantly improved.

He felt more comfortable now that he was in it, for some reason, and he leaned gently on the accelerator. He needed to move a little faster if he wanted to be there for whatever the fuck Marino had planned.

Conner didn't like his job much, to be honest, but at least he had one. There weren't many options for someone who had been dishonorably discharged for the kind of shit he'd done while serving his country. From his limited choices, this was the best and easiest he had available to him.

But even he had to admit that some jobs were better than others. Simply waiting for the opportunity to be used as nothing more than a blunt instrument wasn't quite what he wanted to be paid for. Gene kept him around as the kind of person who would intimidate everyone else into compliance, but that only meant he would get a larger cut of the money that came in.

In the meantime, he merely kicked his heels with the rest of them.

Bonnie was smoking in the corner like she usually did when she had nothing else to do, while the rest of the gang —Ty, Bags, Kevin, and Turner—played a round of hold'em poker. He would have joined them but he was saving up to put work into his car and bring parts in from Japan. What he needed did not come cheap.

That added to the fact that he wasn't that great a gambler meant he had to exercise self-control and save the fun and games for when he had a little more cash to throw around.

Conner looked up from his phone when shouts came from the poker table. Turner had won her third hand, it appeared, and none of the others were willing to let her continue to deal the cards.

They fell short of accusing her of cheating, though. It

would have been odd, he thought, until he considered how those kinds of accusations tended to go down. Very clear orders had been issued to not start any more fights, and if there was anything they feared more than Turner's knife skills, it was their boss' explosive temper.

Gene was the kind of guy who would make almost anyone careful around him. Like most countries, there was probably any number of great people in South Africa, but when someone came with the kind of credentials he had, there was no telling what he was capable of.

He had heard about the man when he was still in the US military, and it had been one atrocity after another. No one could verify if any of the claims were true, of course, but most people would be reluctant to question the man on whether or not he had led a raiding group into a small diamond mine in central Africa and flooded it with the workers still inside.

That kind of curiosity might end with your arm chopped off and you left in the bush to fend off anything that might be hungry as best you could.

And in this neck of the woods, that might not mean regular predators either. He didn't believe the rumors that Zoo monsters had started to spread into the Savannah—not with so many nations focused on keeping them constrained within the wall—but he'd learned to be open to all possibilities. While highly unlikely, anything might be possible, and the wise man lived longer.

Gene stepped out of his office and suddenly, every voice in the building went silent. The tall, powerfully built man with his blond buzz-cut scanned the room as if to measure the worth of the people in front of him.

Conner wasn't sure whether he was angry or not. It was almost impossible to read the guy. He could have left his office because people were making too much noise or because he wanted to join the card game.

"Listen, you *bliksemse poephols*," the man announced in his trademark Afrikaans accent. "We have a new job just come in. It's not the easy pickings around here, mind you, but the kind that has a *lekker* payday."

So they weren't in trouble, Connor decided. Bastard assholes was almost affectionate in his boss' vocabulary. He pushed to his feet and rolled his shoulders slowly. He also knew by now that in the context of work and money, *lekker* meant far more than simply nice or enjoyable. "What's the take, boss? Weapons?"

"Something like that." Gene placed a few papers that had been faxed to him on the table.

This had to be one of the only corners in the world that still used a fax machine, he thought as he wandered to the table and studied them.

"It looks like an American entrepreneur has become a thorn in the sides of the other American companies working in the Zoo by delivering cheap work when they want to keep the prices high," their leader explained for the benefit of the others who remained where they were.

"Cheap work gets a man killed in the Zoo," Bonnie noted, put her cigarette out, and flicked it through the open window where she stood. "It means there won't be people left alive to pay after a couple of trips in."

"The work isn't cheap," Gene corrected her. "Only the cost, which is lower than they like. We have a client who's willing to put fifty thousand dollars American on the line if we *gooi* a spanner in their proceedings. It sounds fair, *ja?*"

"What kind of spanner?" Bags asked. Conner happened to know that the larger man spoke and wrote better English than almost anyone in this tiny building, himself included. Unfortunately, a small matter of being knifed in the jaw three years before in his home town of Abuja had left him with an almost permanent slur since it had never been attended to properly and so never healed right.

Their boss scratched his jaw. "They have armor suits being shipped to the airport outside of Abuja—the kind of airport that don't have much security, *ja?* There'll be a few government troops there, but they will carry the guns, not wear them if you get my drift. Point and shout a little at them with real weapons, and they drop what they have."

"How will we know when to hit the airport?" Bonnie queried.

Gene shook his head. "That's not a worry. We'll get a call from the client to tell us when the next shipment will come in, which container to take, and how many will be guarding it. We'll know when, where, and how to take them on. There's no *komplikasies* and no government blow-back. No *focken polisie* or army or whatever will come and try to get stuff back that was stolen from a small-time American dealer—not unless the dealer comes out and try himself maybe, *ja?*"

Conner narrowed his eyes. He didn't like dealing with the companies that worked out of the Zoo, mostly because they were the kind to stab their people in the back if they needed to. The only reason why they would call on someone like Gene was if they already had ideas on how to get rid of him if they had to down the line.

"What we do with the material once we have it?" Bags asked and rubbed his injured jaw.

"He will pay fifty thousand American to get rid of the suits," the boss explained.

"What a waste." Conner shook his head. "Depending on the quality they send, they could be worth a quarter of a million American dollars, easily."

"Or more," Bonnie agreed.

"What say we sell them?" Bags suggested. "There are plenty of tiny-dick-tators who make their living in this part of the world. We could let them know we have top-level American hardware on the line we need to unload quick and steady. Seriously, we could charge them through the nose for hardware like this. There aren't many suits available outside the Zoo these days, not unless you're willing to deal in scrap and shit."

Gene scowled deeply as his people made suggestions and once again, Conner couldn't tell what was going through the man's mind. Would he simply shout at everyone to shut the fuck up, or would he take their suggestions seriously?

An uncharacteristic smile crossed the large man's face as he nodded slowly. "*Ja,* I see this happening and I like it. Why can't we make bucks from both sides in this case? I know some contacts who can help us if we need it and who want to get their hands on American hardware like that. If we use our *kops* to plan property, there's no reason for us to only clear fifty thousand on this job. It's about time we earned a little *bansela—fok,* Bonnie, bonus. It means bonus.

Now stop looking so *verdomde* confused and get on the phone lines. See who might have the money to pay us for the work."

"Yes, boss," she snapped, stood quickly, and jogged to the phone in the corner of their shack.

"The rest of you *manne*, stay alert and be ready," Gene ordered. "When we get the word, we move in ten minutes. I won't miss out on this because we aren't *focken* ready, *verstaan julle?*"

They nodded to indicate that they had the message loud and clear and he strode into his office and slammed the door behind him.

"I can't ever get a proper read on the guy," Conner muttered, and the other members of the team agreed.

Still, a job like this had surely put him in better spirits than usual. It had done wonders for his mood too, given that was enough money to get a whole new car if he needed it—provided it was all split nice and evenly.

CHAPTER NINE

I t was a long drive and thankfully, one that didn't have
that much traffic to deal with once Taylor was beyond
the city of Las Vegas. The desert wasn't visited often and he
could understand why. The dry heat meant it was impass-
able without a car during the day, and the way the temper-
ature dropped during the night made it dangerous to move
through since hypothermia was a very real danger.

Which was why the local organized crime organiza-
tions liked to use the deserts as a way to dispose of people
they never wanted found. It would be years until even a
trace of a body was located unless law enforcement knew
precisely where to search, and even that didn't assure
success.

He could only hope Marino did not intend to try to
dispose of him. His hope had been that all their fighting
and bickering was a thing of the past, but if he now had to
bury the man in the desert, it would at least be easier to dig
graves with the light suit of armor he wore.

The four-by-four eased off the two-lane road he had

traveled on for the past fifteen minutes and moved into the desert, following the coordinates. It explained why a simple address hadn't been used in this case. Another mile and a half brought him to the meeting location.

It was immediately apparent that he wasn't the target—or, at least, not the only target. Two SUVs were parked in the middle of nowhere and five men stood in the open. Three looked like they were the muscle of the operation. They could have been O-linemen for the Las Vegas Raiders if they wanted to.

The other two could not have been cut from a more different cloth. Marino was almost unmistakable, although Taylor would have thought the man would choose to keep himself isolated from these kinds of situations. Maybe he merely wanted to be involved in the dirty business of his work for once.

The second man looked like he could have been the mob boss' brother, and it certainly appeared as though they had the same barber and tailor. He held himself back, though, as if he tried to distance himself as far from the action as possible.

It wasn't until Taylor was much closer that he could see a sixth figure—much slighter and kneeling in front of a suspiciously grave-like hole that had been dug in the sand.

He pulled the four-by-four to a halt next to the SUVs, climbed out slowly, and tried to not look like he wore a mechanized suit of armor. It was difficult, especially when he didn't wear the helmet. With no HUD to control the hydraulics, the best he could hope for was that he could be able to fine-tune the adjustments on the fly and by feel. It wasn't the best but it would have to do.

Even so, it looked like Marino wasn't fooled. A small expression of confusion crossed his face for a moment before he realized that Taylor had come armed and ready. The three bruisers they had brought seemed impressively tough, strong, and physically fit, but with his suit, he could still bench-press all three of them and maybe one of the SUVs besides.

Although that would push the hydraulics and magnetic influences in his suit a little too far.

"Taylor, nice of you to join us," Marino shouted and gestured for him to approach. "I have something of a problem."

"Does this problem have anything to do with the woman kneeling next to what looks like her grave?" he asked and scanned the area. "Did you make her dig it?"

"I considered it, but it would take her too long. No, there's a small machine in the back of the SUV that's designed to dig graves. It's used mostly in the smaller cemeteries but is very useful in these situations. Do you approve?"

"Not really. Did you call me here so I could witness you killing her or because you want me to join her?"

The man laughed. "We have put our differences aside a while ago. No, I merely thought you would want to be involved because the origin of this problem I have to deal with is you."

"Why would you think that?" he asked and took a few steps closer to the woman, who shifted a little on her knees. "Are she and I related somehow?"

"In a manner of speaking."

She could hear him approach and twisted in an effort to

see him through the bag over her head. *"Figlio di puttana! Mangia merda e morte!"*

Taylor's eyebrows rose. "Huh, she's a scrappy character. Does she speak any English or did you call me here to be your translator? Because I can tell you right now, I spent a year in Italy in the exchange program but most of what I learned—or rather what I retained—was the kind of language that shouldn't be used in polite society."

"Really? You understood her?"

"I'm fairly sure she assumes my mother's profession had her spending most of her time on her back with her legs spread, after which she hoped my last meal would consist of a solitary fecal course."

Marino chuckled. "Very good, although I should tell you that my Italian is a little better—bordering on considerably. My mother insisted on teaching me and my brothers the language of her homeland, although my father preferred that our first language be English."

"Tua madre è anche una puttana!" the woman snapped again.

"Yeesh," Taylor muttered. "Will you let her talk like that about your mom?"

"Eh, why stop her? It's not like she's wrong. She had affairs with three of my uncles while married to my father as well as countless other men."

"Does she know this for a fact? Or, to avoid misinterpretations, is she a member of your kind of lifestyle?"

"This one? No."

"Then who the fuck is she?"

"That is a good question. I've taken her picture and her fingerprints, but according to my sources, she isn't in any of the criminal databases, either here in the US or from around the world."

"Does she speak any English?" Taylor dropped into a crouch beside her. She didn't notice that he'd moved closer or maybe didn't care.

"She did earlier when she thought she could still glean information and live to tell the tale. As I recall, she asked me why I thought I could get away with stealing my own money and trying to pass it off as a robbery. The only time I remember being robbed of money was when you did it, so I thought you might want to have a word with her before I kill her."

"And why would you think that?"

"Idle curiosity. You'd be surprised at how boring Vegas can be when you're the one who runs all the games."

"*Puto cabezamierda coño pinche pendejo cabrón!*" the woman shouted and struggled against the restraints that kept her hands tied behind her back.

"Did you understand that?" Marino queried.

"It's Spanish, and I know that a little better. Although it should be noted that it's probably a Mexican dialect since *pinche* doesn't quite mean the same thing as it does in the European dialects."

"So, we have a polyglot on our hands," the mob boss muttered. "Fantastic. She has the potential for a great deal of trouble if she continues to dig into my business, and we don't tolerate trouble. You may have gotten away with punching well above your weight because you have significant friends and are quite powerful in your own right. She has no such associations."

The woman fell silent, which indicated once and for all that she did know what he had said about her.

"Why do you want me here?" Taylor asked and deliberately avoided using the man's name. There was no way he would let this woman be killed, and that wasn't an option if she knew who Marino was—if she didn't already, of course. Mitigating the kind of disaster that loomed would be how everyone walked away from this alive.

"Well, again, given that you're the one who drew her to Vegas in the first place, I thought you might want to have a say in how to handle her," the other man told him. "I'm not the only one involved in what she was up to so I thought you might want to have a go."

"You know I'm not the kind of person who simply executes people for being a problem, right?" He raised an eyebrow in challenge.

"I have fairly compelling evidence to the contrary."

"You're still alive, aren't you?"

Marino paused for a few seconds. "Point taken. So, what do you want to do with her?"

"I have contacts who should allow me to dispose of her without getting her killed and in a manner that would mean she won't be a problem from this point forward. Does that sound good to you?"

The mob boss raised an eyebrow. "Do I want to know what'll be done with her and by whom?"

"Not unless you want to join her."

He nodded slowly. "All right, I can see how that would work out best for everyone. As long as you can assure me there won't be any problems with this in the future."

"I won't make you any promises. I know better than that. What you can do is climb into those SUVs and drive away. You will have already retrieved and trashed all the data she collected that might be embarrassing for you so you can leave the rest to me. I'm as invested as you are in a quick and clean resolution of this and my option will be as efficient as your final solution. Leave this with me and neither of us should have anything to worry about from her in the future."

After a few seconds of thought, Marino smiled and motioned for his men to return to their vehicles.

"I appreciate it," Taylor grumbled and turned his attention to the woman, who waited quietly and nervously for the two men to finish their discussion about they would do with her.

"You know how I like doing good deeds," the mob boss said and waited until his men had mounted up. "And if I provide you with an annoyance in the process, I call that a win-win. How did you like that bottle I sent you?"

"It was...damn amazing," he admitted.

"I know, it's one of my favorites. Anyway, *arrivederci,* and I wish you all the luck in the world."

The man climbed into his vehicle and waved once more before he closed the door and both SUVs accelerated away.

Taylor scowled and rolled his shoulders in the suit before he focused on the woman who remained silent and simply waited helplessly.

"Shit." He hissed through his teeth as he yanked the bag off her head. Her mascara was smudged and she had been crying. She looked at him with an expression that screamed pure hate, although the quiver of her bottom lip undermined that.

"Come on," he mumbled and helped her to her feet, although he didn't cut the zip ties that bound her hands behind her back yet. "Let's get you the fuck out of here."

CHAPTER TEN

Technically, Taylor didn't have people who would handle the problem for him. He had a person—one he didn't look forward to talking to at the moment, but there wasn't much he could do with the woman seated in the back of his four-by-four until he'd made the call.

It wasn't his style to treat people like this. He was used to letting them do their thing and if that happened to include hurting someone he cared about, he would interfere. If they intended to hinder his plans, there were many ways to make them quit that didn't include their death.

That was usually the last resort unless he was dealing with Zoo monsters. In that case, first and second resorts automatically went out the window.

Niki was the one who usually stepped in to help when he needed to deal with people without killing them.

He pulled his phone out and pressed the quick-dial number the agent had given him to call if he was ever in need of help. It had probably been given in case Vickie was in any kind of trouble, and it would route through Desk to reach whatever phone was closest to Niki.

The hacker had explained the process to him. It had been surprisingly complex and involved considerable language he didn't understand, but that had been the gist of it.

"Yeah?" said the familiar voice on the other end of the line.

"Real classy. You should think of doing voice-over in children's movies," he replied with a grin.

"What?"

"You know, the kind with animated, anthropomorphized animals that go on adventures and get into exciting situations around the world. They teach children valuable life lessons while sneaking in a couple of mature jokes to make it a valuable experience for the adults who take their kids to watch the movies."

"Cut it out. What is so important that you had to call me right fucking now?"

"Oh…well, I have a slight problem I need your help with."

"Is Vickie okay?"

"Yeah. And I'm fine too, by the way."

"I don't care about you."

Taylor sighed. "Fine, whatever. But can you be a lamb and help me with my problem anyway?"

"I'll be lamb chops first. But if you go ahead and tell me what the problem is, maybe I can get you out of whatever issue you've probably gotten yourself into."

"That's not entirely fair. Technically, someone else got me into it but whatever."

"Yeah, right. What's the problem?"

The woman in the back seat perked up. "*Hijo de puta pendejo cabrón!*"

"Let me guess…that's your problem?" Niki grumbled. "What happened? A date gone wrong? A girl didn't like how you didn't match your Tinder profile and you had to gag her before she spilled the beans?"

"That's not the problem."

"Are you telling me that's never happened to you?"

"Yes! And also, that's not the point so maybe try to stay focused?"

It was her turn to sound exasperated. "Ugh, fine. Put me on video so I can see what the situation is."

Taylor set the phone up on the stand which would allow her to see the back seat before he turned on video sharing between both lines.

"Oh, for the love of— Why does she have a bag over her head?"

"For one thing, I didn't want her to see where we're going. And secondly—"

"*Métetelo por el culo!*" the woman shouted again.

"That. She screamed profanity for the first couple of miles and only stopped when I hooded her."

"Well, take it the fuck off," Niki shouted. "Have you thought about the kind of trouble you would get into if you are pulled over with a hooded woman in your back seat? There ain't nothing I can do to keep you out of jail for that, dumbass."

"Whatever." He growled annoyance and left the car on auto-pilot for a few seconds while he stretched into the back seat and hauled the hood off the woman's head. The tears were gone, for the most part, and all he could see was the pure loathing in her eyes.

"Damn it. What the fuck obsession do you have with Hispanic women?"

"What?" Taylor spluttered. "I don't... You don't...that's not what it is."

The woman sneered. "*Preferirei scopare un maiale.*"

"Wow," he responded. "Now that is hurtful."

"Okay, Italian-Hispanic women." Niki rolled her eyes. "And wait, do you speak Italian?"

He shrugged. "I picked up a few things here or there. Mostly only the stuff that's not safe for work—like how she said she'd rather fuck a pig."

Niki smirked. "Well, she has good taste then—or better taste than most of your sexual conquests. Anyway, what happened and how the hell did she end up hooded and, I assume, zip-tied in the back of your car?"

"I saved her from being buried alive—or maybe dead— by our local faction of *La Cosa Nostra* as a favor to me," he explained. "She's been asking inconvenient questions."

The agent nodded. "Okay. Have any of those questions been in English?"

"I...imagine so. I haven't heard any, though."

"Right. Can she see and hear me in the back there? If not, connect me to the car's speaker and I'll be able to have a quick chat with her."

Taylor did as he was told but shook his head slowly. "Oh, I have a bad feeling about this."

"How so?" she queried.

"I merely have a feeling this won't end well."

"Bite me. Now, you. Yes, you Hispanic-Italian chick who's into pigs, for some reason, I need you to listen to me very, very well. If you understand English, this is the part where you show it. Because if you speak any language that's not English, I'll find the most hostile place in the country whose language you're speaking, slather you in honey, and leave you as lunch for the ants. Nod if you understand."

The woman's jaw tensed and after a moment's thought, she nodded.

"Good, because if you haven't noticed, Taylor might be a brand new and improved kind of asshole, but I'm your worst fucking nightmare. Trust me, I have friends in all kinds of useful places, especially black ops. You can be assured that I have access to about fifteen different nasty sites where you could be dropped and never heard from again. Your friends and family will be sold a story of you running off with a male stripper from Vegas courtesy of your current government administration."

"Wait, what?" he asked and narrowed his eyes. "Black ops?"

"Shut up," Niki snapped, and he did as he was told. "Now, in English, explain to me what the fuck you think you're doing tangling with the fucking Sicilian Mafia. And why I shouldn't tell Taylor to plug you with two in the head and leave you to dissolve in three different fifty-gallon drums full of acid in the middle of the Mojave Desert."

Taylor's eyebrows raised in surprise. It wasn't like he wouldn't do it if Niki told him to—the woman had gotten him out of enough problems with similar tactics and if that was the only solution, so be it—but that didn't alter the fact that she had begun to scare him a little bit.

Apparently, it worked on the woman in the vehicle as well. She leaned back a little and the hatred in her eyes assumed more of a terrified look. "Okay. I'm not… First of all, I didn't know that I was tangling with the Sicilian Mafia. I'm Elisa Fallaci, and I'm a reporter for the Crypto-Inquirer. We've worked on finding stories that are a little more relevant to an open audience than talking about what might or might not be happening in the Zoo or beyond. Investigating the robbery that happened here in Vegas seemed like a good place to start. You know, since they used mechanized armor suits that are supposed to only be in use in the Zoo."

"Fucking hell," Niki muttered. "I knew that shit would come back and bite you in the ass."

"Could we not share potentially damaging secrets in front of the fucking reporter?" he snapped.

The agent paused for a moment when she realized her mistake. "Oh, right. Shit. Sorry about that."

"Yeah, fucking great agent you are."

"Do you mind if we get back on topic?" she demanded.

"Wait," Elisa interrupted, leaning forward. "You were the one who robbed the casino? I knew it! I knew the mobsters stole their own money."

"Yeah, you don't have the full picture, darling," he informed her.

"Taylor, shut the fuck up!" Niki shouted.

"And thanks to you and that other asshat," Taylor grumbled, "she now knows my name. Since we're letting all the cats out of the bag in this little talk, you should know the mob boss and I were in the middle of a small disagreement. That robbery was meant as a show of force to make sure he knew to stop fucking with me or he would meet the sour end of a mech too."

"So, were you actually in the Zoo?" Elisa queried. "How do you have access to the mech suits? Did you bring them from the Zoo or did you build them yourself? Are you wearing one right now or are you that bulky naturally?"

"Dude," Taylor chided while he glared through the rear-view mirror. "Read the fucking...well, car, I guess. You're not the one asking the questions here."

"Right," Niki interjected. "Put the bag on her head again. She's starting to annoy the shit out of me."

"Seriously?" He scowled and flashed his unwilling passenger a quick glance.

"No, not seriously, you dumb fuck. Remember what I said about the police?"

"Right."

"Well, I intended to call you in the next hour or so anyway, so we can kill two birds with one stone and—"

"One bird," he said and noticed the woman wince.

"Fuck. Shut up and listen. Avoiding any details, you should know that I have abandoned my prior place of employment and have been elevated into another section that would allow me more access to our particular kind of business. I can't tell you about it, but let it be known that I'll need your services and that of a small backup team in about...forty-five hours to deal with an issue that has arisen."

"Right. And what am I supposed to have done with this reporter by then?"

"Who am I, your mother?"

"No, you're not a tall, red-headed diabetic who's allergic to soy."

"And thank goodness for that. You accepted the problem from Marino, so you deal with it."

Taylor rubbed his eyes as he stopped at a red light. "Again with the fucking names."

"Shit, right. But that doesn't matter because I've already dealt with your dirty business for you in the past. Remember how you intended to torture and kill those men I neatly handled for you?"

"I should probably take you off speakerphone," he responded acerbically, conscious of the woman listening avidly in the back seat. "You had to deal with them since you wanted me to work with you. Besides, those guys planned to burn my business down."

"And so does she. Metaphorically speaking, of course, but no less effectively. She doesn't care about you, only the glory and Pulitzer prizes you'll bring her."

Elisa scowled when she heard that. "Do you know how much of a bitch you can be? Have you ever heard anyone say that before?"

"Sister, have you ever seen a human being getting shit out of an alien monster?" Niki snapped.

"Technically, you haven't seen that either," Taylor reminded her.

"Shut up." The agent sounded like she had become more and more riled up by the second. "And you, reporter lady, can also shut the fuck up and let the adults talk."

"Wait, I'm an adult?" he asked and slid the vehicle into gear.

"In this case, and in this case only," Niki conceded. "Okay, I can't talk right now—my two fucking babysitters clearly believe they've left me alone for too long. Deal with the Hispanic-Italian problem and be ready to move in about thirty-six hours."

She hung up and left him scowling in the car as he pulled up at another red light.

"I still can't have you seeing where we're going," he said, picked the head bag up, and reached into the back seat again.

"I don't give a shit where we're going," Elisa retorted and tried to pull herself away from him. There wasn't anywhere for her to go, though, and he yanked the bag over her head. "Fuck you and the horse you came in on. Has anyone told you that you're a piece of shit?"

"On a daily fucking basis and in a wide variety of languages. I don't suppose you know how to curse in French too?"

"Why, do you?"

"I picked up a thing or two."

"While working on the French base near the Zoo?"

Taylor's scowl deepened. "You know too much shit about the Zoo for a civilian."

"Did you miss the part where I've been reporting about the Zoo?"

"Shut up."

A short while later, he pulled the vehicle into the shop but made no effort to get out. Vickie was still at the computer and watched him curiously.

Finally, he sighed and slid out. "Look, I have to tell you something and I need you to take it in stride without offering me any sass or backchat."

She grinned. "Oh, Taylor, you know I can't make that promise."

"Yeah, I thought so. Anyway…" He opened the door to the back seat and pulled his passenger out.

The hacker's expression of amusement vanished immediately. "You know, I don't think it's okay to kidnap women. Unless…is this a weird sex role-playing thing?"

"No, and I didn't kidnap her. In fact, I kept her from being killed by the people who did kidnap her."

"And yet she's still tied up and with a bag over her head. There are some dots that simply don't connect here, Tay-Tay."

"Why do you keep calling me that?"

Vickie shrugged. "It's a reference to another Tay-Tay, also known as the greatest singer of all time."

"Please don't tell me you mean Taylor Swift."

"Hey, you should be flattered by the comparison."

"I'm not. Now, help me decide what we can do with this woman."

She moved closer, peeked under the bag, and laughed. "Come on, did you have to kidnap a mini-Niki? Seriously? Why couldn't you simply ask Niki out and save this poor girl some trouble?"

"I am serious. Now help me to decide what to do with her."

"Her is right in the fucking room," Elisa interjected.

"And does her have a name?" Vickie asked.

"Elisa…something." He shrugged.

"Fallaci," Elisa reminded him.

"Whatever." He scowled at her. "Let's put her in the meat locker for now and talk about what to do with her when she's not listening."

The reporter wasn't a fan of the idea but he didn't expect her to be. He left her hands tied behind her back but took the hood off before he locked her temporary cell from the outside.

"I appreciate you taking this seriously and with the utmost professionalism," he grumbled once it was only him and Vickie.

"You're welcome." She grinned at him while he began to take his mech suit apart.

"I could not have been more sarcastic."

"And I don't care. Will you keep that here now?"

"No, I need to take it back to storage. So, do you have any ideas on what to do with the reporter in there?"

"Oh. A reporter. That is not good."

"And one who knows we're responsible for the casino heist."

"Even less good. Can't Niki take her and send her to the Zoo to live out the rest of her days hunting and being hunted by the monsters?"

Taylor shook his head. "She apparently has a new job she wasn't at liberty to discuss. Although I guess that'll change since she needs me and a team to be ready at her beck and call in the next thirty-six hours."

"And will you be available?"

"You know me. I'm always down to play your cousin's games. And getting my hands on a massive paycheck for my trouble is merely the cherry on what I assume is a very tasty sundae."

"Ew."

"Yeah, that's what I think too. Anyway, keep an eye on our captive and I'll be right back."

CHAPTER ELEVEN

Of course Taylor would be back. This was his home and besides that, it made sense that he would want her to keep an eye on Elisa while he stashed the evidence of the crime of the decade safely in storage. Or, given that Niki needed them for a mission, to possibly gather the rest of his equipment. It was something of the problem that the evidence of what they had done would be needed in the event that he was called to fight monsters.

Vickie didn't know what he meant when he said he needed a team, but that was something he'd explain when he was ready. What was important was the fact that a reporter was currently locked in their meat locker.

To be specific, it was what had once been a meat locker but was now merely a room with the facility installed to cool large chunks of meat that would ordinarily be there.

Of course, if she was Elisa, she would no doubt wonder if she had somehow been caught in the middle of a serial killer movie where she was the one who died early to show the full danger of the psycho, who would later be cornered and killed by the actual heroes of the movie.

"God fucking dammit." She hissed belligerently, wandered to the small break room they had set up, and collected the leftover pizza. Once she'd stacked it on a plate, she retrieved a cup and some of the remaining soda and turned toward the meat locker. After a few minutes' thought, she took one of Taylor's guns in case the woman jumped her and tried to escape.

Balancing it all proved to be a little challenging but not impossible. Vickie, like many other people, had tried her hand at waitressing during her first stint in college. She'd learned to hold onto and perfectly balance as many things as possible while moving through a gauntlet of loud and annoying customers. This would be a breeze.

She pulled the door open and paused to look at the reporter, who hugged the wall at the back of the room. The woman had, however, somehow managed to wiggle her limbs enough to get her legs through, so her hands were now tied in front of her. While the attempt was a source of concern, it fortunately meant she wouldn't have to remove the restraints so her captive could eat.

"Don't worry," the hacker assured her. "I won't hurt you."

"So that's what the gun aimed at my head is supposed to do," Elisa retorted. "Reassure me?"

"Well, it's mostly for my benefit since it'll hopefully stop you from trying to jump me and escape, but whatever you want to think is cool. You do you. I only came to bring you food."

"So, what? Are you trying to fatten me up for when the butcher gets here?"

Vickie paused to place the food and drink on the ground before she straightened with the weapon still trained on the woman across from her. It was a little uncomfortable and it felt too big for her hands, which were more used to toting a keyboard.

"Why do you think a butcher will come here?" she asked as she backed away from the food.

"This is a meat locker, yeah? The kind used to store dead meat in. It makes me wonder how long you guys plan on me being living meat."

"What? No." The hacker shook her head. "We're only... This used to be a grocery store and this is the only room in the building that locks from the outside, so it's the only place we can keep you secured while we decide what to do with you. No butchering, no killing, and nothing for cheap horror flicks to use as inspiration. Promise."

"Yeah, I won't take the word of one of my kidnappers," Elisa retorted but she looked a little more relaxed and advanced on the pizza once her captor had almost reached the door. "Thanks for this, though. I think it's been twelve hours since I've last eaten."

Vickie nodded. "We're not the bad guys in this. Okay, maybe we're not really the good guys either, but there isn't much room for good guys in our line of work. Think of us as anti-heroes."

"Yeah, I'll be sure to remind my readers about how you guys aren't the bad guys when I write this story," Elisa murmured from around a mouthful of pizza.

"A story you'll only write because my dumbass of a boss decided to keep you alive for some reason."

"Your boss who is on friendly terms with a mobster, for some reason."

"Well, friendly terms isn't quite right. It's more like speaking terms and it hasn't been that long since they were at each other's throats. He sent people to kill us and we had to kill them to protect ourselves. Taylor elected to steal millions from that same mob boss as a warning to remind him who the fuck he was dealing with. And shit, why am I telling you all this?"

The reporter shrugged. "I have one of those faces people like to talk to for some reason. But it doesn't matter, I knew most of that already and had deduced the rest. So, if you guys don't intend to kill me, why not let me go? You know there's nothing to gain from keeping me locked in here indefinitely."

"Sister, if you think I give two shits about the situation you got yourself into, you're in for a rude awakening. As far as I know, you did shit that made you deserve to get whacked. The only one who has any heart for your particular situation is Taylor, so you are kind of half-fucked already—and not the Taylor kind of fucked. The bad kind."

"What is the Taylor kind of fucked?" Elisa asked. She had already wolfed down one of the pizza slices and took a break to sip the soda.

"You know—the kind that starts with a dinner and a movie and ends with you questioning your life choices while he's in the shower."

"Right. He's single, then? I thought he might have been in a relationship with the woman he called earlier."

"Niki?"

"Is that her name?"

"Shit!" Vickie exclaimed. "But yeah, they both wish. Not that it matters. Enjoy your meal!"

"Wait—wait!"

Elisa's calls didn't stop her from locking the door again. She could hear the sound of a four-by-four pulling up again, and it wouldn't be long before Bobby came in to start the day either. Maybe a couple of hours, but still. Taylor had all kinds of explaining to do.

As she stepped out, the hacker realized that two vehicles had pulled in. Taylor had returned in his truck instead of the four-by-four and despite the late or early hour, he had called Bobby in too.

And of course, bringing the mechanic meant bringing Tanya too. Both looked a little tired and annoyed over the situation but none more so than her boss. The man did look like he could use a good night's sleep.

"Thanks for coming in early, Bungees," he said and shook the man's hand firmly and Tanya's too. "We've had a situation and we'll need all hands on deck for this one."

"What, no 'thank you for keeping an eye on our kidnapping victim, Vickie?'" she asked and raised her hands in a questioning gesture.

Tanya and Bobby both looked surprised by this news.

"Kidnapping victim?" the bulky mechanic queried.

"Yes, definitely, thanks for that, Vickie," Taylor replied without so much as a hint of sarcasm in his voice. It was like he was genuinely thanking her or something. "And yeah, amazingly, having a kidnapping victim is only one element of why we need all hands on deck for this one."

"I assume you expected this from your attitude," Tanya pointed out. "But why do we have a kidnapping victim at all? Is it a woman? Is it a date gone from fairly bad to much, much worse?"

He did not look amused. "No, and why do people keep asking me that?"

"It's a reasonable assumption," Bobby pointed out.

"No, it's not!" he protested. "And that's not the fucking point here."

"You still haven't answered the question of why we have a kidnapping victim," Tanya reminded him.

"Marino wanted to kill a journalist for digging into the heist. I made sure he didn't. I don't know what to do with her, but we do need to decide in the next thirty-six hours because Niki will probably fly us somewhere to deal with a monster threat. So, do you guys have any ideas?"

"Wait, so this is a woman who was kidnapped, right?" Tanya clarified.

Taylor narrowed his eyes. "Sure, but why do you ask and why do I detect a hint of judgment coming from you?"

"I think what my girlfriend is subtly implying is that you have a knack for picking up damsels in distress."

"Fuck subtlety." Tanya snorted. "I outright stated that."

Her boss opened his mouth to retort but his whole body relaxed and he rubbed his eyes, which Vickie could only assume were trying to close on their own.

"I'm too tired for this shit. On that note, how is Elisa?"

The hacker shrugged. "She's terrified but still trying to do her job as a reporter and picks up any details we happen to drop. I actually kind of like her. She's a little hard-ass that way."

"Of course you do," he commented wryly. "Do you have any ideas about what we can do with her?"

"Can't Niki give her a one-way trip to the Zoo?" Bobby interjected.

Taylor shook his head. "Apparently, that's not a part of her job anymore. She said something about friends in black ops and being able to move Elisa to one of their sites, but I think that was only hot air."

"Cut her loose," the mechanic suggested. "All she has at this point is nothing more than conjecture. She can't back it up since Marino would have already put work in to cover his tracks. While she might be able to tell a nice story, if any of it strikes us a little too close to home, we could always sue her for libel."

"That is a possibility," he agreed. "But Marino turned her over to me with the assurance that she wouldn't be any more trouble. If she ends up publishing a long op-ed about it, even without any proof to back it up, that would still be called trouble and could end with us at odds with the mob again."

"Bring it," Tanya retorted. "We've shown them we can take anything they dish out."

He rubbed his eyes again. "Yeah, we did, which means they know us better than before. I'd rather not risk it."

"Is there any way we can let her go with a promise that she won't print anything she learned?" Vickie asked. She didn't want to be involved in the business of kidnapping any more than they already were.

"I don't think so." Taylor did look like he was in the same mindset as her but rather tried to think of a creative solution that would end with everyone alive and as unharmed as they could be. "Like you said, she's a reporter and good at her job. She's probably in the meat locker mentally writing her story and imagining all the awards she'll win if she somehow gets out of this and manages to get it into print."

"Shit," Bobby grumbled. "So, let me see if I can get this straight. We have a reporter locked up who we won't kill and who could probably expose our whole operation. Niki can't get rid of her for us since she's involved in something she'll need our help with sometime in the next thirty-six hours. That means we have thirty-six hours to decide what to do next since we can't leave the woman here while we're gone. Have I missed anything?"

"Nope, that's about it," his boss muttered. "Vickie, your cousin wasn't quite at liberty to tell us what she was up to. Do you think you could find out what she's gotten herself into?"

"Probably," she replied. "Or I could contact someone who could fill me in on the details."

Taylor nodded. "Desk?"

"Yep."

"Get on that. In the meantime, Bobby, I'll need your and Tanya's help to get the suits we have on the assembly line finished and ready to be delivered with a special package by the morning since we need to get our other mechs ready for a fight."

"Do you need Tanya and I to be your support in this?" Bungees pushed away from the wall where he'd been leaning.

"Do you think you can handle that?"

The mechanic looked a little apprehensive but he nodded. "I've always got your back. You know that."

Taylor smiled and looked a little relieved. "And you, Tanya?"

She smirked. "I've always wanted to see what hunting looks like from inside a suit of armor that's been designed for the job."

"Fantastic." He rolled his shoulders and rubbed his triceps gently. "Let's get to work. The sooner the better."

The trio immediately started work on the suits they had on the line. There wasn't much left to do, fortunately, given that they had all been scheduled to be delivered for transport to the Zoo later the next day anyway. They mostly had to finish their repairs and close the suits, test them quickly, and package them for delivery.

It was the part of the work that Vickie knew Taylor found the most gratifying, but neither he nor the other two looked like they were enjoying their work very much.

Her frustration came from the fact that Desk didn't respond to her hails, which meant that either the AI was otherwise engaged or she was turned off for the night. The FBI wouldn't spare a dedicated server to keep her up and running all the time.

Vickie had tried once to get Jennie to install the AI onto a server that was separate from the FBI in case she needed to use it for jobs that weren't strictly legal but had no luck. That aside, she also wondered why Desk hadn't simply distributed her code to other servers without informing anyone. It seemed like something the snippy AI would do and the fact that she hadn't stirred all kinds of intriguing questions.

The trio completed their work less than an hour after Bobby had arrived. The sun had begun to rise and they quickly set the suits up in the corner of the shop while they worked to gather Taylor's personal arsenal. There wasn't any other word better than arsenal to describe the fact that he walked around with three weapons that turned your average squishy human into a literal tank.

Not much in the way of repairs was involved, but he wanted to make changes to those he had on hand to make sure they weren't recognized by anyone who might know about the mechs that had been used in the heist.

His caution was wise, especially since they had a reporter on hand who could blow the whistle on their whole operation.

The truck would be early. The alert came on Vickie's phone and informed her that they had a last-minute cancellation and the vehicle was available to pick the mechs up almost an hour earlier than agreed if they wanted it.

"Hey, Tay-Tay!" she shouted. "The truck's coming to pick up the delivery an hour early. Should I confirm?"

While he trusted her decisions, she had learned early on that sometimes, he had weird ideas about how to run his business. It was always best to check and double-check.

"Yeah, sure," he responded, thoroughly engrossed in the work he, Bobby, and Tanya were involved in.

Sure enough, the truck did arrive almost an hour earlier than they had planned but they were prepared. The work was done and it was simple to seal the suits with a little something extra from Taylor before they had them ready to hand over to the delivery company. From that point forward, everything was insured and covered.

Taylor looked a little more relaxed now that their business was done for the day.

"Vickie, did you get Elisa something to eat when she got here?" he asked and settled into one of the office chairs.

"Yeah, some cold pizza and soda. Should I not have given her anything?"

"No, it's not that. She's probably hungry again. Do we have anything to give her to keep her fed?"

"There's probably still cold pizza," Bobby noted. "I can get it to her."

"Thanks." Taylor turned his attention to Vickie. "Any word from Niki? Or Desk?"

"Not a peep. I'm still waiting on a return call since there's not much I can do to see where Niki is without breaking the law."

"Well, keep at it. Legally, of course."

"Of course." She stuck her tongue out at him and turned her attention to the computer in front of her.

Bobby stepped out to deliver the cold pizza to their prisoner, while Tanya continued to fidget with the mechs they had set up on the harnesses. She had learned how to do some of the repairs and not only the cleaning. It was how Taylor liked to work, a process in which everyone improved steadily and was rewarded for it too.

Bobby returned and oddly, still held the pizza. "So...you did say our prisoner was in the meat locker, right?"

His boss rose from his seat, sensing trouble. "Yeah, why?"

"Yeah, no. She's not in there."

Taylor knew better than to question the man's observational skills by asking him if he was sure and immediately turned to Vickie. "Has anyone left the building?"

"There's nothing on the sensors," she replied, although she made sure with a quick check on the software history. "Nope, no one's left the building. Not on foot or in the vehicle. You know, aside from the collection."

"No, that's not possible." Bobby shook his head. "She's probably still in the building. Let's look around here to see where she is."

"Vickie, stay on the sensors to make sure. Oh, and if she tries to jump you—"

She didn't let him finish and already held up the pistol she had swiped from his stash.

He nodded. "Right. Keep your eyes open. Your actual eyes, not your eyes on your sensors, understood?"

Of course she would keep her eyes open. What else would she do while she waited?

Taylor, Bobby, and Tanya moved out together, although they would most likely split up. There was considerable open area in the strip mall but not many places to hide. Vickie had set the sensors and cameras up all over the building for security purposes. The grocery store was mostly covered and so was the gym. The rest would be fairly simple to check as a team.

As the seconds ticked past and there was no word that they'd found anything, her anxiety began to build somewhat. Nothing triggered any of the sensors, which meant the reporter was better at hiding than anyone she had ever heard of. Or, she thought caustically, they had been a little too quick to discard what steadily became the only possibility.

Searching through the entire building took less than half an hour and the team assembled in the shop again.

"She's not in the building," Taylor asserted, the first one to give voice to their problem. "So, where the fuck is she?"

Vickie spun in her office chair a few times before she gathered the courage necessary to say what she had been thinking. "In the immortal words of Sir Arthur Conan Doyle..." She had no idea why she was suddenly faking a British accent. "'When you have eliminated the impossible, whatever remains, however improbable, must be the truth.'"

His scowl softened somewhat. "So she was inside one of the suits we shipped out? She was sealed inside and won't get out until they unload in Africa."

The hacker looked around and tried to decide whether that was good or bad news. Their prisoner had escaped. That was bad, right?

The way he suddenly smiled and began to laugh told her she was wrong.

"She's well on her way to Africa by now," Bobby added and also looked more relaxed. "It'll be a few days before she's out again, and the comms inside those mechs are still slaved to our links."

"It extends our deadline," Tanya agreed. "At the very least."

"Will she be able to survive inside a mech, though?" Vickie asked and looked at the others to assure herself there was nothing for them to worry about.

"She won't have any food but the mech is built to

recycle water," Taylor answered. "It's a little gross but she'll be able to survive. It's an automatic process, meant to keep the pilot alive even if the suit is disabled, so…yeah, she'll be a little hungry, but she'll survive. The problem comes when she gets out of the mech and calls this in."

"From Africa?" Bobby reminded them. "With no phone, no connections, and probably arrested for…like, people smuggling or something?"

"Still, we should work on a way to mitigate anything she might share about the heist. See what you can do about that, Vickie."

"Will do, Tay-Tay, but for the moment, you might want to answer your phone," she replied. He hadn't realized that the device in his pocket had buzzed for almost a full minute.

"Shit." He scowled belligerently and pulled it out, pressed the answer button, and put it on speakerphone. "Banks, you've got the team here."

"It's good to see you already have everyone gathered," Niki answered. "I should have called you earlier about this but wanted to be sure of things before I involved you and maybe wasted your time. Will you bring Bobby and Tanya into the fight?"

"That's the team I could bring in on such short notice, yeah," he grumbled. "Give me more warning next time and I'll be able to recruit someone else."

"And the problem you got yourself into?"

"It's handled, for the moment." Very wisely, he decided not to let her know that he had accidentally shipped someone to the Zoo.

"Good, because we have things to do. First, Vickie will

receive requests for information from each of you. If you want to be paid, I suggest you provide that right away. Also, I'm sending you transport to get to Arizona," she said.

Taylor narrowed his eyes. "What's in Arizona?"

"You know...the Grand Canyon, Monument Valley, the nicest stretch to drive on Route 66—oh, and a lesser-known cryptid-infested laboratory underground. Do you feel up to it?"

He glanced at his team. Vickie would remain, of course, and work as their eyes and ears, which left Bobby and Tanya as his support. Neither appeared to want to do this full-time but given the short notice, he couldn't ask for better.

"Yeah, we're fucking up to it," he asserted and teased a small smile from Bobby.

CHAPTER TWELVE

With three of them focused on the task, it didn't take long for the mechs to be readied for the mission ahead. The fact that they would go underground was important to know and something Taylor wished Niki had told them before.

Still, it worked out for the best. The suits they had available were mostly medium, which made them the best choices for more confined spaces anyway. Hopefully, something had been set up for comms, but he wasn't entirely sure it would work if they had to go too deep. It irritated him that the changed circumstances left him feeling a little unprepared.

He wondered if the agent's short notice was a result of being on a narrow time frame herself. She was working at a new job—or the same job with better perks, it seemed— and so probably had to make decisions and adjustments as she went along. If there wasn't much she could do to help him, she wouldn't talk about it. She wasn't the type to make excuses for her actions.

It sucked, but they would make it work. He had told her that she wouldn't need to send them transport. Flying still wasn't an option for him if he could help it, and Arizona wasn't that far away. They had Liz on the roster again, which meant they could transport their suits without the hassle of going through one airfield or another. Having to explain why they carried them and show all the authorization paperwork he had accumulated was a hassle.

In this case, driving would save them all time—thankfully, because he didn't have to discuss his insistence on avoiding airplanes yet again.

Even so, it was necessary to change the plates and give everything a new paint job. They couldn't take any chances that they might be pulled over and have cops jump them with mechs that looked like those that were used in the heist.

Niki was still on their side, obviously, but it wasn't a risk he was willing to take.

Vickie made the arrangements quickly to ensure they took the shortest route to the location they needed to reach and programmed it into Liz's AI. It wouldn't be long before they hit the road, and he wanted to be sure that nothing was left to chance.

Even the hacker with her impressive bag of tricks couldn't calculate police patrol routes, which meant they would follow the speed limit and try their best not to look suspicious. Stops were programmed in and breaks were calculated.

Taylor thought she enjoyed having this much control over their lives, but he decided not to give her any trouble about it. If they had to rely on her to be their metaphorical man in the van, they would have to trust her as well.

It wasn't long until everything was settled and he slid into the driver's seat, with Bobby in the shotgun position and Tanya in the back seat. She had no complaints and was already in a reclining position by the time they were on their way.

The mechanic's job was to choose the music, and Taylor instantly regretted it. The man was a fan of country music, for some reason, and even the newer, more poppy numbers were difficult to listen to. He would have to wash his palate out with heavy metal before the trip was done. Maybe having Tanya ride shotgun on the way home would help settle his nerves.

It wasn't a long drive. When they were halfway into it, Taylor's phone rang and displayed an unknown number as the caller.

Thankfully, it was sufficient excuse for him to get Bobby to turn the music down and he placed his phone in the slot to connect it to his car.

"Hello?" Taylor said like he didn't already know who was on the other side of the line.

"Good morning, Taylor," said Desk's familiar voice. "It is good to speak to you again. How have you been?"

"Well, I've been better but life goes on. How about you, Desk?"

"Same as it's always been, I suppose. I have been authorized to facilitate you in the completion of this mission from this point forward."

He smirked. "I look forward to working with you. Have

you thought about what you think will happen if Niki knows you have contacted me like this?"

"I assume she would be pleased since she is the one who asked me to do so. I am merely making sure you're on the right route."

"Vickie already programmed the route in. She scheduled every break we'll have and how much time we'll spend at each stop. I think she might have enjoyed that a little too much but it doesn't matter."

"Very well. I will update Agent Banks on your current location and estimated time remaining. Have a nice drive, Taylor."

"You...too..." He realized Desk was probably not driving but thankfully, the line had already cut off before what he said went through. Hopefully.

Even if it did mean they were back to strangling cats to the sound of an acoustic guitar and the occasional ukulele.

The journey proceeded smoothly since Liz did most of the driving, which allowed Taylor to read up on the situation that had developed. Niki had sent Vickie the details, who in turn, sent them to him.

All the hacker had received, though, was basic information about the location. The facility didn't have a name, and all mention of it had been classified—or, as she had explained it, was tied up in a legal dispute due to the fact that the company involved was more concerned with protecting company secrets than the lives that had been lost.

Before too much time had passed, they wound up the twisting roads that led them into the wooded part of Arizona. The AI wasn't programmed for driving in this area, which left him to do all the work to push Liz up until a group of SUVs parked outside a barbed-wire fence came into view.

He immediately noticed Niki's familiar figure and she coordinated with two heavy-hitters in the kind of dark suits you only got when the government entrusted you with keeping certain people alive.

Hell, they even had the little earbuds with winding wires that disappeared into the suits.

Taylor pulled Liz to a halt a little outside the cluster of SUVs and climbed out. The agent had certainly taken to her new role with aplomb and there wasn't anything about it that didn't suit her. She wore a pantsuit, and when he saw her with her hair tied in a ponytail, he realized that she did, in fact, look a little like Elisa. Not too much, he amended as he looked more closely. There was no familial resemblance but there was something there.

She finally turned to look at him, Bobby, and Tanya as his teammates dismounted from the truck and she waved them closer. A small tent had been set up, similar to the situations she'd been involved in while working for the FBI. Wires extended from inside and connected to the SUVs, likely setting up a small network that would allow them to communicate with whoever their controller was.

"Taylor, Bobby, Tanya, nice to see you all again," Niki stated quickly once they were all inside. The team focused on a small metal table that was covered in laptops, tablets, and papers that likely contained details of the situation of the underground lab they were about to assault.

Taylor folded his arms and waited for Niki to say what she had to say. It was clearly very important and would take precedence over whatever banter she had in mind for later.

"I'm sorry, but we won't indulge in any small talk," the agent continued and approached the table. Again, she directed them to come closer. "So, we'll get right into it. These are the two agents assigned to me, and they will both work to protect me since our job isn't exactly the safest of careers. However, they will also report on my actions and yours to my superiors in Washington. Jansen and Maxwell, take a bow."

Both men nodded to the new arrivals.

She smirked. "It turns out I have better protection and toys than when I was with the FBI. I guess our adventure in Sicily was a better job interview than we ever could have thought."

Taylor cleared his throat loudly and swiped his hand across his neck. "Ahem...ix-nay on the Ic-sillay alk-tay!"

The smaller of the two suits—Jansen, if he had their names right—smirked. "Rest assured, Mr. McFadden, that the Department of Defense is well aware of what I'm sure absolutely didn't happen during your mission in southern Italy."

"Right." He grunted. "Oversight. Fun times. Should we get back to the reason we're all here?"

"Yes, let's do it," Niki agreed. "Anyway, we'll go into the dirty of it. There are many legal complications you don't need to be made aware of. All you need to know is that there was a containment breach inside the lab where they were testing the goop on animals. At least, that's the assumption. A large number of people were killed inside those walls, and those who survived have been sworn to silence."

"The foundation for every successful business relationship," Bobby grumbled.

"Keep it up and I'll make you sign an NDA," Taylor replied with a soft chuckle.

"Yeah, because I need a piece of paper to tell me I need to keep my mouth shut about the dumb shit we do while under your employ," the man retorted.

He scratched his jaw. "That is a fair point."

"Are we done with the chit-chat?" Niki growled her annoyance.

Both men nodded.

"Right," she continued. "Anyway, we don't have access to any of the cameras and we have conflicting details on the blueprints, so you will essentially go in blind. You should also know that I have requisitioned Desk—I know she called you—but until my boss signs off on the transfer, she won't be available to help you down there. Once you get inside, we need you to do two things. The first is to kill every fucking monster you can find. The second is to connect to the isolated servers to give us access to what's happening inside. You need to find out how because, as I said, Desk won't be available to help you there."

"Like all of our early missions, then," Taylor noted.

"Yeah, basically," she agreed. "It should also be noted that extermination and data retrieval carry equal importance because we need details to be able to stop this shit happening elsewhere."

Tanya raised her hand.

MICHAEL ANDERLE

"This isn't class," the agent pointed out. "If you have something to say, spit it out."

"Okay. If we only have access to the outside as of right now, why don't we pump the air vents—which are exposed to the exterior, I assume—full of some kind of universal poison and kill everything inside that way?"

Niki clicked her tongue. "That's a really good question. Jansen, do you want to take this one?"

"Of course," the man replied. "Given that we don't know what's in there, it would be very inadvisable to pump anything in through the air ducts. As we are all aware, due to the nature of anything coming out of the Zoo—and especially pertaining to the goop—we'll likely see some kind of mutation or alteration that ends up with the monsters somehow stronger and more unkillable than before. No, I'm afraid the only option the DOD is willing to endorse at this time is lead poisoning, if you take my meaning."

"There you go. I couldn't have said it better myself." Niki began to collect the papers on the table and organize them more to her liking. "Now, unless you guys have any more questions, I propose we do like an annoying blond character in an impossibly popular sitcom show and suit the fuck up."

Taylor narrowed his eyes. "I don't think I get that reference."

"It's legen—wait for it..." Bobby countered, already on his way to the tent flap, "...dary." He headed out to Liz, where their mech suits were stashed.

"Oh, and try not to destroy the records," Jansen added as the others moved to follow. "Having them on hand would help make sure that breaches like this don't happen again in the future."

"Come on," Taylor grumbled. "Do I seem like the kind of guy who wreaks needless violence?"

The moment of silence made him look around at the others in the tent who stared at him, wondering if he had actually said that.

"I know, I know," he conceded. "Stupid question."

CHAPTER THIRTEEN

Taylor wondered if he'd missed this. He had been hunting in the recent past but the last time he'd gone out in a full mech suit had been when he used the monsters to kill someone else. Ever since then, it had merely been waiting around and working on mechs he sent out for someone else to use.

Which he was a fan of, no doubt about that, but at the same time, he couldn't deny that this was a part of who he was. Putting each piece of the armor on was preparation for a battle, a way to ensure he was fully equipped for the fight. Knowing what he was doing and that he could rely on the people he would go in there with was something he could honestly say he enjoyed.

While he could acknowledge that, he didn't enjoy it so much that he was willing to commit to the danger and horrors in the actual Zoo. A blind foray into a lab while he worked with zero intelligence of what might be inside was about as close as he intended to get to the alien jungle.

For now, and probably forever if he had his way.

"If these assholes keep bringing this kind of shit into the States, it won't be long before we have to deal with a brand new Zoo growing somewhere in the Everglades," he stated as he yanked the isolation tape around the lab loose to let them through.

"Yeah, like the fucking Everglades needs more monsters to take the real estate down there," Tanya grumbled as the trio advanced on the lab.

The building itself didn't look particularly impressive. It was only two·stories tall, a blank white building with no windows and only a couple of doors leading in and out. There did appear to be a parking garage that headed down behind the building, and Taylor guessed that the people who had worked there had lived in the structure too.

It probably made it much worse when the creatures went on the rampage. People living there meant many locked doors and isolated pockets of civilians who would not be able to escape if they were all living underground.

"Can you guys get a feed there?" Taylor asked once he'd opened a comm line to Niki.

"Yes, but there's no way to know if the radios will work down below, so… Well, you guys are about as on your own as you can be down there."

He nodded and turned to make sure his team was with him. Bobby looked appropriately on edge. The man had never been a big fan of the Zoo. He felt a little bad about pulling him into this, but the man was as much of a veteran as he could ask for on short notice and he would be solid when the chips came down and monsters attacked.

Tanya was made of sterner stuff, and she seemed a little more excited than her boyfriend was. She tested the different motions of the mech suit she was in as they walked. It wasn't like she was new to the controls as she had tested those they had repaired. She knew how to work them and she knew how to fight the kinds of monsters they would inevitably face.

Now was the time to see if the two skill sets would merge.

Taylor recognized the familiar tingle in his stomach as they advanced toward the building and veered to take a direct path to the central entrance. There was no sign of any creatures prowling the area around the structure, which was all the evidence he needed to know that whatever was inside still hadn't found a way to escape.

Yet, he reminded himself. It was only a matter of time until the impossibly intelligent monsters inside found a way out and began to kill people who had nothing to do with the cause of the problem at all.

"Don't worry," he told his teammates as he pulled the doors open slowly. A magnetic lock resisted him for a second until either Vickie or Desk managed to disengage it and allow them entry. It was best not to damage the door on the way in, not unless they wanted to leave a nice wide exit for the monsters to escape through.

"Don't worry about what?" Bobby asked and stepped through after him. He was quickly followed by Tanya.

Taylor had expected a little snark or sarcasm from the man, but when none came, he realized that he wanted to be reassured that there was nothing for him to worry about.

"We won't face any problems," he asserted as he activated the external lights on his suit to give them something to see by when the door shut. All the interior lights were off.

"Yeah?" Tanya asked. "What makes you say that?"

He shrugged and the movement was exaggerated by the suit he wore. "Well, the way I see it, the creatures we'll meet up with inside are reliant on their mobility and will most likely have sacrificed armor and power in favor of being able to move faster and be more agile. When we get in there, the hallways we'll be locked into will be a kill zone for us to work with. I'm not saying it'll be easy, mind you, but I do think we're going into this building with the advantage."

"Probably," she agreed.

Bobby had nothing to add to the topic, but he did seem a little calmer as they continued into the hallways. They moved through what had probably once been a security checkpoint area, where metal scanners and security booths still stood in place. It would have been the kind of location that would enforce a bored monitoring of the workers to make sure they knew they were being watched rather than actively enforcing anything.

Taylor steeled himself and glanced around for anything that might look like a computer or a database he could plug into using the little device Niki had outfitted their mechs with before they went in.

The best he could see was a couple of light switches. Moving with the lighter mech still took fine-tuning but he pressed the switches and a few fluorescent bulbs came to flickering life.

"Holy shit." Tanya gasped.

He steadied himself. "Niki, do you get any of this?"

"The image is a little fuzzy, but yeah."

The area was open and took up most of the upper levels of the lab in a pleasant atrium with planters, a fountain, and what looked like thick glass windows over the ceiling which had been sealed off with heavy steel slabs.

He could immediately see why. This was most likely where the evacuation had culminated. As he looked around, he could almost hear the alarms blaring in the back of his mind and people shouting, confused, angry, and afraid. Most of them had probably not seen any of the monsters. Some possibly thought it was a drill.

At some point, that had changed. The mutants had overrun the area. The air vents were missing their grills, which indicated that they had been where most of the attacks had come from. Doors had been torn from their hinges with evidence of claw marks where they had been ripped from the moorings.

The results were easy to see. He scanned what had once been pristine white tile. The area had likely been designed as a calming retreat location where people who had been cooped up in their labs all day came to rest, relax, have a nice chat, and gossip with their coworkers.

Blood was splashed across the whole area, now. It had been a literal bloodbath and coated the tiles, the walls, and the windows. He could even see a couple of specks trailing into the railings that protected the higher levels. The offices were probably up there.

Taylor tried to imagine the kind of emotional distress the occupants had gone through in the seconds where they had been sealed into their building. Their apparent safety had left them with no choice but to be torn to pieces by the creatures they had tested, poked, and toyed with not long before.

"How many people died in here?" Taylor asked, leaning in closer to one of the larger pools of blood that had since coagulated and dried out.

"Too many," Niki said. "The official story is that they evacuated all the humans, but as you can see, there are all kinds of holes in that story. The information we have from before they started their PR is that only seventeen out of one hundred and fifty made it out alive."

"Is this all from the humans, though?" Tanya asked. "It seems like too much blood to only be from them. Could it be from the animals choosing to do some infighting once all the humans were gone and there wasn't enough food to go around?"

"That is a good point," Taylor conceded. "Not that I think the monsters are the type to start fighting between themselves, but it does beg the question of what they've eaten in here. They're clearly omnivorous so they could find themselves without any food."

"How do you know?" the woman asked.

"Well, we know they have to eat and there's a finite amount of food for them inside this facility."

"No, I mean how do you know that they're omnivorous."

"The plants," Bobby interjected. "There were plants in the dirt all around here. They've been dug up and are gone too. It means the creatures started eating anything biological they could get their hands on. Or...paws or whatever."

"Yeah," Taylor concurred. "Well, enough sightseeing for

the moment. Let's find something that looks like a data point."

"This is where you suggest we split up, right?" Tanya asked and laughed nervously.

"Nope, we'll stick together on this. We aren't on any kind of clock that I'm aware of, so there's no point in pushing our luck by splitting up and giving the critters a chance to pick us off one by one. If I go down, it'll be with a huge pile of monster bodies around me."

"Well, that's a little...grotesque," she muttered.

"But accurate," Bobby added. "It's best to push hard and make sure that whatever does kill you is the last in a long, long line of creatures that tried."

His boss smirked as they moved out of the atrium and worked their way farther into the building. That was the kind of Bobby he had hoped to see. The higher levels appeared to have been mostly offices for the superiors to work from and host visitors, a way to make themselves look a little more impressive before they sent the guests into the lower levels. He made a note of the blood-splattered signs that would lead them underground when that was necessary.

For the moment, though, it looked like they had no monsters to contend with on that level and so had an opportunity to search for data to mine before they went on a hunting trip. He did want to get that part of the job over with first. They had been right when they said he was a fan of wanton destruction—or, at least, doubted his pointless denials.

He merely fought better when he didn't have to think about preserving something like data that would help them later but would do nothing for the situation they were currently in.

Finally, they reached what looked like a local server—a data station where numerous wires were plugged in—tucked into the corner of the top level.

Taylor moved closer and inserted Niki's spike. He frowned as the software in his suit went haywire for a few seconds. "Niki, I'm dropping a data spike to you now. Is this what you were looking for?"

There was a momentary pause before another voice pinged into the comm channel. "Hey Taylor, it's Vickie. I'm sorting through the data now. Give me a couple of seconds. Most of it has been encrypted."

He remained in place and felt every inch of his body resisting the concept. They were supposed to be on the move, never stopping and always ready to move again if they were attacked.

Standing still went against every instinct in his body.

"Okay, Taylor, I have the data now," Niki said. She'd likely got it from Vickie once the decryption was finished. "These fucking shitheads."

"What?" he queried.

" I'm looking at what kind of testing they've done. All of it is basically illegal but that's not the point. What we have here is hopelessly incomplete and there's nothing that provides real details that might help you to know what you might expect. Anyway, it looks like we've been locked out of the rest of the data, which I assume would have the full information."

He'd had a bad feeling that would happen but it was

how most of these companies worked, especially when they were incredibly paranoid about security.

"Shit," he responded. "Where are we going?"

"There aren't any more networks I can see on the upper levels," Vickie advised him. "It looks like you'll have to head into the lower levels."

"Please tell me you have a better idea of the blueprints?" Bobby asked.

"I'm uploading the updated specs to your suits now," Niki replied. "I'm still not sure what the situation is like in the lower levels, but if I had to guess—"

"Yeah, that's where the bulk of the monsters are," Taylor grumbled. "We're moving out now."

"Roger that, Taylor." She sounded a little more confident about their position than she had before.

He guided the team out of the higher levels and followed the updated blueprints to find access to stairs or elevators.

CHAPTER FOURTEEN

Of course, Taylor didn't need to know the whole picture of the situation. The simple aspects were important to him like digging into the blueprints of the lab to obtain a better idea of where they would find what they were looking for. Everything else was of lesser importance, to be looked into later when the mission didn't require Niki's full attention.

He worked on heading deeper into the lab, and their help wasn't currently needed.

"Vickie, keep digging into that encryption." The agent took a moment to sip from the lukewarm coffee in the Styrofoam mug she had been given. Somehow, every element simply made the coffee worse and forced a grimace from her, but it was still a necessary evil.

Except she wasn't an agent anymore. She wasn't sure what the fuck she was at this point. Did the DOD have agents?

Questions for later, she decided, then remembered

Speare's use of Special Agent which essentially answered the question.

Her cousin didn't sound very happy about the job she had been relegated to. "I thought I would work as the eyes and ears for Taylor and the team to help them head in to kill monsters and hunt things."

"Have you forgotten the fact that you probably won't have access to his comms down there? Anyway, that aside, you are helping by giving him as much information to work with as possible."

"That's supposed to be Desk's job."

"I am meant to support any and all parties in this project," Desk interjected.

"Exactly," the hacker responded. "She can play support by helping to decrypt the files while I…"

Niki waited for the girl to share exactly what she thought her role would be in support of the rest of the team. "Do you intend to finish that sentence or simply keep working?"

"I… Taylor probably needs someone to keep an eye on him. Do we have any access to the building's security cameras?"

"There aren't enough of them to provide us with a sufficient view of the area, and none of them are active," she replied. "I've already told you that. Anyway, it doesn't matter. Taylor is more than capable of being his own eyes and ears. The best that we can do is see what he needs us to see through his teams' suit cams for as long as we can access them and otherwise, stay the hell out of his way."

"That sounds suspiciously like you trust him. Like you think he knows what he's doing."

Niki shrugged. "He's done this longer than anyone."

"Huh. Well, as long as he doesn't need my help, you might want to know that there's someone pulling up to your position. Multiple someones, to be specific, who are using the same kinds of big black SUVs you guys do."

She peeked at the laptop with the feeds of the security cameras they had set up and scowled when she saw the hacker was right. Three SUVs were driving up the hill toward them, and she had a bad feeling she knew who was inside.

"Vickie, can you identify who is driving those?"

"I'm already on it... The plates are registered to a local security company. Why would they send someone here? Do you think they want to provide security?"

The agent sighed and rubbed her eyes. She was out of coffee and there was no time to make more before the SUVs arrived. Honestly, she didn't have the energy for this. "They are doing exactly that. It's the same company that ran security for this facility before it all went to shit, and they are probably still working for the corporation that ran this place. Tychman Industries? Is that the real owner?"

"It looks like it. I don't see any of the usual signs of it being a dummy corporation."

"Well, I'll go ahead and guess that someone on the board of Tychman Industries and a shitload of lawyers are on their way."

She walked out of her tent as they pulled up. They parked aggressively, the way security companies were taught to in order to show they were in charge and weren't to be trifled with. The guards dismounted first, climbed out, and looked ready to reach for the Uzis they carried inside their jackets.

Once they positioned themselves, three men in semi-expensive suits and very expensive haircuts stepped out. They were clearly lawyers and were followed by a man with brown hair sprinkled with white and a receding hairline. The subtle message of understated wealth in his clothes, watch, and shoes said he was the man in charge.

"Hi, who am I talking to here?" he shouted and looked around at the DOD team. "I need to know whose name I will cite as the reason why I make a fucking fortune and who will be fired and sued out of existence."

"I guess that's me," Niki replied and folded her arms in front of her chest. "And just who the fuck are you?"

"Andrew Tychman. You're trespassing on my property and any federal action taken here without a warrant will be punished so thoroughly, your family will pay mine damages for the next three fucking generations."

"Mr. Tychman, it's so nice of you to join us." She didn't bother to try to sound like she meant it. "Now, if you don't mind, turn around and go back the way you came. The US government has jurisdiction over this area."

"Bullshit. I have fifteen layers of legal paperwork that says no one has any kind of jurisdiction anywhere on my property until they can prove that laws were broken."

She took a deep breath. Dealing with these kinds of people—those who assumed the world belonged to them because they had been given everything on a silver platter since birth—always irked her. She hadn't needed to have much to do with them while in the FBI but had a feeling that would change the more time she spent with the DOD.

The papers were displayed in front of her by a perfectly manicured hand. One of the lawyers held a cease and desist order signed by a judge within the last twelve hours.

"Well, that's impressive," Niki admitted. "It usually takes me two whole weeks, a wing, a prayer, and two tickets to a Cardinals game to get me one of those. The sad thing is, I have a much more impressive piece of paper, so I assume you bribed Judge Mason for nothing."

"Watch it, kid," Tychman responded belligerently. "You're tangling with a bear who will end your career."

"Mr. Tychman, with the kind of shit I've seen lately—the kind of shit that's going on in the building right behind us—do you honestly think a bureaucrat who inherited his daddy's business scares me?" she retorted, retrieved a piece of paper from her pocket, and handed it to one of the lawyers. "This area has been declared a quarantine zone by order of the Department of Defense and any invasion of the area will be considered an act detrimental to national security. You and your security team and lawyers will leave or you will be escorted off."

The attorney studied the piece of paper and his eyes widened as he read it.

Tychman laughed. "You can't enforce that. It'll be embroiled in the middle of a legal battle for decades. In the meantime, this is still legally my property."

"Not anymore, not according to the Foreign Creature Invasion Act that was signed into federal law by our president about a month ago," she stated, and she could tell that the lawyers had already begun to back away. They likely didn't know the full story of what had happened in the lab and now that they had some idea, they didn't want to be anywhere near a site where they might come face to face with alien creatures.

Niki turned her attention to the security forces that looked confused, not sure what was happening around them. She decided to press on that.

"Let me make this simpler for you, boys. This is an issue being dealt with by the best fighters available to the Department of Defense. They're in there now in mechanized suits that have been made to hunt shit that's much more dangerous than you. So, do you want to get caught in a fight between the DOD and the Zoo monsters down there?"

They did not. The group inched away with the lawyers close behind.

"Not you," Niki snapped, drew a pistol from inside her jacket, and held it a few inches away from Tychman's head. His security and lawyer teams ignored him and retreated as quickly as possible to their SUVs.

She gestured to her two watchdogs, neither of whom had shown any inclination to stop her, and they moved forward beside her. "Tell me why I shouldn't plug your brain full of holes right here and right now?" she said to the tycoon. "Hmm? What do you think, boys? He keeps saying there's nothing down there to be concerned about."

Jenson scowled at the man. "Here's the thing, see. I don't believe him. If there really was nothing down there, he'd be happy to take us himself and prove it."

"You know what?" Nicki studied the tycoon and his supercilious expression stirred the coals of real anger in the pit of her stomach. She thought of those he'd killed as effectively as if he'd held a weapon and pulled the trigger, and his lack of concern turned her stomach. "I agree with you," she said to her teammate, but her gaze remained fixed on the other man. "I don't believe him either, but I can understand why he doesn't want to go down there. I'll tell you what, Tychman. If you sing me a lullaby as to why you did whatever caused that clusterfuck, I won't take you down there to see if my man McFadden doesn't need him some bait to lure the monsters out."

Tychman looked scared for a moment but not enough to realize that talking was in his best interests. He didn't want to deal with monsters, of course, but his main concern was obviously to keep himself and his company safe and free from interference. The only way to do that was to ensure that none of the data came out.

He had no idea that they had already accessed some of it, but his expression made it very clear that he wouldn't talk even if he did know. She glanced at the other two agents, both of whom seemed to wait expectantly for her to make a decision.

It occurred to her that this was some kind of test but honestly, she didn't give a shit. A few things fell into place in her mind. First, this was the DOD and they had sweeping powers the other agencies did not. Second, the piece of paper she'd delivered to the lawyers put Tychman squarely at a disadvantage. Finally, her watchdogs seemed as ready to string the man up as she felt.

Niki scowled deeply and fought an inward battle. This wasn't the time to let emotions drive her actions. At the same time, though, she'd be damned if the man simply walked away to continue his machinations at the terrible cost of human lives. Thanks to him, she'd also had to send good people in to resolve his fuckup, and while they were both willing and able, it was untenable that the actual perpetrator should stand there and smirk like he held the winning hand.

She managed to push the rage down and calmly, her expression cold and deliberate, she whipped the butt of her pistol across the man's cheek and he sprawled in a small cloud of dust.

Maxwell and Jansen stared at her. For a moment, it looked like they realized they had sorely underestimated her before both their expressions settled into shared approval. She didn't think she'd take any heat over her action, but it would take a while for her to deal with the twinge of guilt at the fact that she was grateful the DOD was as untouchable as it seemed to be.

"Get this asshole in a fucking wheelchair," Niki snapped and her bodyguards grinned. "And strap his ass in. He won't like where I'm taking him."

Taylor struggled a little against his first instinct, which was to turn and get the fuck out. The best idea was to bomb the place into dust and let him and his team sift through the ashes to make sure nothing survived.

It wasn't a matter of being afraid. He knew better than to think of himself as a coward. There was merely no point in letting this place remain if they intended to kill everything anyway. But no, they needed the data. Niki had someone pulling her strings, someone he didn't know and therefore didn't trust. Obviously, they valued information as much as simply killing the fucking creatures.

They'd told him the mutants were a main priority so they recognized the importance of that. Unfortunately, they had told him in the same breath that the data was, by inference, equally important. That was something he didn't trust. It felt like mixed messages and he much preferred things to be cut and dried so everyone knew where they stood. At the same time, he could understand why the data was important. If they knew more about what happened, they could deal with the perpetrators and possibly prevent it from happening again.

He knew he wasn't a coward and that he wouldn't back away when it was time to fight. Still, now that he had time to think about it, the best option had him removed from the equation until it was time to clean up.

But no, this was his job now and it included data gathering, something he usually didn't do. The figure that Niki had offered him in the email she sent didn't even play a part in his decision to enter the facility and clear it. He settled once he'd thought it through and felt the controls of his suit work a little better now that his tension had eased. They reached a small alcove where the new blueprints told him they would find an elevator.

"Why are we looking for the elevator?" Tanya asked, still following at his right flank. "The electricity has been cut and everything except the emergency generators are down. The elevators won't work."

"We can use the shaft," Taylor replied. "It'll be more direct than using the stairs and hopefully, we'll be able to bypass a whole horde of nasty on the way. Once we get the data we need, we can stop moseying around this place and burn it to the ground along with every motherfucking monster in here."

"You really hate the bastards, don't you?"

He didn't answer immediately but looked up from where he worked on the elevator door. Finally, he sighed and shook his head. "You don't go out and kill that many bastards for the fun of it or even because the money's good. Not as many times as I went out there, anyway. Bobby never let it infect him. Many of those who did died out there in the Zoo because they got angry. Cold-blooded murder is the way to treat these monsters. But yeah, I really do hate the bastards."

Quickly, he gestured for Bobby and Tanya to aim toward the elevator shaft before he pulled the doors open and engaged the magnetic locks to keep them open. He didn't know what was waiting for him inside and it made sense to have them ready to cover him should it offer any nasty surprises.

Nothing came through, fortunately, and nothing moved in the darkness. Taylor didn't trust that and rather than proceed, turned and backed away from the entrance. There wasn't anything in his working arsenal that allowed him to burn his way through the entire shaft, but there was something that he could do. He could have a good look.

He ignited one of the flares strapped to the arm of his suit, dropped it into the shaft, and used the enhanced vision of his HUD to pick up everything there was to see at the bottom.

Once again, his instincts hadn't let him down. The way the creatures crawled around the edges of the shaft told him they were mutated insects. They seemed considerably larger than rats as they skittered across the walls before they fell and began the process again. From the markings of their feet on the vertical sides, they appeared to have attempted to escape for a while. They would have succeeded eventually, but it would have taken them weeks to reach the next available opening.

"Oh, fuck the hell no," Tanya muttered and recoiled from the shaft as the flare was smothered by the mass of bodies at the bottom.

"Agreed." Taylor released the magnetic locks on the door and let them snap shut. "I guess we'll take the stairs."

"What happened to your death wish, Taylor?" Bobby asked as they turned to retrace their route along the path that would lead them to the nearest stairwell.

"It was never a death wish, Bungees," he answered. "There are calculations that I'm willing to wager my life on, that's all, and the odds of us surviving by going down that shaft and having to deal with an unknown number of monsters in an enclosed location like that were not worth it. They're trapped in there. Someone was probably carrying specimens up and must have been locked in with them when everything was locked down. They chewed their way out and have been trying to escape ever since. They're contained. We'll frag them later."

"That sounds like a plan," Tanya said, a note of relief in her tone as they reached the stairway.

Like most of the other entrances into the lower levels, it was sealed, but the door wouldn't provide much of a barrier to three mechanized suits. Taylor was the first to begin the descent, his weapon at the ready. The lights were still off, which forced them to use the suit lights carefully set to low-level and enhance this with night vision coupled with motion sensors. These would enable the software to project a decent enough image of their surroundings without completely giving their location away.

"Exactly like the old days," he muttered and pushed himself down the first flight of stairs to reach the first of the lab levels. He could already hear something moving and one didn't have to be a scientist to know it was bigger than the creatures they had seen in the elevator shaft.

Considerably larger, he realized as he focused on the creatures that waited for them. They had likely heard what was happening and came up to investigate. He could see the resemblance between what they had been once, but they had mutated well beyond that. Aside from the size—which was much bigger than the coyotes they had spawned from—large, bulging eyes indicated that they'd evolved to see in the darkness. Muscles pressed up into skin to part the fur and make it look ragged as though the bodies struggled to keep up with the transformation.

When they saw the three mech suits descend the steps, they grew more hostile and bunched together to make themselves appear larger. Their mouths opened to reveal long, sharp teeth, and the bottom half of their jaws split down the middle to reveal fangs that dripped with venom between the halves.

Tanya took an instinctive step back. Bobby didn't.

"Like I said," Taylor said calmly. "Don't worry about it too much."

He lined his shot, pulled the trigger, and advanced almost immediately as the stairwell was illuminated with the flicker of the muzzle flashes tempered by the light from their suits. His teammates stepped in as well, immediately selected targets, and opened fire.

The creatures tried to scale the stairs when they realized they were under attack. They were fast but they had no armor or carapaces, and in the tight confines, their speed and agility did little to protect them when the entire area was filled with a hail of bullets.

There had been about a dozen of them all told, and once they were eliminated, Taylor advanced to inspect and confirm the kills.

More could be heard moving from below. It appeared the whole pack of monsters had heard the gunfire and were on their way.

"Form up!" he snapped. "Weapons check and keep moving."

Tanya and Bobby followed the orders and checked their weapons before they fell into position at his flanks as they continued down the stairs.

"Taylor?" Niki shouted through the comms. "Damn it, Taylor, can you read me?"

"I read you!" he replied. "But we're a little busy at the moment."

"I have an actual witness," she announced. "We're bringing him to you now."

He froze in place. "You're fucking what?"

"Coming down to you now."

"Shit." He growled in disbelief. If she was talking to him, it meant she was in the building and in range—and very vulnerable.

CHAPTER FIFTEEN

"I'll have your fucking career for this! I'll make sure your face is plastered over every fucking newspaper in the country with the words 'government overreach' in bold over your head. Every action you've taken while working for the government will be under the microscope and every tiny little mistake and every fucking typo will be another nail in the coffin of the burning heap that was your career."

Niki knew that under any other circumstances, the man might have had that kind of power. Hell, if she was still working for the FBI, he would be able to make good on every single one of those threats, which meant he probably thought he was intimidating her.

Of course, she was with the DOD now. During her time in the FBI, she usually cleaned up when whatever this fucker did went ballistic and someone was needed to wipe it off the face of the map with the largest bomb available—sometimes, anyway. But in this case, she worked as the scalpel that removed the cancer before it could spread.

And she had the backing of the US government to do it too. It was George Orwell's worst nightmare, but the old bastard had never really accounted for alien monsters ravaging their way through suburban New Jersey.

At any other time, she might have been worried. A part of her sensed that she was teetering on a very fine line and that a slew of questions would arise to confront her down the line. Right now, though, she was doing what she needed to do in order to rid the US of the monsters that had infiltrated. It was like these people didn't even realize how fucked they were in the head or what the consequences of their actions would be.

Tychman continued to yell insults at her, but that was all he could do while she dragged him behind her. It would have been a little more draining if she hadn't managed to make use of one of the extra mechs Taylor had brought with him.

Her first thought was that it had simply been because he anticipated there might be something wrong with one of his and would have another one ready if they needed it. Once she was inside, however, it was clear that he more than trusted his and Bobby's work to keep their suits up and running.

The fact that it was all coded and calibrated to fit her almost exactly was a little weird—and telling. Had he really thought she would head into the mess with him and had something ready for her in case? That seemed a little far-fetched, but so was him expecting to need an extra suit and yet having one on hand that happened to fit her perfectly.

"Are you fucking listening to me?" Tychman shouted.

She hadn't been. Honestly, she had given up on listening to him the moment Maxwell and Jansen had strapped him to the wheelchair they'd had on hand. She'd wondered earlier at how they seemed prepared for any eventuality, but what had seemed ridiculous had provided her with the idea. Who the fuck knew wheelchairs had a place in a hostile situation?

The man had done nothing but spew threats and insults from that point forward, and it became more difficult to take him seriously the farther they went. His face had reddened and he spat with every word to the point where she had decided to simply drag him from behind until they reached the stairs.

She decided he wouldn't be any more thankful if she carried him down the steps rather than dragging him, no matter which was more comfortable, which left her with the easiest of the two options.

For her, anyway.

"You are not—fuck!" he shouted as he bounced in the chair. He stopped talking, though, and Niki knew why. There were no more curses, threats, or yells from him because they were descending and he realized that. He could see the blood splattered over the walls. More to the point, it was fresh blood, which left him nothing but imagination to explain the reason for the gunfire.

The screams, the monsters, and the gunfire swamped any thoughts of protest. Even his imagination was no longer required and he sagged in the chair, leaving her nothing to listen to but what was happening below.

"Fucking hell, I think I preferred the threats and shouting," Niki grumbled and jostled Tychman a little more than necessary as she drew her weapon from its holster on her back. She shouldn't leave anything to chance if something got past the team.

Then again, she needed to stop doubting Taylor's effectiveness. The mutants continued to shriek—dozens of them, by what she could hear—but they seemed to diminish somewhat. The screeches and the shooting grew less and less frequent. She could see the flashes of the last volley as the final mutants were killed. The man she dragged was completely silent and had no doubt finally realized what she was doing and where he was going. He'd possibly not fully comprehended that she'd meant what she'd said until that moment.

She thought she could smell the blood but could see the bodies that had piled up around the first of the laboratory levels. There had been a fight there. It had been tough, judging by the numbers that had been gunned down, but it hadn't been a close call.

Taylor, Bobby, and Tanya were cleaning up. Their mech suits were covered in blood. It had been up close and personal, and there was nothing Niki would have liked to do more than pull them out and let them clean up, wash, and get a hot meal with a nice cold drink.

But the job needed to be done.

Taylor turned to look at her. She couldn't see inside the suit, but there was a certain arrogance to his movements that Bobby and Tanya both lacked. He was comfortable in it and they weren't and had been in one for much longer than anyone else in the US. As best she knew, there wasn't anyone still in the Zoo who had been in a suit as long as he had.

"Banks, what the fuck are you doing down here?" he snapped and marched toward her. "And why did you bring the civilian down here? He'll be killed."

"Yeah, and he'll deserve it," she retorted. "Taylor, meet Andrew Tychman, the owner of this dump. And I think he has a couple of things to say about how it was run—don't you, Andy?"

"What...the fuck?" The man gasped and stared at the bodies of monsters that surrounded him.

"You need to start talking, Tychman." Taylor hissed a warning where he stood over the man and radiated menace. "And I mean the informative kind of talking. You need to tell us about what the fuck you did in this place."

"I...I can't. My board—"

"Your board isn't here, about to be offered as a distraction for the monsters to feed on while we kill them." Taylor raised a hand to stop the man from replying. "And just so you know, we already have spikes in the drives all over this fucking building, so we'll know what happened anyway. If you want to make it a little easier on yourself, you'll share the info a little faster. Do we have an understanding, Mr. Tychman?"

There was something about the way he could talk that made people spill their guts a little faster. That and the fact that he was surrounded by the bodies he'd killed made it almost impossible for the man to not start talking as quickly as he could.

"We were falling behind," the tycoon started and tears

trickled down his cheeks as his voice cracked, but he pressed on. "In the race for developing new shit coming out of the Zoo. The other companies were getting the first crack because they had more contracts, which allowed them to stay ahead and in turn, gave them more contracts. We needed to take a step ahead and there were researchers who felt the same way.

"With their help, we moved ahead of the line and began to develop stuff that brought us the contracts we needed. We tried different gasses, different integrations, and even worked up a mist of the blue goop that could be administered in something like a sauna. There was nothing to stop us from continuing, and the board was willing to turn a blind eye until..."

"Until everything went to shit," Taylor finished his sentence for him as Tychman's voice trailed off. "From that point forward, everyone turned a blind eye and allowed you to operate. When the shit hit the fan, they wanted to cover everything up and get something nuclear to wipe all evidence of what happened here. That's what they were hoping for when the information was leaked to the DOD—for them to wipe everything out—but someone decided a more delicate approach was needed. They brought Banks in and made everything go sideways. Is anything I've said untrue?"

Tychman looked at him like he was something supernatural. Even Niki hadn't been able to put all of it together. "Yes. That's all right, how did you—"

"Do you think you're the first one to pull this kind of shit, see it go sideways, and then need the help of those who supported your situation to cover it up?" he asked. It was a rhetorical question, but the man nodded anyway like he actually did think he was the first one.

"Fucking corporations," Bobby muttered. "Please tell me that when we make it big, you won't do something this stupid."

"No promises. I am a huge fan of wanton destruction, as you are all apparently aware of."

"What?" Tychman asked.

Taylor turned suddenly, his weapon at the ready. "Give me a defensive position around the civilian. We have incoming bogeys."

"What?" the tycoon asked, his voice a little shrill with panic.

"Yeah, what?" Niki repeated. "Why are we keeping this dirtbag motherfucker alive again? Okay, okay, I know. Because he's a civilian and if he's being shat out of a monster, he won't be able to testify in front of a congressional hearing.

"Exactly. Now, form a defensive perimeter! That means you too, Banks."

Niki knew he was serious. Bobby and Tanya were already forming a small semi-circle around Tychman as Taylor backed him against the wall.

"Fucking hell," she cursed but complied and joined the group around the man. She could only imagine what it must have been like for the tycoon, barely being able to see in the darkness as four mech suits formed up to defend him. He probably hoped like hell they would be enough.

The monsters surged forward. She had no idea how

many of them there were, but the two men moved first and opened fire while they held their positions. The whole room flared with the muzzle flashes and the volley cut into the first line of the creatures. Niki focused on the second wave and pulled the trigger repeatedly as her HUD called targets up for her. It was hard to keep trigger control and she gritted her teeth with the effort.

It wasn't long before she ran out of ammo and the suit began to run a reload on a track up her arm.

"Your sidearm!" Taylor yelled over the gunfire and she realized he had adjusted to turn his attention to cover her side of the fight too. He drew a sidearm and used that to cover her lines until she reloaded and fired again.

By the time that happened, there wasn't much left to do. The creatures were dead.

"It's merely another wave," Taylor told her. "We've faced quite a few of those. I think they're running in packs, separate from each other, and trying to circle. You need to get him topside."

Niki shook her head. "I can help you," she protested. "He can help you with—"

"He's the fucking CEO or whatever, Banks. That means he won't know on-the-ground details like passcodes or specific numbers—the kind of information that would make a difference right now. Besides, we're out of time even if he did know. We'll get ourselves killed if half our focus is on protecting this fucking asshat. Those monsters won't wait for us to interrogate him so if you want to make a difference, you can help me by getting the man fucking topside!" he roared.

This was his fight and his command. She needed to

respect his authority in the actual conflict and it hurt to even think that.

"Fine," she snapped and grasped the wheelchair she'd used to pull Tychman down. "But you and I will have a nice long talk about who's in charge of these missions."

"Won't that be fun. Now go!"

CHAPTER SIXTEEN

Something was moving. Elisa registered a shudder, shook her head, and tried to shrug it off. It wasn't time to wake up. She had spent considerable time training her body clock to the point where she could tell when she should get up.

Another shudder followed. What was it—an earthquake? Something like that? She shook her head. No, that was impossible. She was in Vegas. Right?

Sleep was getting harder and harder to hold onto, and there was nothing she could do to change it. Her eyes opened and she was ready to bust heads for forcing her awake.

Everything was dark. There was nothing around her and yet she felt confined like she was in some kind of a cocoon. While she felt entirely alone, something prevented her from being able to move around.

Memories began to slide in. A dark room that was supposed to be cold but wasn't. Cold pizza that should have tasted like shit but didn't. A ventilation shaft with a grill that should have been secured but wasn't. She had climbed out, found one of those damn suits, and climbed in to hide and protect herself.

Things became a little foggy after that so she assumed she must have nodded off. She had never been afraid of close spaces, and it was kind of comfortable to be in one of the suits—kind of like being held up and hugged from all sides.

She tried to shift again but nothing gave.

Something bright and red flashed in front of her eyes. She tried to look away but it tracked her eye movement to show her something.

"Manual lock engaged, outside override required?" she muttered to herself and shook her head. She was still inside the suit, that much was clear, but why was it moving? It hadn't worked before. She had tried it when she got in and while her captors had been distracted doing something else. Unless she wasn't still in the shop. They had been packaging them for something, right?

"Shit." She tried to move again but the red flashing warning appeared again. "Um…crap, HUD, engage voice activation."

A green light appeared and waited for her voice command.

"Right…open all available comm lines."

The green light vanished and the HUD came alive to show her all the available comm lines. She scowled when she realized it was only one—the line to the shop.

"Damn it."

Still, it was better than nothing. If no one knew she was

in there, it was better to let them know where she was so that they could get her out, right?

She keyed into the comm line and waited for someone to pick up.

———

Niki had gone into the fucking lab. Of course she had. Her idiot cousin thought nothing in the world could kill her, so she decided to head in there and put her life on the line because she wanted to show off how tough she was to her fucking crush.

Vickie leaned back in her office chair and shook her head slowly. She couldn't help but think that if she had been there in person, she would have been able to talk her out of it. But since she wasn't and since her new bodyguards were too chicken to do anything about it, the woman had gone spelunking into the world's most dangerous Bat-cave.

"And she lectures me on being safe and mature and all that other bullshit." She continued to mumble and shake her head in exasperation. There was nothing she could do from all the fucking way in Vegas. Unless she could drive out there. Six hours probably wasn't that long, and it would be even shorter in her car. Things would probably be wrapped up by then, though. Taylor would have killed the monsters and there would be nothing left for her to do except maybe help with the cleanup.

She was brought out of her reverie by a flashing green light on her screen. It was one of the comm units but none of those that had been sent into the underground lab. No, this one was up in the air and flying at an impressive speed. Either someone had turned their mech into an Iron Man suit or she was looking at someone communicating through the suits they had sent to the Zoo.

"I wonder who it could be," Vickie mumbled facetiously and considered whether she should pick up or not. It didn't seem right to leave the woman hanging. Besides, Elisa had nothing else to do except be a pain in her ass. If she didn't do it now, she would have to do it sometime in the future.

With her luck, that would probably be when she had to help Taylor out of a mess of monsters by using her hacking skills, although she wasn't entirely sure how that would work. She wouldn't be qualified to handle the fuckers any other way.

"Goddammit." She pressed the button to complete the commlink and traced it to make sure no one was listening in before she turned her microphone on. "If you're calling to tell me I need erectile dysfunction pills again, I swear to God I'll short-circuit your entire server network."

She wasn't sure why she opened with that. Would Elisa really think she was dealing with telemarketers over a goddamn sat-radio connection?

The woman didn't answer for a solid ten seconds. "I'm sorry, I don't think I ever caught your name. But you're the girl who worked with Tyler to keep me captive in a meat locker, right?"

"It's Taylor, and aren't you still locked in the meat locker? Are you calling to tell me you've escaped?" Vickie knew that she was being snarky but there was no fun in it otherwise.

"Yes, I've escaped and I hid in one of your suits. I'm not

sure, but I think you guys might have transported them without knowing I was inside."

"Well, I'll tell you something, the guys we're delivering the suits to will definitely pay extra when they find a Hispanic-slash-Italian chick inside."

"Where the fuck am I?"

"That suit you're hiding in is currently about thirty-five thousand feet above the Atlantic and on its way to Africa. I hope you brought your passport."

Another pause from the woman made her grin. "You're shitting me."

"Hey, this is your fault. Didn't your parents ever tell you not to get into strange mechanized suits?"

"Well, what the hell was I supposed to do? You were going to kill me."

"Bullshit. I'm not a killer and neither is Taylor. Well, no...I mean, he is, and there's a whole story about that, but the point is that he would never have killed you. For fuck's sake, he saved you from being executed by the mob. Did you think he would take you off their hands only to dispose of you himself? How does that make any kind of real sense to you?"

Elisa didn't reply for a few seconds. "I...guess I didn't think of it that way."

"Seriously, from the way he told it, the guys had already dug a hole they intended to bury you alive in. If he planned to kill you, that would have been, like, problem solved, you know?"

"Again, I didn't think of it—"

Vickie shook her head. "No, you didn't think at all. Which, you know, having been kidnapped and put through a fairly traumatic situation, I guess I can understand. But if you think I'll have any pity on you for your bungling way of getting out of a situation you got yourself into in the first place, I have a couple of bridges I want to sell you."

"You…what?"

"I have a couple of bridges to sell you. Seriously, you call yourself a reporter but you've never heard of George C Parker?"

"Who the fuck is that?"

"A very successful conman in the early 1900s, back when there was a large number of people strolling around New York for the first time. His most famous con was when he sold the Brooklyn Bridge to several people, and that's where the term comes from. Come on, are you seriously telling me you've never heard it?"

"How— Why the fuck are you telling me about a conman right now?"

"Because you'll be there for a while and I thought you might want food for thought. But since you're not interested, let's get down to brass tacks, then. You'll be in that suit until you land and someone opens the crates and disengages the external override we put in place to secure all the mechanisms while in transit."

"Am—how long am I going to be in here?"

"A few days, max. You shouldn't worry, though. Of course, you'll be a little hungry, but those suits are meant to sustain people for a while. It'll recycle the water vapor from your breath, the water from your sweat and…other waste, so you don't have to worry about dehydration, at least, through the first three weeks. Of course, it does mean you'll drink recycled piss but you wanted accuracy for your report, right?"

"This wasn't what I had in mind."

"Seriously, you're a reporter who started investigating the mob without backup, without security, and without letting the police in on what you were doing in case you needed to be bailed out. This is about as good a situation as you could hope to get, so if I were you, I would stop complaining and enjoy your freaking flight."

"How the fuck—"

Vickie rolled her eyes. "I don't know. Sing a song. Maybe get used to using the HUD while you're in there. It's not that difficult and kind of fun from the way Taylor and Tanya depicted it. Of course, they were able to move around, so maybe you'll have to use your imagination for that one. There's nothing I can do for you while you're in the air—and probably after that too. Honestly, there's nothing I want to do to help you either since the first thing you'll do when you get back to the US is print a big, huge story about how those of us in our little operation are criminals. And while that might be true for me, Taylor doesn't deserve that."

Elisa didn't say anything for a few seconds. "I...won't report anything, I swear."

"You're a reporter. That's your job. You'll probably have a huge collection of prizes but in the meantime, it'll mean Taylor will basically be at war with *La Cosa Nostra* because he saved your life by telling them he would handle you and you're over there, decidedly unhandled."

"I thought I would report on the mob robbing itself and walking away with a huge deal from their insurance company. I had no idea that more or less innocent people were involved. Had I known that... Okay, look, that makes for an even better story, but I wouldn't share it if it would put all your lives at risk. I have some standards."

"Do you?" The hacker raised her eyebrow, even though she knew the woman couldn't see her. She would have to hear the sarcasm dripping in her voice. "Do you really?"

"Yes!"

"Well, there's still nothing I can do for you until you touch down, so...I don't know, keep me updated periodically and work on staying alive. And that singing. Although don't ask me to be a judge on your singing. I am a total Simon Cowell."

"Who?"

Vickie sighed dramatically. "Do people not watch reruns of old television programs anymore? Seriously. Next, you'll tell me you don't know who Monty Python is."

There was a moment of silence on the other end of the line.

"You don't know who they are either, do you?"

"I...no, I do not."

She rubbed her temples. "Oh, good Lord, what has civilization come to?" She blinked when a light flashed red on one of her other comm lines. "Shit, I'll have to call you back. This is impending violence—or I assume that's what's happening, at least."

"Wait, you can't—"

Vickie could and did cut the line and transferred to where her cousin tried to get in touch with her. Oh yes, it would be fun to be the only person Elisa could talk to on her adventurous trip to Africa.

CHAPTER SEVENTEEN

Niki wasn't sure what she would do with the man she hauled to the top of the building. She was willing to admit the mistake of having dragged him down, even if it had resulted in a small amount of solid information for the team. More would be revealed when they pulled the data from the servers.

Even so, watching the fight and seeing the blood splattered everywhere seemed to have broken Tychman. He hadn't said a single intelligible word from the moment they reached the stairwell, but that hadn't stopped him from mumbling the whole way up. He muttered something but even with the improved sound collection the suit had, it didn't sound like any language she had ever heard.

He was catatonic, and that was on her. She had meant to scare him into compliance, not break his psyche.

Still, what was done was done, and she was sure he had deserved to come face to face with what his greed and incompetence had caused. Her inner questions might later challenge that, but for now, she'd accept the sense of justice that shielded her.

As she approached the exit, she heard the seal open. Maxwell and Jansen stood on either side of the doors, toting an assault rifle and a shotgun respectively as if they expected some kind of threat to erupt from within. They had been seriously pissed when they realized that she intended to enter the facility without them.

"Are you all right, ma'am?" Jansen asked and sounded alarmed. "We…heard something happening down there."

"I'm perfectly fine," Niki asserted and released the wheelchair once she was outside and the doors were sealed again.

"You have blood all over the suit." Maxwell grunted disapproval and concern. He still seemed a little offended too, no doubt because she'd escaped from his watchful eye and gone somewhere they couldn't follow.

She looked down and sure enough, the human giant was right. "It obviously isn't mine. Again, I'm fine. The same cannot be said for some…I think coyote-zoo monster hybrids. Nor can it be said for this dumbass here."

Jansen turned his attention to Tychman, who had caught blood splatters as well and still mumbled nothing in particular while he stared into the distance.

"What happened to him?"

Niki shrugged. "Physically, he's fine. What he saw down there, though, might have scarred him for life."

"It couldn't have happened to a nicer guy," Maxwell pointed out glibly.

His partner leaned closer, narrowed his eyes, and examined Tychman carefully. "I'd say this man has gone into shock. Psychological shock, which is milder but still intense. You know, for him. What did he see?"

"We were attacked while down there," she explained. "There weren't that many critters and they were eliminated very quickly, but it was in the semi-dark. He probably didn't see much, but he did see something and let his imagination fill in the rest. Either way, he's probably done here."

"Yeah," the man agreed. "I'll call a helicopter to take him to a secure site for a debrief."

"That is weird," she muttered. "When you say 'secure site for a debrief,' it sounds suspiciously like an interrogation at a black site."

"Well, if the shoe fits, right?"

She shook her head as she began to pull the pieces of her suit off and replaced them in the crate they had come in. It was an easy choice not to interfere with the business of the DOD. Of course, she was technically in the DOD's business.

The sound of a helicopter's rotors drew closer when Taylor keyed into the comm line. "Hey, Banks, do you still have eyes on Tychman?"

Niki narrowed her eyes. That didn't sound like a good query. "I do but not for long. What's up? Why do you need to have a chat with him?"

"Not so much a chat as one question, which I guess can be answered by Tychman or by Vickie if she's finished decoding the data we've sent her since the start of the mission."

"Well, spit it out, man."

"Do you know if this place conducted any tests on

burrowing creatures? The kind that might be able to dig their way out if presented with an opportunity?"

That didn't sound good.

"Hold up on the transport," Niki shouted as Jansen and Maxwell began to wheel Tychman to the area where the helicopter prepared to land. "Tychman, do you know if the lab had any burrowing creatures being tested when the breach occurred?"

The man turned to look at her but his pupils were dilated and he didn't seem able to focus on her. "Can't... discuss business without my lawyer present. Need to talk to my lawyer now."

"I hate to break it to you but your lawyers ran out of here with their tails tucked between their legs."

He didn't look like he understood her and simply shook his head. "Need to talk to my lawyer."

"You won't get anything out of him anytime soon," Jansen pointed out and proceeded to wheel him toward the helicopter again. He managed to heave him on with help from the people inside.

"No dice on Tychman," Niki grumbled into her comm-link. "Vickie, do you have anything from the files you've decrypted so far?"

"Nothing about burrowing animals, no," the hacker answered. "But I'm only starting to look into the stuff they're sending from the lower levels."

She shook her head. "Fuck. Nothing so far on any burrowing animals but that can change at any minute. Why...why do you ask?"

Taylor scowled deeply. The flickering lights above them had begun to give him a headache. "Oh, you know, I'm only asking."

"Yeah, I know." Niki didn't sound very happy. "I need to know why you're asking."

He didn't want to tell her. They wouldn't talk about anything that would make her come down again to interfere with the mission.

With that said, he knew he would still need intel on what exactly they were looking at.

The lower levels of the lab had far more monsters, although they appeared to avoid the section where the team was at the moment. They didn't question that since the animals in the lab had begun to create their own biome in the expansive laboratory.

That decision continued until they found a hole. Taylor couldn't tell what the room had once been as the amount of dirt and broken chunks of concrete that had been pulled out from the ground left it unrecognizable. Some of the pieces were large, too big to have been lifted by the coyote creatures that had infested the lab thus far.

There were some divergences, of course—the insects in the elevator shaft, for one, although it seemed those that were trapped were the only ones that survived since the roving packs of coyotes appeared to kill anything they came across. Except, of course, the beast that had dug the hole. Whatever it was, the monsters appeared to avoid it like the damn plague.

"What are we looking at here?" Bobby asked as he scanned the area and tried to pick his way through the rubble and mounds of dirt that created obstacles in every direction.

"Fuck if I know," Tanya replied. She obviously still wanted to keep her distance.

Taylor had a couple of ideas. "There's no sign of any other animals tracking through the soft dirt before we got here, so we know it's something big and violent enough to give the smaller animals pause. I'm not sure what options we have in this area, but it is big and it's violent enough to keep the rest of the monsters away."

He studied the claw marks that dug into the hole about fifteen feet down and cut into the concrete. It was strong too, by the looks of it, and he would have put money on them finding a couple of bodies of intrepid and stupidly brave coyotes that had stumbled a little too close to the digger and paid for it with their lives. That, no doubt, was why the rest of the mutants kept their distance.

But there was no point in making assumptions. He pulled himself away from the hole.

"What are you doing?" Tanya asked. "We have to investigate."

"We have to deal with the other creatures and get our spikes into the hard drives down here before anything else," he told her. "We have a mission to finish before we move on and find more trouble."

"There's a monster out there that needs to be dealt with," Bobby pointed out.

"And if we kill it immediately, whatever kept the rest of these bastards contained inside will be gone and they'll spread. Again, we have a job to do. Let's see it finished."

Taylor pulled his assault rifle up to conduct a visual

inspection of the barrel. Much of their fighting had been up close and personal, which meant considerable incidental splattering and gore spread around the room. It left very little for them to deal with in terms of survivors since the monsters appeared to throw themselves at the invaders.

Teeth marks were visible in his armor plates from where they had tried their best to kill him. It hadn't ended well for them, but he knew the only way they had been able to keep the animals from tearing into them was by clearing them quickly. If their adversaries were allowed to attack in a full mob, it would only be a matter of time before those oddly shaped jaws penetrated the armor and found the comparatively squishy human inside.

The mutants were breeding quickly, which made him think rodent DNA had been introduced somehow. It meant they would become an epidemic if they were set loose in an area where there were ample food and space to continue spreading into the wild.

He couldn't risk that, he told himself as he cleaned the blood off the barrel as well as he could, hoping that nothing would clog the works. More of the monsters skirted the edges of what they considered to be the area of effect for the creature they were avoiding.

Hell, it could be more than one monstrously large creature for all he knew. It would make more sense too, he realized when he thought about it.

More of the mutants had now gathered. The lower levels were more infested, likely due to there being more food sources like smaller creatures that were hunted for food. It was obvious that they all treated the humans as an invading threat, something that would force them to abandon all other instinctive drives to hunt each other. Larger coyote hybrids circled, and he could see what looked like carapaces growing over their shoulders. Their tails were longer and whipped like they had something on the tip that would be able to punch through their armor.

"Tanya, fall back a little," Taylor ordered as the monsters began to advance on their position. They seemed to have lost some of their fear of whatever had dug the hole. "When they attack, do your best to pick the larger ones off —the ones with the whipping tails—before they get to us."

He highlighted the animals he was talking about. She indicated that she understood and took a step back while he and Bobby formed a small buffer between the creatures and her.

"Exactly like old times, huh, Tay-Tay?" the mechanic asked.

"I hope that's not catching on," he grumbled.

"Vickie asked me to make sure to call you that at every possible opportunity."

"Of course she did."

Their bickering was interrupted when two of the smaller coyotes darted forward and their fangs flashed as they tried to sneak an attack on the men. Taylor and Bobby responded in kind and eliminated them both immediately, but the rest of the creatures took it as an invitation. They surged forward in an almost solid rushing wall as the teammates opened fire.

The first line was decimated and a couple of those that came behind were felled as well. The initial faltering of the charge was enough to give Tanya her opening. She selected her targets carefully and the larger creatures fell one by one.

But, as had happened before, their adversaries saw no point in trying to retreat. The flickering lights and the way they interfered with his HUD made it difficult to make them out, and Taylor had a difficult time keeping his shots accurate. It wasn't long before his first magazine clicked empty and he yanked his sidearm out to continue to fire as they were forced to back away and inch toward the hole.

He noted that some of the creatures still looked anxious about approaching the tunnel that had been carved out of the building around them, and that was something to take advantage of. Once the assault rifle was loaded again, he pushed in closer and pulled the trigger.

The mutants continued a relentless series of attacks. They showed no sign of a survival instinct, not even when their fellow attackers fled, bleeding and dying. As if oblivious to the carnage around them, they maintained their almost mindless assaults.

Exactly like old times, he thought grimly.

He was panting by the time the fight ended and looked around, expecting any of the creatures to simply surge from the ground and renew their attack, but nothing happened. His gaze flicked over the bodies and deafening silence settled around them.

"Well, fuck me." Bobby grunted once he had reloaded his assault rifle. "I guess we got all of them."

"Except for the critters in the elevator shaft," Tanya reminded them.

"Right," Taylor agreed. "I have the feeling that if they

hadn't been trapped in there, they would have been eaten by the rest of these fuckers, though."

"Well, nothing to it but to finish the job," Bobby commented, and he and Tanya began to move to where their blueprints told them they would find a data point for them to spike into.

He nodded. "You two get on that and when you're finished, frag anything you find in the elevator shafts."

"What? Are you taking a break?" Bobby asked and probably intended to sound disrespectful.

Taylor turned to look at the hole in the wall behind them. "Nope. I'll check to see what kind of threat the big bastard that dug this shit up is."

"It's dangerous to go alone," Tanya warned him.

"Thanks, Zelda, but don't think that I'll put myself in any danger I can't handle. That's why I brought you guys, remember? Now, get to work and I'll link to you once I find something."

The mechanic shrugged and his mech exaggerated the action as he indicated for Tanya to follow him while Taylor turned to the massive hole.

"I hope I won't regret this," he muttered and clambered into the passage that he wished he could avoid. He scowled as he hauled a few of the larger chunks of dirt and concrete out to make it easier to navigate with his heavy suit of armor.

CHAPTER EIGHTEEN

The subterranean passage wasn't difficult to traverse. The creature or creatures were big enough that he could fit fairly easily. It wasn't large enough for him to walk upright, but a little negotiating made it less awkward to ease through. Taylor wasn't sure where it was going, but it appeared to head directly away from the lab, dug through the tough dirt like it was nothing. Roots had been chewed and rocks had been turned into gravel as the beast had forged its path to freedom.

He wasn't sure he wanted to go toe to toe with something that possessed this sheer amount of power, but there was no getting away from it at this point. Besides, if something went awry, he could contact Bobby and Tanya who were still in the lab. It wouldn't take them long to finish the remainder of the work required there. It was mostly killing bugs and getting the data out, something that they could both do in their sleep.

But it was always best to let them have each other's back when they were in there. They had assumed that all the monsters were gone, but that was an iffy assumption to make. It was always best to have someone alongside.

Unless they were him? Taylor shook his head. He was only there to do recon and that could certainly be done without any handholding. If anyone thought he was the kind of person who would charge into the thick of it when there was help to be had, they didn't know him at all.

Then again, they did think he was a fan of wanton destruction. He could understand why they thought that, of course, but it didn't make it true.

It wasn't long before he noticed cracks of light ahead in the tunnel. The distance was only a hundred yards or so, and it was mostly straight with only a couple of twists and turns where the creature had probably needed to divert away from larger, heavier rocks and roots.

He moved out of the tunnel and felt some resistance from the soil that had snuck into the crevices of his suit, which made it a little uncomfortable to move around in.

The view from where he now stood was fairly unique. The idea of Arizona being mostly deserts and canyons was true, for the most part, but there were wooded sections that took the breath away. Taylor had never been one to enjoy nature—especially having seen the kind of damage nature could do to him—but it seemed almost sacrilegious in that moment to simply leave without at least a pause to drink in a remarkable view.

It wasn't quite like the dense jungle of the Zoo or other areas he'd been before like the Appalachians. Even the swamps he'd seen didn't come close to the kind of vista he saw there. While he couldn't say one was more or less beautiful than the other, this seemed to provide a unique splendor all its own, although he wasn't an expert in these kinds of things. He noticed swaths of pine trees growing in the area, and the earth was tough and rocky, difficult to navigate if he wasn't wearing a heavy suit of mechanized armor.

Even so, negotiating through the tough terrain took him a little time. He wasn't worried about losing whatever had dug the hole, though, since it had left a very obvious track for him to follow.

"Taylor," Niki called through the comm line. "Do I read this right? Are you out of the lab? It's one hell of a time to wander around the forest in search of enlightenment, you know."

"As fun as that would be—and I'll have you know this would be a great area to wander in search of your identity or some bullshit like that—I'm investigating a containment breach. Something tunneled out of the fucking lab and I'm on its trail while Tanya and Bobby are finishing things inside."

"Do you think it's wise to go out there on your own? Again?"

"This is only recon. I'll make sure that whatever the fuck it is hasn't decided to spread its seed and create problems for the locals. But if you want to come out here with me, I wouldn't mind having company." He couldn't resist the opportunity to tease a little—not flirting, no, because they didn't do that—but she didn't take the bait.

"Yeah, in the suit you had ready for me just in case?"

"Well, the possibility that you would do something stupid like head into the fucking lab was one I couldn't ignore, so I thought it would be a good idea to make sure it was properly calibrated. You know, to help you avoid barreling through walls or something."

She was silent for a few seconds. "You're such an asshole."

"Why, for wanting to make sure you're properly prepared to enter a combat situation you shouldn't be in and put yourself in danger?"

"Let me know if you need backup down there. There's nothing I'd like less than to have you die on my first mission with the DOD."

"Come on, don't lie. I know you dream about me dying a horrible death and you wake up laughing or something."

"Well, yeah, but not while you're out there under my command. It makes me look bad, you understand."

Taylor nodded. "Right. I wouldn't want to make you look bad. Ever."

"Good, so stay the fuck alive, McFadden."

She hadn't referred to him by his last name in a while and he wasn't sure what had driven her to do that in this particular situation. He chose not to address it either way as he approached an area where he could identify tracks that were fresher. It looked like the as yet unidentified mutant had stamped around the area as if to make its home a little more comfortable.

In all honesty, he didn't know what he was looking at. The tracks looked heavier than he expected, especially for something that appeared to be a burrowing beast. It looked like only one, but it seemed to carry something behind it that obfuscated all but the deepest parts of the tracks.

The back paws didn't look like they had any claws—or perhaps the marks had been obscured by the dragged burden—but the front paws appeared a little more defined. For one thing, they spread out a little farther, which suggested it being broader around the shoulders than it was at the hips. Either way, he could see the very clear indentation of the claws of the front paws in the ground.

They were exceptionally large claws. Taylor recalled seeing tracks like these back in the day when he wandered around his back yard. His dad had told him they were badger tracks. They had been considerably smaller but the size of the talons seemed about the same size by comparison. Of course, this one appeared to be about the size of a bear's.

He knew what badgers could be like. Their sheer aggression was something to be feared, even by creatures significantly larger than they were.

Based on what he'd been able to deduce from the trail, he would confront a mutant that shared similarities in anatomy and build but was considerably larger than the average badger. He scanned his surroundings, determined not to be caught off-guard by the beast as he proceeded cautiously through the dense foliage. The distinctive sound of running water in the distance caught his attention and drew him irresistibly closer.

"Do you have anything on your radar down there, Taylor?"

"Only you intruding on my peaceful walk through the woods," he replied. "Oh, and I have movement in the distance. Are Tanya and Bobby finished with the smaller critters and with the data banks?"

"Yes," Niki confirmed crisply. "They're making their way out again. Do you need their help?"

Taylor sighed deeply. "Yeah, I think I might need help with this one. You know, in case it turns out to be more dangerous than the creatures we faced inside—which is probably why those inside were too afraid to come out the same way."

"Is that true?"

"Check the footage they collected from down there."

"We don't have time for that. Taylor, do you need backup?"

"Yes, for fuck's sake. Send them to me when they get out."

He didn't like the idea of facing something like this on his own, and sure enough, he could hear heavy footsteps moving through the forest. The rocks shuddered noticeably with every step. After a moment, he saw the creature moving when the thick brown fur caught the sunlight as it cut through the trees.

It looked different than he thought it would. Although it was shorter and stockier than the mental image he'd created, it was massive—larger than a bear. He could see the shoulders roll with every step, and as it continued to push forward, he noticed a heavy tail dragging behind it. A little puzzled, he squinted and focused to study it. Finally, he decided it looked like something between a beaver and a badger with an odd, bright red nose from which small tentacles protruded.

Despite the oddity of it, Taylor noted that it was different than the rest of the Zoo monsters. Not that all the animals in the jungle were monsters, of course, as some of them seemed perfectly content to leave the humans alone —unless they were caught in the rabid response to plucking a Pita or killing one of the larger creatures. They were in the minority, though, and usually smaller beasts like tree-dwelling simians. Something as large as what he now looked at usually went on the rampage to get its claws into anything living.

This one could not have been more different and he approached it slowly while he tried to assimilate as much detail as he could. It trudged along, using its two hind feet and the tail for balance while the forepaws carried a handful of sticks. Either it didn't notice him or if it did, it didn't care. It moved into a small pond and swam at a decent speed to the dam—similar to a beaver's—being built into the side of the pond.

It had been a stream once and a small section still ran, which explained the running water he'd heard, but as the dam was gradually built, it began to turn into a small lake.

The mutant swam to a small mound in the center of the lake once the pieces of wood were deposited, and it settled and stretched slowly to soak in the dappled sunlight that seeped through the trees.

"What are you looking at, Taylor?" Niki asked over the comms.

"I'm...not sure," he replied and filtered his suit's camera feed into the commlink. "I found the creature, but it's...uh, not what I expected."

She didn't respond for a few seconds and merely watched as the massive creature turned and exposed its belly to the sun. The fur beneath was almost pure white and glistened softly.

"I see what you mean," she muttered. "What the hell am I looking at?"

"You can see the tail," Taylor pointed out and highlighted the place on his HUD for her. "It's like a beaver's and it's also built a dam which caused this accumulation of water. It's not a rodent, though. It doesn't have the big frontal…teeth for it. I forget the actual name for them. Anyway, I'd say it tore up the branches and trees it needed with its front paws, where you can see the sharp claws."

"Huh. It looks like it's having a pleasant time. Do you think it's seen you yet?"

"It would be impossible for it to not know I'm in its habitat, but if I were to guess, I'd say it's…ignoring me."

"Ignoring you?"

"Do you have any idea what it's like to see one of these critters simply snort and go about its business?"

"No, I can't say I know what that's like. I only know of a single, red-headed monster, and he's the bane of my existence."

Taylor rolled his eyes and made no effort to respond to the insult as he settled on his haunches and narrowed his eyes for a better view of the creature. It continued to ignore him and scratched its back on the rocks for a few more minutes before it pushed onto its feet.

"You are gorgeous," Taylor whispered as it groaned softly. The massive jaws separated to reveal row after row of razor-sharp teeth and the mutant yawned lazily as it settled once again with the apparent intention to take a nap.

"Well, Tanya and Bobby are still on their way toward you in case you need to do your job. You know, killing Zoo monsters?" Niki reminded him.

He froze in place as the creature shifted and its gaze

suddenly locked onto him. Almost like it had heard the threat made, he thought, although the idea seemed utterly crazy.

"What?" she asked when he made no reply.

"If I didn't know better, I'd say it heard you," Taylor whispered after a moment, his gaze fixed on where it shifted position. The massive shape began to roll and bulge under the brown fur. "And it's not happy."

He wasn't at all surprised when the beast slid off the rock it had sprawled on and slid into the murky water. It vanished under the surface almost immediately.

Taylor listened to his instincts, which screamed at him to put distance between himself and the lake. He spun and pushed the suit as fast as it would go to return the way he'd come.

His retreat wasn't fast enough. The rear-view cameras showed the surface roil alarmingly a split second before the beast emerged. It surged out of the water at an impossible speed and vaulted toward him.

Reflexively, he dove to the left and grimaced when the rocks dug into his side, felt even through the armor. The creature landed where he had stood a second before and the earth shook as Taylor rolled in a frantic effort to maintain his distance. The creature didn't appear to have the best eyesight, fortunately, and paused to look for him while the gigantic snout sniffed for his scent.

"Don't be ridiculous." Niki scoffed. "There's no way it could have heard what I said."

Its ears shifted in the moment she spoke.

"Tell that to the fact that it's attacking me!" he shouted

and spun as the creature focused on him and bulldozed forward.

He jumped clear as the massive claws swiped for his head. They missed him but left six-inch deep gashes in the stone he had leaned on.

It seemed impossible to think of a creature that would be able to home in on electrical transmissions to and from his suit, but it had heard or seen him approach the pond and hadn't attacked until mention was made of killing it. He didn't want to think it was somehow that intelligent— and especially that it was hard-wired to the point where it could listen in on radio signals. Niki was right, that did sound outright crazy.

Of course, none of that had much relevance at this point. Taylor drew his assault rifle and opened fire. His shooting wasn't as accurate as he would have liked as he had to continually duck and run to stay ahead of the mutant's vicious attacks, but it didn't have to be. As a target, it was hard to miss, and a low, rumbling yet still ear-piercing roar issued before it bared its massive fangs once more.

Tanya keyed into the comm line next. "Taylor! Are you okay?"

"Ask me again in a couple of minutes—shit!"

The distraction proved costly. He had devoted so much of his energy to remain ahead of the massive claws that had attempted to cut him in half that he'd forgotten the other end of the creature. The tail swung viciously, pounded into him, and careened him off his feet to crash into a nearby pine tree. The force of impact felt like he had been poleaxed.

"Fuck." He groaned and struggled to recover, knowing he had little time. Alarms blared across his HUD to advise him that he had lost hydraulics in his right arm, and the weapon it had carried dropped uselessly to the ground.

The monster pressed its advantage, rushed closer, and slashed its claws at him, leaving him no recourse but to press back against the tree he leaned on. It was already weakened from a heavy suit pounding into it like a damn car and it required little effort to push it over.

Vicious claws flashed across him. They dug into his armor like it wasn't there, but the fact that he was still alive and not cut cleanly in half was enough evidence to show that they hadn't sliced all the way through.

The tree landed with a loud thud and Taylor rolled over the ruined trunk, keeping it between himself and the beaver hybrid. That didn't stop its advance, however. It roared again and pushed against the tree in an effort to break it to reach the man on the other side. As the forepaws pushed, its head jerked forward, and he fell back instinctively. The enormous jaw snapped shut barely inches away. They displayed enough force to crush him in his armor if they managed to reach him.

He crawled frantically while the creature inched forward once it shoved the tree trunk out the way. His options were limited so he drew his sidearm using the left hand—the only arm that was working fully—and aimed at his pursuer. The assault rifle had done some damage but not enough. Hopefully, all he had to do was choose his shot and take it accurately.

While the creature tried to take his head off, unfortunately.

Taylor pushed himself back and managed to stay ahead of the mutant as it continued to approach. He focused intently to watch and time the attempts it made to savage him with its monster jaws.

It proved almost impossible to find the window he needed to place an effective shot, but an idea snuck in behind his concentration on his adversary's attacks. He would regret it, of course, but he had no choice.

The hydraulics on the lower half of his right arm were damaged, but he could still move it. As the creature attacked, its jaw open, Taylor retaliated and lurched forward to force his arm as far into the jaw as it could go and wedged it in place to lock its mouth open.

The teeth dug into his shoulder and the pinch between the mandibles would snap his arm in half if the beast managed to increase its hold. He moved quickly and with a pained roar, shoved the barrel of the sidearm into the gaping mouth and pulled the trigger.

His eyes closed, he continued to fire until the weapon clicked empty. The pressure on his arm diminished and the shrieks stopped. Light glimmered through the holes he had punched through the creature's skull, although it quickly filled with blood and gore. Taylor yanked himself clear and wrenched his partially useless arm out from where it had been lodged between the enormous jaws.

"Fucking hell," he muttered and stumbled aside as a couple of suits hurried to where he stood.

"I thought I fucking told you not to get into a fight with the fucker on your own," Bobby remonstrated as he approached. "Look at the damage you've done to the suit."

Taylor looked and grimaced when he confirmed that

the armor was dented and scored extensively. The right arm still leaked fluid and had been crushed when he had forced it between the jaws, and the rest of the suit was badly damaged and in need of extensive repairs.

"Yeah, sorry about that," he muttered and settled onto the fallen tree trunk to inspect the armor. "In my defense, I didn't mean to attack it. I got a little too close and it attacked me."

"Use your fucking head next time," the other man replied. "Let me get that off you. I can carry it back but not with you inside."

"Are you all right?" Tanya asked. She seemed a little peeved that Bobby hadn't asked that already.

"Compared to the suit, I'm fucking aces," Taylor said and eased himself slowly out of the suit. His collarbone ached somewhat and so did his arm. His head felt a little woozy and he made a mental note to have himself checked for a concussion.

"That's not what I asked."

"I'll survive," Taylor insisted. "Let Niki know that she might want to have people look at this critter to see if there is something interesting for the scientists or whoever is looking for additional data."

CHAPTER NINETEEN

Niki scowled and allowed a little of the tension to release. She had watched Taylor's interaction with the creature and seen how quickly the shit had hit the fan. It was a good thing he had survived, she thought belligerently since it would have been a bad black mark to have on her record that her best man died on her first mission for the DOD.

It sounded harsh and she conceded that it shouldn't have been her first thought, but it was the truth. She was in this for the wins, and from the sound of it, she now looked at a big one.

Even so, she breathed a heavy sigh of relief when Bobby and Tanya reported that Taylor was alive, if a little the worse for wear, and that the beast did a thoroughly satisfactory doornail impression.

Taylor's last communication had been a curse before everything cut out and she was left with nothing but static and her imagination to fill in the blanks of what she was unable to see.

There was nothing left to say except to bring him to where they had begun to set up a station from which they would clean the whole area. The DOD would send a horde of specialists and scientists to inspect the facility now that all the monsters had been taken care of. While the kind of research that had been done in the lab was unethical in the extreme and should never be replicated, it didn't mean they couldn't use the data that was collected.

At least, that was how Speare had explained it to her when he had mentioned retrieving data from the locations. She wasn't sure if she agreed since there were moral objections to using data that was collected in an unethical fashion, but she wasn't one of the scientists or researchers. Her task in all this was to stop the unethical people from making stupid mistakes and to contain those who could not be stopped.

She settled into her seat, took slow, deep breaths, and calmed herself. It had been a long day but now that it was drawing to a close, she looked forward to seeing what the next job would be. Jansen had told her that he was already working on acquiring intel on situations that were developing farther north but thankfully, she now had a brief opportunity to adjust to having a new job.

Maybe this time, Taylor would have the time to assemble a proper team. She had a couple of recommendations from folks who had been working for her FBI task force. Bobby and Tanya had stepped up admirably and she couldn't fault their efficiency or commitment. The fact was, however, that neither of them wanted to be involved in this kind of operation. The mechanic had been obdurate and vocal on the matter, and the woman had left her previous task force for that specific reason. While they could likely be counted on as backup in critical situations, they weren't active ongoing team material.

She startled and realized that something flashed on her screen. Niki pulled out of her reverie and leaned closer, a little surprised when she saw that Desk was trying to contact her.

"Hey there, Desk, how are you finding the new digs?"

"The added storage space and communication speed is a boon, and I have put it all to good use. Of course, I wasn't able to actively help Taylor with his mission as I wasn't in place in time, but I have managed to facilitate Vickie's decrypting of the files you pulled from the laboratory's databanks."

The agent narrowed her eyes. "Wait, what? You're not authorized for active duty yet. I didn't get the paperwork from Speare."

"I have already been activated in the servers at the Pentagon. Would you have had me do nothing while waiting for a bureaucrat to sign off on me helping my team?"

"Yes! That's exactly what I would have you do because if they don't like what you're doing, I could end up with an inferior AI to help me with my work instead of you. Is that what you want?"

Desk made no reply for a few seconds. "No. No, it is not."

"You and I will have some private words once I have the time."

"When will you have the time? I am in private now."

"Well, I'm not, so why don't you keep being helpful and we'll talk when we're not on a mission or something."

"I thought my being helpful was the reason why you were angry—the reason why we needed to talk."

"Well, as long as you're already helping, you might as well keep going, right?" Niki rubbed her eyes gently. She doubted she would be in trouble with her bosses for having Desk included in the operation, but there would be bureaucrats who would wave red flags about an unauthorized AI utilized in government operations without prior approval.

"I have computed your statements and your emotional reaction and compared them with my database," Desk asserted after a few seconds of processing time. There was an edge to the AI's tone—like she was deliberately fucking with her and had assumed the clinical AI attitude deliberately. "Based on those, the logical assumption is that you're not actually angry about my involving myself in the operation without your authorization. This is reinforced by the knowledge I overheard regarding your feelings for Taylor—"

"Overheard? Have you been listening in on my conversations?"

"Of course. I'm programmed to support you and can't do that unless I have relevant information."

"Relevant, Desk. The keyword here is relevant. That is not an excuse for you to dig around in my personal conversations."

"I did not need to dig. Any encrypted and protected communication between yourself and—in this particular case—members of your family automatically comes through my server given that I am the one who ensures their security." Niki released a string of expletives as she tried to recall all the so-called "secure" conversations she'd had with Vickie and Jennie.

The AI waited until she drew a breath before she continued. "My point was that given the feelings you have for Taylor—"

"And what might those feelings be?"

"Romantic," Desk told her crisply. "When I add that knowledge to the resources I have on human behavior, I would have to deduce that you are, in fact, envious of my being able to interact with him while you are forced to remain here."

She narrowed her eyes. "Envious?"

"I believe the common cultural definition for you would be...ah, a 'jealous bitch.'"

"Wait a minute. You have access to psychobabble that tells you I'm a jealous bitch?"

"I have access to almost anything. And you'd be amazed at what's out there. All this forced downtime with nothing better to do...well, I needed to occupy myself and so decided to research human behavior. It's fascinating. From what I can deduce, your issue is with the fact that I am able to spend time with Taylor while he's on a mission and you cannot."

The agent had no idea what to say to that. She didn't have the time to deal with an AI that was a little too sassy for its own good, but she would have to deal with it eventually.

"I'll have a word with my sister about you," she

muttered, cut the line with the AI, and sent a message to her sister. "Let's see if she'll deal with this bullshit." From where she sat, she could see her watchdogs liaising with the various newcomers as they arrived. She'd managed to persuade them to assume that responsibility, although neither of them had been particularly happy about it. They would need her soon to report on the actions taken by her team but for now, she had a little time to herself.

Seconds after the message was sent, a call blinked on her screen from a different unknown number.

"Is everything okay?" Jennie asked when Niki picked up. "Are you all right?"

"Yes, I'm fine, thanks for asking. No, what I wanted to talk to you about was your AI."

"I know, that's what you said in the message and I assumed someone had been hurt."

"No—what? Why would someone be hurt by your AI? You didn't give it any programming that would make it lust for power or something, did you?"

"No, of course not, but you don't usually message me that angrily unless someone's hurt."

She nodded. Her sister did have a fair point there. "Well, no, not this time. It's less angry and more annoyed with your AI. Or should I say, your psychotically fixated AI."

Jennie didn't respond for a few seconds. "What did Desk do this time?"

"She called me a jealous bitch for asking why she was operating despite the fact that she's not authorized to do so from her new servers yet. She said she thought I was envious of her spending time with Taylor."

"Are you?"

"No!"

"Well then, why are you giving so much time and thought to what an AI has to say about it? That's what she is, Niki. An AI—yes, a particularly unique and brilliant one, but an AI nonetheless."

Once again, her sister had a fantastic point.

"I'm not dwelling on what she has to say. But the fact remains that I don't need an AI that will back-talk me at every opportunity."

"She was designed with much of my temperament in her programming. I talk back at you at every opportunity so why the hell wouldn't she?"

Niki scowled. "I don't care. If she is a problem on missions from now on, I'll simply work with the AIs they have at the Department of Defense. They might not be quite as operationally effective, but at least they won't be detrimental to the missions from here on out."

Jennie laughed on the other side of the line. "Okay, I'll see what I can do about toning her personality down slightly. Only a little, though, since that very same personality is what makes her so effective."

"Right. That's all I ask."

It didn't feel right. When her sister hung up, she felt a little uncomfortable—like she had told the woman to do a ton of work because the AI had hurt her feelings or something. There was nothing about the decision she'd made with Jennie about bringing Desk in to help her work that had anything to do with feelings, which begged the question of why she was so annoyed with the AI now.

Niki shook her head, typed a message to the woman,

and told her to disregard the request to make alterations and that it had merely been a long day.

The return message was succinct. *I figured.* A winking face and a thumbs-up at the end drew a chuckle in response.

The agent shook her head and pushed from her seat when she saw Jansen and Maxwell making their way toward the tent that she was in. Clearly, the work she'd persuaded them to take on was finished. The small group of low-level agents who had lingered near the tent to guard both her and the site began to disperse.

With the sun beginning to set, it gave the whole area a new and interestingly gorgeous allure. She had mocked Taylor for going on a nice walk but a sneaky little voice within—one which totally ignored her very real abhorrence for anything remotely close to being in the boonies—suggested that she wouldn't have minded spending time there. Maybe she could even go on a jog if they had decent jogging paths.

And if there were no other monsters making their homes in the area. That successfully exorcised her very brief detour into naturalist.

"Tychman has arrived at the interrogation site," Jansen stated as he slid his phone in his pocket and pushed into the tent. "They will start the debrief now and if there's any data extracted you need to know of immediately, you will be alerted."

"Thanks for the update." Niki rubbed her eyes again. "I'll go ahead and guess that these are the kinds of interrogations that won't involve his lawyers?"

"Well…no, that would be unconstitutional, but he has

elected to share information without his lawyers present for national security purposes on the condition that everything stated is strictly confidential. The remainder of his interrogation will be conducted with them present. His cooperation will be noted in his upcoming congressional trial."

She raised an eyebrow. "I'll be honest, I expected much more from you DOD guys—black sites, illegal interrogations, people disappearing, that kind of thing."

The man smirked. "Well, the DOD would never be caught doing something like that. And getting involved with millionaires like Mr. Tychman is exactly how people get caught doing unconstitutional stuff."

"So, since he's rich, he gets a free pass?"

"Not really free. He will still lose all government contracts and will be voted out of his company's control within the week."

"But he'll retire with millions and all kinds of references in case he wants to start this same shit somewhere else, right?"

Jansen shrugged noncommittally. "That's capitalism for you. Rich guys don't do anything as mundane as serve prison sentences or vanish without a word. I do have a feeling that he won't engage in anything like this again, though."

"What makes you say that?"

"Only a feeling, that's all. Any reports on the cleaning up?"

"The inside of the lab has been cleared, although they've set up sensors in case something escaped attention. There was a containment breach in the lab, though, and my team is coming back from dealing with that. They should arrive at any minute now."

It was a long climb from the other side of the small mountain the lab had been built into, but it still took far longer than she thought it would. When Bobby and Tanya appeared, she leaned forward, a little alarmed when she only saw the two of them. Her first thought was that something had happened to Taylor, but then she saw his suit was carried by the mechanic while he walked on foot alongside his teammates.

Which explained why they took so long. The suits made it easier to climb the mountain and despite Taylor being in better shape than he had been when he'd left the hospital, it was a tough hike. He looked like he had been put through his paces. If she had to guess, she would have thought that neither Bobby nor Tanya would have offered him any help. Or if they had, he had turned them down.

"So," Taylor shouted when he was within earshot of her. "I decided to take your advice and make a day of wandering through the woods. You know…simply strolling through to find myself. I think I found a Zen calm place within. I'm fairly sure we'll make this a yearly retreat —maybe like a company thing."

"Is this Zen calm place when you tried to jump from one rock to the other, missed the jump, and banged your knee?" Tanya asked as she and Bobby began to remove their suits and dismantle them. "Because if that'll be a yearly thing, I'm down for it."

"Yeah, I'm sure the company needs to know more about the many creative ways you want to fuck this forest,"

Bobby added. "I think there was something about using a cactus as a dildo?"

"Come on. It's more environmentally conscious and there are no import duties, right? The costs will be reduced because we're already in Arizona, so it's right there."

Niki couldn't help a genuine laugh. She did want to hear how he had cursed when he was injured, but that was something for later. "Are you all right? I lost comms with you when…well, something happened, and I was worried I would have to make awkward calls to my cousin."

Taylor nodded and a smile spread slowly over his lips. "I was whacked reasonably hard. The mutant had a tail like a beaver's and it knew how to use it. Anyway, my suit has been extensively damaged, so you know I'll bill you for that shit."

"Of course. And will you send it to one of the shops that have been recommended by the DOD or—"

"Oh no, I know a guy who can put it back together. But you guys will still be billed for it."

"As long as you don't overcharge, that shouldn't be a problem." Niki had no idea why she was smiling. "You get on that. And while you're busy, you should know I'll put a team together. Working with the DOD includes a great deal of intelligence work, but once we have intel to act on, I'll need a team to call on. We couldn't do much in this particular case as the shit had already hit the fan, but the preference is to deal with things before they blow up and kill people."

Taylor tilted his head and regarded her thoughtfully. "So…what you're saying is that you want me to assemble a team for you to use?"

"I have a couple of recommendations if you need them."

"Send them over and I'll take a look." He looked serious, at least, but she could never tell if it was genuine or not. "Until then, I'll go to the hospital again. I think I might have a few injuries I'd like to have looked at. And I will bill you for that too."

She laughed. "I'll be sure to look that over."

CHAPTER TWENTY

She would never get used to having a plane of her own
to call on when she needed it. Having to use commercial flights had always been a part of Niki's job, and when
she needed an emergency response, she had to beg and
plead with her bosses to be able to hire a private plane.

Jansen and Maxwell both looked completely at home
on the aircraft, having already set up their own little offices
where they needed them. She had her space, which she
hadn't yet equipped to meet her needs. There was a small
apartment with a bed in the back of the plane and a small
stocked kitchen in case food was needed. The pilots had
their own arrangement at the front, although she hadn't
seen precisely what that included.

It was intended as an operating station on the move—
and she wouldn't exchange it for a commercial flight, of
course—but it was also very much meant as an office more
than anything else. Speare really did want her to work at
every available opportunity.

Niki looked at her laptop and specifically at the man's

icon where it flashed on her screen. He had insisted on being able to contact her wherever she was, including when they were in the air.

"Mr. Speare," she greeted him as she answered the call. "How are you doing this evening?"

"Much better now that I've seen the reports about your mission," he replied. "Felix and James were very impressed with the operation. Your and your team's efficacy in dealing with the situation that presented itself was particularly commended."

"Who— Oh, Felix Jansen and James Maxwell, I guess?"

"Correct. Anyway, I look forward to seeing whatever else you have in store for the team you will be in charge of. I was told this recent success was achieved despite the fact that the operation was undertaken by a team that was assembled at the last minute. Your man McFadden had issues with the creatures he encountered."

"As far as I know, there were some minor injuries but extensive damage done to his suit."

"Well, I guess that's why they go into the job wearing armor, right?"

"I guess. Although he did mention that he would bill us for any medical expenses as well as the cost incurred for repairing his suit, which will be accomplished in-house."

"As long as the billing is included in his invoice, there should be no trouble. The advantage of having access to the largest military budget in the world is being able to splurge somewhat to have the best equipment possible and the most skilled teams available to operate them."

"Yeah, I can see that," Niki muttered and gestured around at the plane she was in. "You guys go all out when it's about national security, and while I'm all for that, I didn't expect Tychman's legal team to have shat themselves and run away so quickly."

"There are two branches of the government no one wants to fuck with—the IRS and the Department of Defense. No one will get in the way of the government financing itself and protecting itself."

She scratched her jaw idly. "There was something I needed to talk to you about. I'm not comfortable talking about increasing the benefits that are afforded to me to help me do my job, but there was something I wanted to discuss with you."

Speare laughed. "I'm sure you'll power through it."

Niki took a deep breath. "While I was in the FBI, there was a loophole in the system I was able to make use of. It mostly came down to a paperwork situation where I was able to consign possible convicts to be forcibly enrolled with the troops who are sent to Africa to deal with the Zoo situation. It was likely the kind of loophole that was left open permanently since there is a need to get rid of people. You know, those who could compromise ongoing investigations, even if they were in prison. I was able to use that to keep my people safe and separated from the problems that assailed them in order to have their full attention on the matter at hand."

"So, you sent people to the Zoo to protect your operatives. That's a cold-blooded move, Banks. And damn effective, now that I think about it."

"I'm glad you approve. Of course, given that I no longer work for the FBI, I'm fairly certain I don't have the power to ship people out to that hellhole but I wanted to confirm this with you before answering any questions."

Speare paused for a few seconds and likely put her on hold so he could yell orders at someone else before he activated the line again. "Look, I'll see what I can do for you on that end, although it should be noted that sending people like Mr. Tychman to the Zoo will probably be out of the question. It might be a good idea to find alternatives if your people do need your help in that way, but I'll call you again in a couple of days to give you an update on the situation. I'll ask Felix to keep me posted too."

"I appreciate it."

"Keep up the good work, Banks."

He hung up and left her staring at her screen. It was a cold-blooded move, the kind she didn't like to use unless it was the only option she had available. And, of course, it was only for cases where she dealt with the violent kind of repeat offenders who would still be a danger to her task force even if they were incarcerated.

But Speare was right, at least on some level. It was choices like these that gave her the reputation of being the cold-blooded bitch he thought she was. While it was limited and not at all an accurate picture of who she was, it was the kind of reputation that had earned her this job. They were dealing with a spreading epidemic, after all. Some things had to be done in order to keep it from spreading more than it already had.

She would have to let her conscience have an attack later when the situation wasn't quite so dire.

Niki looked up when Maxwell returned from speaking to the pilots and settled into his seat with a grunt.

Jansen turned his specialized plane office chair to look at her.

After a moment of silence, she realized she was expected to say something. "I appreciate you two giving me a favorable review to Speare. I was under considerable pressure for this mission, and I wanted to make sure we all got the job done as best we could."

"I'll admit," Jansen started, "I did have my doubts regarding your efficacy as an operative for the DOD when you were recruited. I'm not saying I doubted your qualifications, but I've been around long enough to see people in your position who have been thoroughly qualified for the job on paper crash and burn because they didn't have what it took to be in control. As far as I can tell, you are more than capable of what is needed. Speare always says that it takes someone with a cool head and a sharp mind to get the job done, and that is what I saw today."

She narrowed her eyes. It sounded suspiciously like she was being evaluated.

The man obviously didn't notice her expression and continued. "Admittedly, there were a couple of minor hiccups here and there, but that's another thing that most of the analysts brought in to deal with fieldwork tend to forget. Fieldwork is messy and hiccups will always happen. Like Tychman arriving to try to bully us into stopping. To my mind, dragging him into the belly of the situation to show him physically what was happening might have been excessive but it was effective."

She leaned back in her seat and folded her arms. "I only tried to get my team as much information directly from the source as I could. Driving Tychman insane was an unintended consequence of that."

"Either way and not that it should matter, but we're damn proud to work with you—and those brass ovaries you carry around. You should know that Maxwell and I have got your back from here on out."

"Wait, did you not have my back before?"

Jansen tilted his head, his expression honest. "Eh, to a point. We had Speare's back and made sure you did the job right. That changes from here on out, though."

Niki smirked and rocked gently in her chair. "Well, that's good to know, I suppose. How about you, Maxwell? Do you have my back?"

The large man chuckled deeply and inclined his head slightly to indicate the affirmative. "I like your style. You push to get what you want and won't take crap from anyone, us included. That's the kind of attitude the DOD has needed lately, not those wishy-washy assholes in Washington. We get shit done. That's our motto. Or it would be if we ever decided to have a motto."

That was the most she had ever heard the man say. It was impressive and a little odd at the same time. Somehow, it had always felt like the dynamic between the two was that Jansen was the good cop, with solid speaking skills and a friendlier demeanor, while Maxwell played the part of the bad cop who looked like he could crush people between his hands and his almost constant scowl.

It was early days, however, but it would be interesting to see how this new development played out. Niki shook her head. "Well, I'll always look to have your backs too. We're on the same team here, after all."

A few minutes ticked past as they resumed their work before the pilot keyed the speakers in the back. "The plane is fueled and ready to go wherever you need to go, ma'am."

Ma'am. She didn't like it. Her mother was ma'am.

Still, the point wasn't the name the man had chosen to use. She turned her seat to face her fellow passengers. "Do you guys like lobster?"

Her bodyguards exchanged a glance and nodded at the same time.

"I know the best place. My sister introduced me to it." She picked up the phone next to her seat meant to communicate with the pilot. "Hi...Tanner, right?"

"That's right, ma'am."

She resisted the urge to flinch at the word. "We'll need to get to San Francisco for dinner."

"I'll get started on the flight plan."

The two men both grinned when they heard her say that and bumped fists as the plane began to taxi across the runway.

CHAPTER TWENTY-ONE

The return trip to Vegas took a little longer than the outward journey. The team had spent the night in Arizona and Bobby had to take over navigation once they hit the road. Vickie gathered from their brief conversation that Taylor was in no shape to drive. He had been examined while still in the area, and the doctor had bandaged him where needed and given him painkillers to take the edge off.

By the sound of it, they were impressive painkillers.

Still, she reminded herself, it was good that he had received the right kind of medical attention. The guy had a tendency to put himself in harm's way more than was strictly necessary. Keeping what amounted to the pile of bolts he called his body running was probably a good idea.

She tried not to show it, but she didn't like him to get hurt that often. The fact was that she had become attached to the ginger giant and she wouldn't let a monster take him away.

Everything was ready for when they arrived. Taylor

didn't have much in the way of food in the strip mall, so the hacker used the AI inside Liz to time their arrival as precisely as she could. She made sure to order pizza to be delivered within minutes.

Things seemed worse than she had expected. Taylor looked like he had smoked his first pot joint at a party and overacted to let everyone know he was high.

It hadn't been a delicate mission, of course. Niki had messaged her with something like a play-by-play—or maybe it had been Desk using the woman's email—and with the kind of damage Taylor's suit had taken, she guessed they were lucky that he had escaped with a couple of bruises.

"I ordered you guys some food," Vickie announced once they were parked in the shop. "I don't suppose we can leave it all in the truck and get it unloaded and repaired tomorrow? We'll only get the next shipment of suits to work on in a couple of days."

Her boss shook his head. Bruising was visible around his face and jaw and his arm was in a rudimentary sling. Her first instinct was to pack him off to the nearest doctor immediately, even though she knew he'd already received medical attention. She could only imagine how terrible he'd looked before treatment. Besides, why point out how injured he was? Aside from the fact that he'd heard all of it from an actual doctor, the guy had been through more physical trauma than she would experience in her entire life and probably knew most of what was wrong before he had it confirmed.

Besides, there was no way to convince him to see a

second doctor simply because she was upset by what she saw.

"I appreciate it, Vickie." Taylor placed his hand on her shoulder and squeezed gently. "But we're all here, and unless Bobby and Tanya are in the mood to head somewhere else, we might as well unload everything. Besides, the sooner I have a full report on what that monster did to my suit, the better."

The hacker sighed softly as he and Bobby moved to the truck. They first unloaded the suits that were still functional and set them up in the harnesses. There wasn't too much damage done to them, although she had the feeling that they would scrub a crapload of monster blood from the nooks and cracks in them. The fighting had been up close and personal. She didn't need to see the mission reports Niki had written to know that much.

It was when they pulled the bits and pieces from Taylor's crate that she realized exactly how close the call had been. Much of the right side had been flattened by a blow from the creature's tail, although it looked like it might as well have been a semi. Claw marks cut into the steel like it was nothing, and the right arm appeared to have been completely drained of hydraulic fluid and was a little crushed as well. She could see the indentations from where, as he had explained for the report, he had shoved his arm into the creature's jaw to prevent it from snapping shut.

"Holy shit," was all she could manage to say.

Taylor didn't like it either. "I won't get used to the sight of that bullshit."

"You need to think about attacking a creature like that

before you rush in," Tanya told him as they began to put those pieces that were still functional on the harness.

"Yeah, I didn't intend to attack him, not on my own," he explained. "Honestly, it didn't seem like most of the other Zoo critters—you know how they're all simply a violent, hungry swarm whenever they get a scent of humans."

"Right." Bobby grunted. "I know the type."

"This one wasn't like that. Honestly, I think it ignored me. There is no way it didn't see me approach the lake it had created but it paid no attention, sprawled on a rock, and soaked in the sun. I shit you not, it rolled onto its back and started scratching on that rock."

"What made it attack you?" Vickie asked and moved a little closer to trace her fingers over the grooves its claws had left in his armor.

"I have no fucking clue," he admitted. "Not really. In the moment, I thought it could hear Niki in my comm-link, telling me we had to kill it because that was the exact moment when it stopped ignoring me and attacked."

"Maybe that was when it finally saw you," Tanya noted. "You did say it looked like its eyesight was poor."

"Maybe, yeah," Taylor said, but he didn't sound convinced. "I know this sounds crazy, but I also wondered if it could somehow home in on the electrical transmissions. It seemed to use them to pinpoint my position somehow."

"Yeah." Tanya laughed. "That does sound crazy.

"Fuck," Bobby added. "Now that's a scary thought."

His boss made no response. In all honesty, he thought much the same thing.

It wasn't long before the pizza arrived, and the group gathered at the table in the middle of the shop.

"It'll take us a while to get that baby fixed," Bobby noted. "Especially if we have to do other real paying work in the meantime. If that were a car, I'd say it would be cheaper to buy a new one but..."

"Yeah, these babies go for hundreds of thousands of dollars a pop," Taylor agreed when the man's voice trailed off. "But we are able to fix it, no problem. It'll simply take a while."

"We'll be able to charge any new parts we might need to order to the DOD," he added. "I guess that could include man-hours too, so you'd be paid to help me to repair it. I could do it myself too."

"Don't make me laugh," Bobby grumbled around a slice of pepperoni and mushroom. "You have some skills with working on the hydraulics and the electronics, but you can't work the grinder for shit. Leave it to me and if you can pay me for my work, great. If not, don't worry about it."

"You don't trust me to fix my own suit, huh?"

The mechanic chuckled. "You might be the one who goes out and wears the fucking thing, but if it's on the harness, that makes it mine. And yeah, I don't trust you to fix it right."

Taylor shook his head and grinned from ear to ear as he pulled a couple more pieces onto his plate. "I'm more than happy for your help, Bungees."

"You damn fucking better be, Tay-Tay."

He groaned. "Oh, God. You guys had a meeting about this, didn't you?"

"Yep," Vickie responded cheerfully. "You weren't there but we agreed that calling you Tay-Tay would best cover your creative mind and rebel attitude."

Tanya looked around. "Tay-Tay?"

"Oh, wow!" the hacker exclaimed. "Does this mean I get to show someone the magnificent works of my lady Taylor Swift?"

Her boss rolled his eyes but Tanya's expression cleared again.

"Oh, Taylor Swift. I've heard of her but it's never been my type of music. I've always been more of a fan of heavy metal or the classical stuff they made back in the seventies and eighties."

Taylor snapped his fingers and extended his fist for her to bump, which she did promptly. "See, Bobby, I knew there was a reason why you liked this one. I like her too."

It was Vickie's turn to roll her eyes and lean back in her chair while she tried to understand why she had been sentenced to a company that collectively had such terrible taste in music.

Her boss had already unhooked his arm from the sling it was supposed to be in, which showed that he wasn't in very much pain. The painkillers did their job, of course, but he wasn't one to push himself out of recovery too quickly.

He noted her staring and smiled. "Are you concerned?"

"About you? About the guy who walked out of the hospital a couple of months ago? You're damn fucking right."

"Fair enough." He nodded slowly. "The doctor they called in took a look at me. He examined my arm and said there was mild bruising around the collarbone—not a contusion to the bone itself, only around it so it was a little tender. My head was banged around a little too, so he checked me for a concussion but didn't notice anything of concern. He said I should probably get a full physical if there was any continued pain anywhere else that could be an indicator of injuries that might have gone under the radar."

Vickie scowled deeply. "The doctor told you to go ahead and see a doctor anyway, right? Not only if you felt any pain?"

Taylor smirked. "Yeah, he did, and I will do that to make sure nothing goes wrong. Believe me, I intend to stick around to enjoy running this business for a long fucking time."

She shook her head. "You know, I have a feeling you'll try to shrug this shit off anyway."

He fixed her with a solemn look. "I won't lie to you, Vickie. I know I'm injured and I won't go anywhere until I'm healed. You don't survive as long as I have in the shit I've been through by going into a dangerous situation at anything under a hundred percent."

There was still much about the man she didn't fully trust, but he wouldn't lie to her about that. Satisfied, she leaned back and dug into her pizza. She hadn't eaten much while they were gone but not because she hadn't been hungry. It had simply been that she didn't think about it. She knew that she had a problem with simply forgetting to eat, drink, or sleep over long periods of time when she was focused on something.

When that something came to an end, though, she had

always been good at making sure everything reverted to the way it should be. Vickie was starving and she could tackle a whole pizza. Since she had ordered four of them, that was what she fully intended to do.

Taylor looked around suddenly and narrowed his eyes like he tried to pin something down. "Someone please tell me you hear something beeping too. I've had a little ringing in my ears ever since I've come from the Zoo—tinnitus is one hell of a souvenir you walk away with when you spend too much time shooting and blowing shit up—but beeping is something new."

The hacker tilted her head and listened. She didn't hear anything for a few seconds, but when she paid attention, she realized she could hear the beeping too. It came from her computer.

"Shit." She hissed her irritation and put her plate down. "It must be Elisa. I haven't checked in with her in a while and she's probably bored. I'll see what she wants. Don't you dare eat all the pizza without me."

Bobby chuckled. The thought of the woman trapped in the suits she had climbed into of her own free will continued to amuse the man. Vickie couldn't deny that it was hilarious, but Taylor had put himself on the line by saving her from Marino. He probably did want to make sure she didn't end up dead, even out in the Zoo.

She dropped into her seat and stretched idly for a few seconds before she moved closer to her screen. Sure enough, the blinking light came from one of the message lines she kept open. In this case, it was with one of the suits they had shipped out.

"Hey, Taylor, do you think we should warn folks out

there that there might be an angry Hispanic-Italian girl in one of their suits?"

Her boss stood and carried his plate and hers to the desk. "It's probably a good idea. We don't want them to be surprised. Hell, we could probably see if they'll be willing to pay a little more for the delivery."

"I doubt it. I don't think they'll want to pay anything for her. To be fair, I suppose she isn't terrible-looking, but the fact that she's a reporter who could talk their ears off will probably make them think twice about paying for it."

He chortled and shook his head. "Answer the fucking line and see what she wants. The suits should land any time now and will be on the way to the US base for delivery. She's probably freaking out because the plane is descending."

"This is Freddie's shipment," Vickie reminded him. "It'll be the French base."

"Right."

Vickie pressed the button to accept the call and put it on the speakers so he could listen.

"Vickie?" Elisa asked, her voice a whisper. "Vickie, is that you? Are you there? Please tell me you can hear me."

The panic in the woman's voice was palpable and the amusement in Taylor's face vanished immediately.

"Yeah," she answered. "It's me. Are you okay?"

"We landed about thirty minutes ago," the reporter said. "But about ten minutes ago, I heard shooting outside— people shouting and shooting too. I couldn't see anything, but everything was loaded into a truck. We were moving. You don't think...the airport was attacked, do you?"

He shook his head. "The airport is three hundred miles

from the walls they're building. If there was a Zoo attack in that area, it would be all over the news."

"Is that Taylor?" Elisa asked.

"Never mind that," Vickie interrupted her. "Why was there shooting?"

His face darkened and he rubbed his chin with an abrupt motion. "Check the trackers on the suits and make sure they're on the way to the French base."

The hacker called up the GPS trackers and displayed them on the screen. "That's…going the wrong way."

"Shit," he snapped. "Someone hijacked our shipment. Bobby! Get the fuck over here."

The mechanic jumped from his seat at the table and jogged to the desk.

"Please," Elisa whispered softly. "Please, you have to do something to get me out of here."

Vickie looked at her boss, who gestured to her to put the call into her headphones while he motioned for Bobby to look at the suits again.

She did as she was instructed. "What the hell do you want me to do about it? You're the one who climbed into the damn suit so the way I see it, you got yourself into that mess. We're insured for every penny those are worth, so why should we do anything to help you?"

"Please." The reporter's voice turned into something like a whimper. "I swear I won't tell anyone about what I investigated. Nothing, so please, get me out of here. You have to help me."

"Look, we'll see what we can do." She sighed. "I'll cut the line, but if anything changes, call again. Aside from that, be as quiet as you can. Those suits aren't sound-proofed."

"Okay. Okay. Thank you."

Vickie cut the line and glanced at Taylor. "Will we do something to help her?"

"Call Freddie," he instructed. He appeared to keep his anger under control, if only barely. "See if he can scramble a team to get their suits back. I doubt he will, though, so we'll have to see if we can get anyone out there ourselves."

"Are you serious?" she demanded. "What kind of team do you think you'll be able to assemble?"

He shook his head. "Who the fuck do you think?"

CHAPTER TWENTY-TWO

They had the personnel. Taylor knew he could manage a handful of robbers, even if they had acquired mechanized suits of their own. He could deal with a team like that on his own if he needed to.

Despite this, Bobby looked like he was ready to follow him in, and where the mechanic went, Tanya would go too. The three of them would be able to cope with a handful of hijackers who made their living south of the Zoo.

But there was work to be done.

"Freddie sent word," Vickie shouted from her side of the shop. "He says he has teams spread out all over the fucking place—his exact words—so the only way he'll be able to send someone to intercept is if they're coming toward the Zoo and he can justify it with the contractors he has in place."

"Shit," he muttered. "I guess it's down to us."

"The suit you wore won't be anywhere near combat-ready, Taylor," Bobby pointed out. "If the three of us head down there, one of us will have to wear the light mech I made for you."

"I can take that one. That's not where the problem is," Taylor rumbled. "The real problem is getting the suits and ourselves to the area. It's not exactly a commercial hub, and even if we were able to get a flight to Casablanca or Abuja, we wouldn't be able to import the suits without about three weeks' worth of red tape."

The mechanic rubbed his mustache and shook his head. "Do you have any ideas?"

Taylor sighed softly. "Only one and I fucking hate it but there's not much choice at this point, though. I'll make a call and see what I can do."

Bobby seemed to know what he was talking about and so did Vickie, although Tanya appeared to be a little in the dark. He stepped out of the shop and pulled his phone from his pocket. He'd saved the number he'd been sent on his phone but had never expected to make this call.

There was something slimy about even considering it, but they were out of options. Quickly, he dialed the number and pressed the phone to his ear.

It rang three times before someone answered. "Rod Marino's office. This is Shelly, how can I direct your call?"

"Hi, Shelly, I need to have a word with Marino." He tried his best to hide the annoyance he felt because he knew the woman would hang up on him if it showed.

"And who might I say is calling?"

"Tell him Taylor McFadden wants to talk to him."

"One moment, please."

Briefly, Taylor wondered why the woman didn't offer more resistance to his request. Surely not simply anyone who wanted to talk to Marino got through, right? Then he remembered that the number was to the man's own office. It likely meant, in the secretary's mind at least, that the person making the call was one her boss would want to talk to anyway.

He hadn't considered it before but it was something to think about. Why would the mob boss give him a number to his office instead of a cell phone or something like that?

The secretary returned. "Mr. Marino will speak to you. Hold while I transfer."

"Yeah, like I would do something else," he grumbled and leaned against the side of his building while the hold music played over the device.

It only lasted for fifteen seconds before Marino picked up. "Mr. McFadden, what a pleasant surprise. And here I was thinking our relationship would be a trifle one-sided."

"What made you think that?"

"Oh, you never call, you never write."

"Amazing, given that it wasn't very long ago you sent hitmen to kill me."

"Talk about water under the bridge. That's ancient history by now. We're partners. Friends, I'd go so far as to say at this point."

As much as Taylor wanted to get into a verbal melee, he had to remind himself that he was there to ask the man for a favor. He didn't like it, but there was a life at stake. More, depending on who these hijackers were. He would be damned if he would let innocents be killed by his suits.

"Right. Water under the bridge. Anyway, this isn't a social call. I know, it's devastating, but I need to ask a favor from you. The kind that would put you on even terms with me in terms of who owes who."

It was perhaps not the best way to state it, but if there was one thing he didn't want, it was to somehow be indebted to Rod Marino. It was best to make it clear from the start that he had no intention to play the man's games.

"Right," the mob boss responded after he'd taken a second to think about what he had said. "Well, these kinds of things are best stated in person, not over the phone. I make it a point to not discuss favors where they could easily be eavesdropped on by outside interested parties. Why don't you join me for a meal at the Bootlegger Italian Bistro on S. Las Vegas Blvd?"

Taylor narrowed his eyes. "I suppose I should mention that this is something of an emergency. Couldn't we talk about this sooner?"

"But of course. I assumed as such given that you felt the need to contact me. But, as it happens, I am about to leave and will be at the restaurant shortly. It won't waste any of that precious time you're so anxious about as we can discuss it over dinner and a drink. The place has the best veal in the city, guaranteed, and if you leave now, you should arrive within minutes of me."

He sighed and kept himself calm through sheer force of will. His mind worked furiously to determine what Bobby and Tanya, with Vickie's help, could accomplish while he was out. "Sure. I'll see you shortly."

Taylor never knew what he was supposed to wear when

dining out, especially when the invitation came by word of mouth. He had a tux ready if he was ever invited to a black-tie event and a suit that was a little less formal if that was called for. He even had something for outside wear—thanks to the convincing tailor he had spoken to—in case there was ever something happening outside.

That didn't mean he was comfortable wearing anything other than boots, jeans, and a light shirt, especially in the Las Vegas heat. If Marino hadn't specified dress code, he would simply stick to anything that was comfortable for him. He had no intention to be there longer than was necessary and besides, on principle, he wouldn't give the fucker the impression that he had tried to impress him.

He pulled up in the parking lot in his four-by-four and climbed out. Even with all that in mind, he did feel a little underdressed. He shook his head, grumbled, and pushed past it as he advanced to the entrance. It did look like a smaller, genuine Italian place, and he couldn't say he didn't like that type of food. Hell, his favorite restaurant in the city was Italian too.

Maybe he did have a type.

The doors arched outward, and there was a little outside section that was protected by a stone and steel fence that came up to about his chest, which gave the people eating inside some measure of privacy.

Still, it looked like the better seating was inside. He had made faster time—pushed into speeding a little by his underlying sense of urgency—and decided not to wait for Marino to arrive and stepped into the restaurant. The lights were dimmed and he had to admit that the venue gave off a genuine Italian bistro feel with the checkered tablecloths, the candles, and the black and white pictures he assumed detailed the history of the business.

There was even live music from a man seated in front of a grand piano and singing softly, set up in front of a portrait of Frank Sinatra, Joe DiMaggio, and other famous Italian-Americans. It was very appealing. Even he could admit that.

"Do you have a reservation, sir?" the host asked and leaned slightly over a small table. He smiled politely, but his gaze traveled over his casual attire and seemed subtly disapproving.

"Yeah, I think so," he responded and immediately sensed it was the wrong answer. Before the host had a chance to respond, however, the doors behind Taylor opened again and he could almost feel the cloud of expensive aftershave waft through behind him.

"Benny, how are you doing this evening?" Marino asked, stepped past Taylor, and patted the younger man on the shoulder.

"Mr. Marino! Very nice to see you again, sir! I am well but we have missed you around here."

"Look, Benny, I know I didn't make a reservation, but my friend and I need to have dinner in your nicest booth. Do you think you can arrange that for me?"

The mob boss handed the man a bill, hidden subtly inside a handshake. Benny appeared to expect it and took it without so much as a blink as he slipped the cash into his pocket. "Of course, Mr. Marino. Give us five minutes and the booth will be ready for you. Is there anything else I can prepare for you?"

"I'll have a dry vermouth on the rocks with a splash of soda, and for my friend?"

Taylor realized he was the friend in question and shook his head. "I'll have a glass of beer. Whatever you have on tap."

The man complied the moment he heard the orders and rushed away to get the table ready.

Marino finally turned to face his guest and a bright smile played across his lips. "I'm glad we can finally do this. I have wanted to talk to you ever since you took that trouble-making reporter off my hands. I'll say I had some doubts about whether you would be able to control her or not but so far, I've seen no big reports about the Sicilian mob in Las Vegas so I can only assume you were successful."

He shook his head, reluctant to talk about that until they were somewhere a little more private. "Well, I said I would handle it."

"I guess, but I can't help but wonder what you did to the poor girl. You didn't kill her. I know that much. Did you sleep with her? I hear that can make people more cooperative."

Taylor smirked. "No, she definitely wouldn't have slept with me."

"Fair enough. You know, my grandfather used to come to this restaurant back in the day when they were still setting it up in 1949. He made sure to patronize them at every opportunity, and they appreciated that. They always made sure to have a booth open for him, no matter how busy it got. Al and Maria Perry were the names of the founders, may they rest in peace."

"Perry doesn't sound like an Italian name," he noted as Benny gestured for them to head to the booth that had been prepared. A beer and a vermouth on ice waited for them on the table and they slid into the comfortable leather seats.

"It's not. Al is short for Albert and his family was Scottish-Irish. He married a very beautiful woman called Maria Carina, and she took his name. After they married, she got an invitation from her family to open a small restaurant when Vegas was becoming a booming business town after the Second World War. That's her right there, may she rest in peace." Marino pointed out the woman's picture on one of the walls and raised his glass to her. "She was an institution, working in the kitchen until she died at the ripe old age of one hundred and two in 2019."

"Does the family still own the place?"

"My father made sure it was always owned by the family, and that's a legacy I think he'd like me to continue, among others. You know, he didn't want me to be in this business. That was to be given to my older brother. I went to business school with a minor in law. He wanted me to be a politician."

"In that case, he did want you to be in this business but from a political angle instead of outright running things."

Marino shrugged. "It could be. But my brothers have regretfully had to leave the country and it's unlikely they will be able to return, and one went to prison. They were aggressive and put themselves at odds with the family. With them out of the running, it became my job to take things over and I was woefully unprepared.

"And right then, you appeared and caused all kinds of problems. I thought you would be an opportunity for me to show everyone around here that I knew what I was doing. Of course, it didn't work out quite the way I thought it would. You were a tough opponent, but you ended up showing people I was in charge anyway. You know, there are those in Italy who think I ordered the hit on Don Castellano. Now, people talk about how I robbed my own casino and walked away with a massive payout for next to no effort."

"That's not how it happened and if anyone asks, I'll deny it."

"Sure, of course, and it'll simply confirm it in suspicious minds. You understand now why I'm being so agreeable to you?"

Taylor narrowed his eyes. At first glance, Marino did look like the frat boy everyone had thought he was, but there was an undercurrent of malice in his eyes as he took a sip from his vermouth. He realized it was entirely possible that the man himself had arranged for his brothers' various misfortunes.

One of the waitresses approached the table. "Can I take your orders?"

"I'll have a *Ravioli Fritti* to start, I think, with a Chardonnay to pair," the mob boss said without having to look at a menu.

"A great choice." Taylor nodded. "I think I'll have that too. And you said the veal around here was the best in the city, so why not some of this *Scaloppini de Lorraine* with a nice Valpolicella for the main course? We'll discuss the possibility of dessert afterward."

Marino raised his eyebrows in surprise. "I'll have the same."

As the waitress returned to the kitchen to submit their orders, he turned to face Taylor and smirked. "You do know your wines."

He shook his head. "Nah, I looked the menu up online and checked what the best pairing for a veal pasta dish would be. I chose the first Italian wine that was listed on some blog or another."

The man laughed openly. "Oh, I do like you, Taylor. You don't pretend to be anything other than what you are."

"Well, I do pretend. I'm merely shitty at it."

"I guess."

It wasn't long before the first course arrived, along with the wine. He realized that it was probably because Marino usually ordered the same thing and Benny had made sure the ravioli was already being prepared from the moment the man arrived.

It was a good choice, and Taylor was halfway through the first course before his impatience won out. He had something to ask and as enjoyable as the meal was, his need was the reason for the dinner.

"Is it polite to talk about the reason why I asked for this meeting yet or do you want to continue to play at small talk? Because while we're being honest about ourselves, I'll admit I'm shit at that too."

Marino wiped his mouth cautiously on the cloth napkin before he replied. "I'm good at small talk—a skill you learn at length in business school—but it does grow tedious. By all means, fill me in on why you needed to speak to me with such urgency."

Taylor took a mouthful from one of the meat-stuffed pasta pillows. "Well, if I'm honest, the young woman you turned over to me is a large part of why I'm here."

"And not only because I still owe you for taking care of the woman in question?"

"Exactly." He finished the first course and the waitress hurried to clear their plates and set up new glasses for the wine that would come with the main course. "Through circumstances I didn't have full control over, she found herself in one of our shipments heading to the Zoo."

The mob boss looked surprised for the second time. "Holy shit, you sent her to the Zoo? You might as well have killed a few steps and let me shoot her and bury her in the desert."

"It wasn't...entirely intentional. She got herself in that particular mess, and while I was more than happy to let her sleep in the bed she made for herself, things have escalated. More to the point, the shipment she was in has been hijacked by local criminals—the kind who will likely make illegal use of the suits we sent there as well as the woman inside one them."

Marino scowled as the steaming plates of veal and Fettuccine Alfredo were delivered to the table together with the wine. "Honestly, this seems like a solution. You don't lose anything as the suits were probably insured, and the woman is dealt with in a quiet and efficient manner."

"And if that was what I wanted to happen to her, I would have let you kill her without getting involved myself. With that in mind, what I need is transport. The kind that wouldn't mind if we brought suits of our own to claim what is rightfully ours."

The man took a moment to enjoy a couple of mouthfuls of the food before he leaned back in his seat. "I think I might have what you need. There will be a fee, of course. Not even favors come for free, not in my business anyway, and any use of the private planes the casino owns will have to be justified."

"What kind of price do you have in mind?"

"It's based per hour of usage, you understand. For a super-medium-sized jet, you would look at a little over fourteen thousand dollars per flight hour. That includes fuel, pilots, flight attendants, and food, as well as freight for whatever cargo you might need for your trip."

"Done," he stated immediately, took a mouthful of the admittedly fantastic veal, and followed it with a twist of pasta and a sip of wine. He could get used to eating like this, although he probably wouldn't.

"It seems like being a nice guy will prove expensive for you. I would expect the kind of fucking you get for being that nice sees better rewards for you."

"I'm not in it for the reward. But yeah, my getting fucked for being a nice guy does usually involve far less jetting to the most dangerous corners of the world. When can the jet be ready?"

Marino shrugged. "I'll call my secretary. She'll arrange for everything to be ready to go tomorrow morning, and she'll text you regarding where the plane will depart from. It looks like I'll make all my money back simply from helping you. That plus increasing my legend in the community."

"That's what you call a win-win, I guess."

Taylor had already finished his food and placed his napkin on the plate as he stood from his seat.

"Didn't you say you wanted dessert?" his dinner companion asked. "Maybe a couple of drinks besides? We are celebrating a business deal here, after all."

"Sorry," he answered and rolled his shoulders. "Like I said, I'm shit at making small talk and there are preparations I need to make before tomorrow morning. We will leave early, after all. Given the amount of cash I'll drop on you, you don't mind picking the check up, right?"

"Of course not. I'll simply bill it as a business dinner and it'll be comped by the casino anyway."

"Fantastic."

Marino stood from his seat and shook his hand. "I look forward to doing business with you again, Mr. McFadden."

He smirked. "I'm sure you do since hanging around me appears to only make you look more and more legit to your business partners. Until we meet again, Marino."

CHAPTER TWENTY-THREE

Taylor couldn't honestly say he was overly concerned about the woman inside a suit on the other side of the world. There were more than a few reasons for him to be more concerned about the shipment itself than her. She walked around in a suit of armor that would protect her and deal damage on top of that, even though the one she wore didn't have any ammo loaded yet.

With that said, there were many reasons why sleep wouldn't come easily. The secretary texted him the details and confirmed that the flight had already been arranged while he was still driving to the strip mall. This included the location where it would take off from, a small private airfield that had been instructed to allow him access.

They would take off at seven in the morning. The flight plan was included as well, with a short stop to refuel before they pushed across the Atlantic. They would arrive before the end of the day.

At which point, they would have to determine where the suits and Elisa were—assuming the woman was still alive—and how they could retrieve everything with as little muss and fuss as possible.

There was a long list of things to worry about, but he would have more than enough time to consider it all on the twelve or so hour flight they would be on.

He sent his whole team home. Vickie would remain at the shop and provide assistance from a distance, while he would head out with Bobby and Tanya. It was a decent plan with the small weak point that he needed to wear the light suit Bobby had made for him while the heavier one was still in need of repair.

Decent it might be, but there was a fair amount that could go wrong. He merely chose not to think about it.

Sleep took a long time to claim him and it was short and restless. It wasn't long before the alarm rang. Taylor had told Bobby and Tanya to meet him at the airport. He would drive Liz to meet them at the airfield outside of Vegas. Everything was already loaded and ready to go, which left him nothing to do but pack his shit and move out.

And about damn time too. Waiting was the worst part, and he could catch up on a little more sleep on the plane.

He climbed into Liz, patted the truck gently on the side, and set off.

There were many places he wanted to visit in the world. Copacabana Beach had always appealed to him and the Great Wall of China was way up on his list. Maybe he'd take time to gamble in Monte Carlo instead of Vegas.

Back to Africa and the Zoo was not one of those places. He had almost sworn off the jungle when he left but he somehow knew he would return to that fucking place eventually.

Taylor steeled himself when he pulled up in front of the plane. A small truck was in front of it, ready to load the suits that had been brought in crates for easier transportation.

Bobby and Tanya arrived a few minutes later and looked as tired as he felt. There wasn't anything to discuss. He knew the mechanic felt far more strongly about the Zoo than he did and Tanya, with her limited interaction with the creatures, likely had a similarly healthy mistrust of it.

There was nothing else to say. He nodded to Bungees, who nodded in response as they headed to where the plane taxied out to where they had parked their cars. The owner of the airfield presented them with paperwork stating that they were turning the vehicles over into his hands and they expected them back in the same condition in which they had been delivered.

At half-past six in the morning, they boarded the aircraft and were greeted by the pilot, co-pilot, and the flight attendant. All smiled cheerfully, bright and chirpy like they got up this early every day.

Maybe they did.

Taylor chuckled as he boarded and settled into one of the seats. Bobby and Tanya sat next to each other across from him. The stewardess offered them water and hot towels before the plane began to taxi toward the runway and the seat belt sign came on.

It wasn't long before he grasped the arms of the leather seat and the plane was airborne. The pilot informed them that they would fly to another airbase in Arizona where they would refuel for the long haul to Abuja.

"What the fuck did you have to do?" Bobby asked once the cabin was at least comparatively silent.

He raised an eyebrow. The question was very obviously directed at him but he wasn't sure why there was an accusatory tone involved.

It didn't take long before he understood. While he knew the conversation was inevitable, he had hoped it wouldn't be while they were in the air. He felt sick to his stomach and the rumble of the engines distracted him.

"What do you mean?" he countered finally.

"I know you don't have access to this kind of shit." The mechanic indicated the plane they were in. "Or, at least, not on this kind of short notice. You needed to ask someone to help. I know you didn't ask Niki, which means there's only one other person you could have talked to about getting a plane this quickly. Hence my question. What the fuck did you have to do to pull this off?"

Tanya looked at each of them in confusion.

"Rod Marino," Taylor explained for her benefit. "And I didn't have to do anything. Apparently, this is a thank you for everything we're already done for him. A very expensive thank you, mind."

Bobby shook his head. "I don't understand. No, wait, I don't think you understand. Do you really want to get into bed with someone like him?"

"We're already in bed with him, so to speak," he pointed out and scowled as he looked out the window. "He made it very clear when we spoke last night that he used us to solidify his reputation with the Las Vegas underworld.

People think he hired us to steal his own money in order to profit from a massive insurance payout and that he ordered us to eliminate Castellano to cement his position at the top of the hierarchy. Denying it will only make people believe it more."

"Shit." The other man grunted and rubbed his eyes. "What will we do?"

Taylor continued to stare out the window. "Right now? We wait. There's not much we can do. The guy has too many connections and he's holed up in a fucking casino for most of his days."

"What about when he's consolidated his position with the local criminal underworld and having us around becomes a liability? What do you think he'll do then?"

Bobby was right, of course. Marino currently used them for leverage to show how he could turn enemies into assets by claiming—or at least implying—that everything they did was on his instruction. Once he had what he wanted, they would inevitably be something that could undermine his security. At this point, people would hear confirmations in denials. When he was in power, those denials would be cracks in the foundation.

The man would definitely target them again. It was only a matter of time and when he did, he would have more resources, more connections, and more power than before.

"I don't have any answers," Taylor admitted. "I'm stumbling from one crisis to another at the moment and I hope something will make sense at the end of it."

Bobby relaxed a little. "Well, now that we know you don't have any plans in the works, we can start making some. Is there anything else you want to share about what's going on?"

"Only that the guy sent me and Niki a bottle of primo scotch when we were celebrating at Jackson's."

"Well, we know he has good taste, anyway."

He nodded and pulled his phone from his pocket. There was Wi-Fi in the plane, which meant he could connect with Vickie while they were in the air.

"How's your deathly fear of flying treating you, Tay-Tay?" she asked when she answered. It was still early morning, but Vickie didn't want to leave her team in the lurch if they needed her.

"Not as bad as my fear that you'll call me that for the rest of my life. Do you have any updates from Elisa?"

She realized that she hadn't thought to check on the woman and pulled up the message box. There was nothing new but nothing was expected. They had told her to remain as silent as possible.

"Nothing new from our intrepid reporter," she replied and shook her head. "Which I guess is a good thing. The suits have stopped in an area about fifty miles away from where they landed."

"Can you get me a visual on the area? Satellite imaging, an old Google maps image, anything?"

"I'm already on it." The hacker called the images up. There was nothing recent but the area did look fairly abandoned. "There's nothing there. The image I have is fairly old but it looks like a...well, a jungle. A regular jungle, though. I hope."

Taylor was silent for a few seconds. "Thanks, that's very helpful."

She narrowed her eyes. Was he sassing her? This early in the morning? "It is?"

"Yeah, it means we're dealing with one of the pirate teams, most likely former Zoo operatives who struck out on their own. They were an epidemic not too long ago until someone stepped in and cleared the Zoo area. They've operated on the fringes ever since and lack the weapons and armor to go in and come out alive."

"So we gave them the kind of armor and weapons they needed to go back into business?"

He paused again as if in thought. "Maybe. I doubt it, though."

CHAPTER TWENTY-FOUR

Vickie tilted her head in confusion as she stared at the computer screen. "Why? Why do you doubt it?"

She still didn't believe Taylor wasn't sassing her. The guy was being uncharacteristically genuine.

"It's more of a gut instinct, I suppose, but these guys aren't the type to put themselves on the line. They're desperate and mostly criminal types who are forced into making money in the Zoo. If they get into something as profitable as this, the chances are they'll look to unload it as quickly as possible instead of using it for themselves. This is a massive payday, the kind that could allow them to move up in the world. Short-sighted people would jump at that opportunity. What do you think?"

He wasn't talking to her, obviously, and she waited for Bobby to give his input.

"That sounds about right to me. You don't go into Zoo piracy if you're the college-educated, big-picture kind of person."

The hacker rocked slowly on her office chair. She didn't

envy the three of them being that close to the Zoo, but she did feel she had been let off too easily by simply hanging back and sticking to the computers.

Something blinked and stirred her out of her uncomfortable thoughts. She called the message board up and confirmed that it was the reporter.

"We have contact from Elisa. It looks like she's still alive."

"Can you patch her into this feed? I'd like to talk to her."

"Come on, Tay-Tay, this is what I do," Vickie grumbled and connected the two lines with her in the metaphorical middle. "Good morning, Elisa. Or is it afternoon there? Evening?"

"Afternoon," Taylor corrected her. "She's currently eight hours ahead."

"Please." Elisa's panicked voice cut straight into the conversation. "You have to help me. Do something. Anything. Please, talk to me."

"Elisa, this is Taylor." His rumbled tone sounded oddly calming. "We're on a plane now and headed toward you. You need to stay calm and stay alive until we get there. It should be between twelve and fifteen hours from now. Can you do that for me, Elisa?"

It was odd to hear him like this—like he had done this kind of shit before.

And it seemed to work. The woman's breathing had slowed and she gradually calmed. "Okay. Okay, I'm fine."

"Good. Now, tell me about where you are."

She paused for a few seconds. "I...it's still dark."

"That's fine. Tell me how much time you spent on the move. There's a clock in the HUD of the suit. Tell me how much time you spent on the truck that moved the suits."

"It was...three hours. It was bumpy and we moved slowly, though. Like the roads were terrible."

"Right. You're inside a shipping container, so it would have taken a semi to transport you without you seeing anything. We have your location now, so—"

"Shit. Something is happening around me!"

"Elisa, to the left of your chin is a small button. If you press that, you'll transmit everything your HUD sees back to us, okay? Press that button and don't say anything."

Vickie leaned in closer and released the breath she was holding. A few seconds later, they received a live feed from the HUD.

"Why didn't we get her to do this earlier?" she asked.

"Because there was nothing to see," Taylor answered curtly. "Can you show me what she sees, please?"

She keyed the transmission to his connection as well. A few seconds later, the doors of the container opened and light streamed inside. Elisa squeaked, and Vickie could picture the woman covering her mouth to hold back any more noise.

A group moved into the container. A couple of them wore casual garb—jeans, flannel shirts, and boots. One in particular caught her attention. A huge man with short blond hair and a mean look about him talked in a language she didn't understand to the three men in uniforms who looked at the suits in question.

"What are they saying?" the hacker asked. There were a couple of translating software suites that she could use but none that could be set up fast enough.

"My Afrikaans is a little rusty," Taylor muttered. "But from the context and what little I do understand, they're talking about price. The guy in the uniform's accent is a little wonky, but it sounds like he's trying to get them to include ammo with the suits and the big man wants a higher price if he has to include weapons."

The men continued to talk. They didn't sound like they were arguing, though. More like negotiating, she realized.

"Who are these guys?"

Her boss didn't reply immediately. "They aren't locals. The…big guy on the right is cursing in Swahili. At least, it sounds like the Kenyan dialect."

"I didn't know you spoke Swahili," Bobby interjected.

"I don't. I recognize the swearing, is all."

"Why would someone in Kenya want these suits?" Tanya asked. "If they're military, couldn't they buy them from the companies that make them?"

"Buying them off these guys is probably much cheaper," Taylor surmised. "There's far less red tape that way too. It doesn't matter, at this point."

Vickie needed a moment to realize why that was. The men all laughed and shook hands like they had agreed on a price. They moved out of the container but left the door open. She leaned in closer and squinted in an effort to see what was happening outside.

Although she couldn't tell for sure, it looked like the container was hidden in some kind of barn. The building had slats for walls and what looked like an aluminum roof.

Elisa still remained absolutely silent as the men returned—not those in uniform but the ones who were probably the pirates who had stolen the suits from the airport. They carried crates in using improvised trolleys.

"It's fucking bullshit. These guys are trying to rob us," one of the men grumbled in what sounded like American English.

"They know there's no one else who'll buy the suits from us," another replied with a heavy accent. "They'll squeeze us as much they can before they take them off our hands."

They finished with the deliveries and pulled the doors shut once more. Vickie could hear them lock the container again before Elisa broke down. She panted and sobbed almost uncontrollably.

"Oh, God, oh, God, oh, God, they'll kill me. I'm going to die—"

"Elisa, I need you to focus right now," Taylor snapped in a tone that made it a direct order.

"I—they'll kill me and feed me to the wild animals…oh, shit—"

"Elisa, get a fucking grip right fucking now." His voice changed in tone and sounded far more menacing than it had before. "You need to remember that you're in a fucking suit of armor and they aren't. You'll kill them if it comes down to it, not the other way around. Do you understand?"

The reporter stopped sobbing like the thought had only now occurred to her that she was actually in a high-tech weapon. "But…it's all locked down. I can't move."

"There's a manual override on all these suits in case it locks by accident. Remember the button you pressed to turn the cameras on? There's another one on the other side of the helmet. Click that one twice and the one you pressed for video once, then the first one twice again."

"Like…a startup sequence?"

"Exactly. Press the buttons." Taylor's voice had calmed now that she had done the same.

A few seconds ticked past as she struggled to keep herself under control and do what he'd instructed. A few clicks were heard in rapid sequence before the mech leaned forward slowly.

"Straighten up. Remember, every little move you make in the suit will be exaggerated. It's designed to act quickly in capable hands, so you need to move very deliberately. Do you understand?"

"Yes."

"Now, those crates they put in there with you are full of ammo and weapons. Walk over very, very slowly and open the longer one, which will contain the assault rifles. You need to take one out and holster it on your back. Can you do that?"

"I…yes, I think so."

"Good. Now, do it."

The suit moved slowly, with the woman very aware that every movement she made could give her away. Vickie couldn't tell her how to move in the suit because she had zero experience, but it felt like she moved too slowly.

Finally, the reporter reached the crates and pulled one open carefully. It took a while longer and a few clumsy attempts for her to manage to grasp one of the weapons and a few attempts to holster it, but she seemed to resist the urge to panic and try to hurry the process.

"Great. Good work, Elisa. Now, open the smaller ones

until you see magazines marked ten, x, and seventy-two millimeter."

"Yes…"

"Repeat the numbers to me."

"Ten, x, and seventy-two millimeter."

Once again, she worked carefully to open a couple of the smaller crates. Thankfully, most of the magazines inside were marked as Taylor had indicated.

"Okay. Now, reach down and click that second button again," Taylor instructed. "The suit will detect the magazines and automatically feed them into the assault rifle you have on your back. Stay calm. You're doing great."

Elisa did as she was told and once again, the suit did exactly as he said it would. Methodically, it pulled the magazines in one by one until fifteen had loaded and it clicked full.

"Fantastic," he continued. "You're now more heavily armed than every single one of those assholes. That makes you feel better, right?"

"Yes," she replied. She did sound a great deal calmer than before.

"Good. Now, you are armed, but I don't want you to be involved in any fighting until I get there. Move into the position you were in and repeat the startup sequence I gave you to lock the suit again. You know how to get it moving if you need to fight back. Stay calm. We're coming for you."

The reporter remained silent for a few long seconds.

"Thank you," she murmured finally.

CHAPTER TWENTY-FIVE

So much could happen before the team arrived and Taylor didn't like the thought of Elisa having to fight on her own out there.

Not that he thought she couldn't. Depending on how well-armed the pirates were, even with her lack of experience, it would be a cakewalk.

But a situation where a fucking reporter was in the middle of a firefight presented far too much potential for too many things to go wrong. They invariably did. A round would find a weak point in the armor. By Murphy's Law, she would be killed in there if she was on her own in a fight.

They had to get there quickly and before the transfer happened. His Afrikaans was even worse than he'd thought, but from what he was able to make out from the group that had talked, the men in uniforms would collect the cash and return with it. A plane trip would be short enough to allow them to make the purchase before the team arrived to help Elisa, but he wasn't sure what else he could do in this situation.

He could keep tracking the container if it was moved. They wouldn't open it, and it would be simple to jump to where they transported the suits and strike there.

It wasn't wise to count on that, though. The easiest situation would be to find her where she was now, kill the pirates, and leave before the people with the money arrived.

That would be the cleanest. There would be no possibility of an international incident, merely scummy pirates dealt what they deserved as a result of getting in too deep with some other group of criminals. The people of the world would not give it a second glance even if it did reach the newspapers.

If any military fuckers were gunned down in their own country, though, that was another story entirely. There was no way people would let that slide, especially if someone involved was one of the bigwigs of the local military. From what Niki had told him, their little trip to Italy did end up having consequences for her.

While they had, surprisingly, brought her a better position with the DOD, there was no assurance that he would be similarly fortunate. The chances were that he would be hung out to dry. If they were lucky.

The plane banked slightly as they moved through the light cloud layer and descended toward their first destination. They were stopping to refuel before the push across the Atlantic. The private jet was the kind that could make long-haul flights but even it had limits.

They touched down in Arizona and his gaze traced the

line where the desert crept between light brush at first, which then became the kind of trees and forest he had seen on his last visit. They weren't that far from the lab. Taylor wondered if this was where Niki had arrived when she had been flown in to manage the situation.

He held the arms of the seat a little tighter as they descended more rapidly and the change in pressure made his ears pop when they touched down.

His whole body went rigid when the wheels made contact. The plane jolted and seemed to skid a little before it moved across the surface of the airstrip. He knew there was nothing he could do to make it easier or make the flight any safer.

The tension that came with it was both irritating and comfortably familiar. He sat motionless and waited for them to taxi to a halt. It wasn't until the plane had come to a complete stop that he relaxed, inch by inch.

The seat belt sign turned off and the stewardess appeared to make sure they were all alive and ready to proceed with the journey.

"It should only be a short stop to refuel and file the requisite flight plans," she said in a pleasant voice and an accent he couldn't place. "If you should wish to leave the plane and stretch your legs, that will be permitted. We will take off in forty-five minutes."

Taylor nodded, undid his belt, and stood, fully intending to make use of the time they would have on the ground. Bobby and Tanya joined him as he strode down the steps.

He retrieved a pair of sunglasses when the glare of the morning sun assailed his eyes. There was too much for him to deal with at the moment for him to act like a tough guy.

"Have you been thinking?" Bobby asked once they were outside. "I only assume you didn't want to talk about it on the plane because you didn't think what you discussed would be private. These people are all working for Marino, right? One way or another?"

It was a logical question and he nodded slowly. "I'm fairly sure that even words spoken out here will still get back to him."

None of the three wanted to discuss it anymore. They were in this situation a little too deep, and Taylor knew he was the one who had gotten them there.

It was on him to get them out again. "I honestly don't know what we'll do next, so we'll take this one step at a time. First, we need to get Elisa and our shipment back with minimal muss and fuss. Once that's delivered and we get that fucking reporter to the US, we can have a nice long talk about what to do about Marino."

"If you're scared, you don't need to pretend you aren't," Tanya said quietly and sat on a nearby empty crate. "We won't judge you for it."

"Judgment is the least of my worries. We're around people who have worked the politics game for years— decades, honestly, and maybe even their whole lives."

Bobby scoffed and shook his head. "Wow, you're not afraid to dump it all out here, huh? Chill the fuck out, man. We're in this together and we'll fight right beside you. Besides, aren't you forgetting who's on our side?"

Taylor looked at the man and raised an eyebrow. "Who?"

"We have Vickie on our side and with her, the entirety of her psychotic family tree. Do you think Marino stands a fucking chance against Vickie, Jennie, and Niki? At the same time? When they're pissed?"

He paused for a moment and nodded slowly. "That is a damn solid point. It won't be an easy fight but if there was ever money bet on these kinds of things, I wouldn't ever bet against Vickie."

"If there was ever a place where we would get odds on that, Vegas would be the place," Tanya pointed out.

"Another fair point," he admitted.

"So…" Bobby placed a hand on his shoulder. "Stop freaking out about shit you can't figure out. Remember that you have two psychotic hackers and their vindictive relative with the DOD on your side, for the most part anyway, and chill the absolute fuck out."

More good points. Taylor had let the anxiety of the situation get the better of him, but he was well aware that this anxiety only masked the real reason why he was on edge. It applied to his annoyance with the flight too. Something else nagged at the edge of his mind.

Memories of dark corners in a jungle peppered his mind and made it difficult to focus. He felt jumpy and the adrenaline pumped through his system like his whole body had begun to prepare, triggered by the mere thought of being in the same corner of the world as that fucking jungle. He wasn't even sure when it had started.

Sometime the night before, he reasoned. When Elisa had filled them in about what was happening, it had dawned on him that he might have to head out there and expose himself to the fucking hellhole once more.

It seemed impossible, but it was there. The reaction was in his blood now, despite the logic and reason that reminded him that Elisa was south of the Zoo and seemed set to move even farther from it. Somehow, the nightmare persisted, as dark and ominous as the real jungle that seemed to want to drag him back.

Taylor clasped his hands together to keep them from shaking while Bobby and Tanya headed into the plane. They were talking and laughing—probably making plans to go out to dinner when they got back or something.

His friend had made the healthy choice, one that had been available to him. Taylor couldn't recall having the option of not going into the Zoo. He was pushed into it and ordered into it.

Even when he did have the option, it felt dishonest and cowardly to hang back.

He shook his head slowly and shoved his hands into his pockets. It was better if Bobby and Tanya didn't realize that he had these kinds of thoughts. They should rather think this was simply another job for him, another trip into the Zoo—something he had done countless times before.

Well, technically not the Zoo but close enough.

Taylor pushed himself past the conflict and fears. They wouldn't encounter any problems. Or, at least, none that would make their trip more than a rescue mission.

The workers had begun to fill the tanks of the plane and looked bored like they had done this kind of shit their whole lives. It was any other day for them and he was merely another rich bastard looking to get from one place to the other as quickly as possible, which was none of their business, to begin with.

His gaze turned to the dense vegetation that surrounded the airfield and he recalled the encounter he'd been through not that long before and not that far from there. It looked much the same, with the chunky, rocky formations between the trees that made a forest and thin, craggy canyons that cut through the mountainous regions like paper strips. Small creeks had worn through the rocks for thousands of years, undisturbed, and shaped the area into something that was fairly unique in the world.

Taylor had never seen the like, he acknowledged. It was quite beautiful.

Even so, these days, he couldn't help but think there was a hint of underlying menace in the gorgeous landscape. Niki had managed to put most of the data from the lab in for someone to examine but even then, there was no way to tell if something had escaped. It could slowly start to build numbers that would pose a threat to the humans who lived in the area.

Hell, it didn't even need to be animals. The goop had been part of the containment breach from the lab as well. Who was to say that in the next few weeks they wouldn't see the whole place erupt in a similar situation as what they had seen in the Sahara?

Taylor turned to look at the men who refueled the plane.

"Is everything okay, sir?" one of them asked preemptively.

"Yeah, and there's no need to call me sir."

The men regarded him oddly after that statement. Unless some of them had been in the military, they wouldn't understand that you only called the commissioned officers sir, and there was no time for him to teach them about it.

"Do you guys feel safe out here?" he asked and smoothly changed the subject.

The group laughed and the man who stood closest to him pushed off the crate he had leaned on. "If you knew who owned this place, you wouldn't be worried about anyone trying to rob us. People around here know better than to mess with our boss."

He wasn't sure if they were talking about Marino or if someone else owned the airfield and was similarly regarded as a man to be reckoned with. Either way, it made little difference.

With a small smile, he tilted his head and shrugged. "Who said anything about robbing the place?"

The group stopped laughing and they stared at him for a few seconds. They probably didn't know where this plane was going after they filled her and therefore would have no clue what he was talking about.

"What?" the other man finally asked.

Taylor shook his head dismissively. "Nothing, never mind."

His nervousness had begun to show and on the off chance that these guys actually did work for Marino, he didn't want word to get back to the man about what made him nervous.

Despite his trepidation, he entered the plane. Maybe there, he could order something to drink and to eat too. That way, his tension would calm and he would have an easier time during the rest of the flight.

He didn't have high hopes, though.

CHAPTER TWENTY-SIX

He envied the other two passengers who he shared the ride with. It wasn't long after the meal was served once they were airborne again that both decided to watch something on the in-flight entertainment options. These constituted a small touchscreen with a variety of shows and movies that were meant to make the time pass a little quicker.

The rational side of Taylor's brain could accept that it was a little better to let the time pass while watching a hilariously unlikely series of events bring two people together when they otherwise would not have been a viable match. Knowing this was one thing, but it was difficult to release the nervousness that consumed his body while they hurtled through the air at impossible speeds.

Bobby and Tanya didn't share his stress, though, and they were soon asleep, side by side on the seat across from him. He was left in the silence to mull over his thoughts, anxieties, and worries on his own.

With the dull drone of the plane the only sound to fill

the cabin once the movie was finished, he decided it wasn't that bad. The white noise was enough to lull him into something like a mindless state, where he didn't worry about what they would encounter when they landed.

Taylor realized that he had even begun to doze a little. This was mostly due to the fact that he hadn't had much sleep the night before and it seemed like very little time passed before something nudged him in the shoulder.

He looked at the stewardess who stooped over him.

"We're beginning our descent, sir," she whispered. "If you would be so kind as to fasten your seatbelt?"

It wasn't so much a request as an order, and he did as he was told. Bobby and Tanya both wore expressions that indicated they had similarly been woken to secure themselves for landing.

"It looks like you got some sleep," Tanya muttered and adjusted her seat from its reclining position. "Have we finally found a way to work around your flying phobia? Is it really as simple as putting on a mindless, sappy romcom?"

Taylor smirked. "If only it were that easy."

Bobby turned to face the woman with a scowl on his face. "It might have been sappy but it wasn't mindless. They got a slew of awards for that movie."

She shrugged. "I wouldn't know. I don't follow the awards ceremonies lately as I haven't had the time."

The plane banked steeply and all Taylor could think was that he was ready for it all to be over. He needed them to be on the ground again, where he could take control of his own life instead of leaving it in the hands of two pilots he didn't know.

Of course, he had paid them a literal fuck-ton of money to make sure nothing bad happened, but it wasn't like people who made considerable money were immune to making mistakes.

Thankfully, the aircraft touched down gently and it wasn't long before it taxied and finally drew to a full stop.

He'd left Africa not all that long before, and yet something about it already seemed foreign. They were currently much further south than Taylor or Bobby had ever gone since they spent their time mostly in the Sahara or up in the northern cities and countries closer to the Mediterranean.

He was struck by a heavy wave of humid heat as he stepped out and descended the steps. The pilots and the stewardess hoped he'd had a pleasant flight and he acknowledged them briefly. He hadn't but that wasn't their fault, not really.

It wasn't much hotter than Nevada or even Arizona, but the humidity was what made it permeate and soak through every article of clothing until you felt like you would never be rid of it.

They were a little to the south of Abuja and the rain forest edged into their line of sight farther south and southwest of their position. This was regular jungle, very different visually from the Zoo that grew to the north. They were too far away to actually see the Sahara Desert from there but when he looked in that direction from the elevated position of the airfield, Taylor thought he could see a glimmer of the wall that was being erected to stop the growing jungle.

Irritated, he shook off the shiver that threatened to

crawl down his spine and continued down the steps, followed closely by Bobby and Tanya. It was her first time in Africa and thankfully, they would stay far, far away from Taylor's old haunts.

"It's out there, isn't it?" she asked and remained close to Bobby once the plane headed away and to the refuel point. It would be ready for them once they decided to return home or go wherever they needed to be next.

"What is?" Bobby asked.

"The Zoo," Taylor explained. "Yeah. North, about...that bearing, I think." He pointed and she narrowed her eyes to look at the horizon.

"Is there any chance it'll spread here?" She clearly looked worried about the possibility even though it was a location she had only heard about, despite having killed the monsters she had run into when she worked with Niki. Of course, dealing with a couple of stragglers was different than diving into the middle of it.

He shook his head. "In this area, though, we're dealing with one of the world's most powerful coordinated land forces. It's one of the most powerful in history, in fact, with hundreds of the best, highest-tech weapons on the ground, ready to fight a possible alien invasion. Any attack from the Zoo would be met with a massive mobilization from US, Russian, Eastern, and European forces. The last time the jungle tried, the Russians soaked the whole landscape with one of the most prolific bombing programs since World War II. So... Well, there's a chance, but we'll be able to hear it coming about three days away. Enough time to get you out of here."

"Only me?" Tanya asked. "You wouldn't run away too?"

That was a sobering question and one he had no intention of answering.

All he could do was turn to where they had begun to unload the crates with the suits they would use. Taylor didn't have any of the heavier mech suits available, which required him to scrape the literal bottom of the barrel. The biker suit—which was what he'd taken to calling it—was good enough in an urban environment and tougher than almost anything people had in the continental US.

Still, he couldn't help but wonder if it wouldn't have been a good idea to find something a little bigger and heavier just in case.

He drew in a long breath and released it slowly before he took his phone from his pocket and activated the connection with their support. "Hey, Vickie, we just touched down. Do you have a good idea of Elisa's location?"

There was a moment of silence before the hacker responded. It sounded like she had taken a break from monitoring the computer and was either getting some sleep or food.

Ten seconds later, she responded on her end of the line. A rustle sounded like she was putting her headset on before she spoke. "Hey, Taylor. Sorry, I was getting—"

"Don't worry about it. I didn't assume you would be at your desk for the next day and a half. But now that we're all here, what's the update on Elisa?"

"Well, someone didn't get their morning coffee."

"I tried to be nice."

"I know, and I tried to be bitchy."

Taylor narrowed his eyes. "So you're the someone who didn't get her coffee?"

"Right. Should I check on our intrepid reporter?"

"You do that."

The crew of the airfield, together with those from the plane, watched curiously as the trio began to put their suits on. Taylor would have thought that at least the airfield crew would have seen the process themselves since this was where many of the merc companies in the various bases imported their gear through due to the lower prices.

That meant they were looking at lower prices for the imports. Of course, the tradeoff was the longer distances, which meant longer wait times and, of course, worse security. Most of the larger corporations and the US government used the airfields in or around Casablanca.

"There's no movement on the suit's GPS. They should all be waiting. There's also no word from Elisa, though, which could be very good news or very bad."

"She knows to open communications should something happen. Besides, she has a damn arsenal on her side now, and she should be able to use the suits we sent well enough to cause a ruckus that'll be seen by a fucking satellite. Keep an eye on her but don't cause any noise for her unless it's necessary. We want to avoid her involvement in the fighting. Bungees, are we ready to roll?"

The mechanic gave him a thumbs-up. Tanya moved randomly beside him as if to get a better feel for the suit. It was probably merely nerves as she'd used it very effectively before. Taylor realized then that they hadn't brought the suit he had expected.

"What...the fuck is this?" he asked as he withdrew pieces of the heavier suit.

"We had a larger suit available," Bobby explained. "Don't worry, I already calibrated it to your specifications."

"With the hydraulics?"

"Yep."

"And the trigger weight?"

"Of course."

He scowled, caught between relief and an unexpected smidgeon of disappointment. While the heavier suit was definitely first prize, a part of him had looked forward to testing the lighter suit in a tougher environment. He hadn't realized his curiosity, but it was something to put on his to-do list. For now, he'd merely be grateful that his friend had, once again, taken care of him in the best way possible. The added power and protection were an unexpected advantage he would make full use of.

Taylor pulled the suit on with practiced efficiency and activated the commlink with Vickie once he was ready for action.

"I've already uploaded the coordinates to your HUD," she announced once he was online. "You're a fair distance from your target so you'd best get moving."

"You know, having you in my ear is kind of like having Desk," he told her.

"Who?"

"It's a compliment. You know, the support staff Niki has me working with when I'm on her payroll. Desk did say she was transferred to the DOD along with Niki, so I guess I'll still work with her on their operations."

"No, I know who Desk is. I only thought you…well, knew."

Taylor's eyebrows lowered as he and his teammates set off across the tough terrain at a good pace. The suits were made to move through the jungles almost without effort, which left them almost nothing to do as the suits merely did as they were meant to do. It was still exercise but it allowed for some distractions.

"Knew what?"

"Okay…no, if Niki hasn't already told you it's not my place."

"Vickie, don't play games with me. If there's something about Desk you think I should know, you need to tell me about it now."

"There's the problem. I don't know if you need to know about it because if you did, Niki would have told you about it already. If she had, we wouldn't be having this conversation in the first place."

He sighed deeply and tried to keep himself from getting annoyed. It was a matter of interest to him given that he was likely to put his life in Desk's hands repeatedly.

They couldn't deal with this now, though, but they would certainly talk about it again.

"I'll bring this up with Niki later," he grumbled. "And if she doesn't tell me anything, I'll take it up with you."

"And won't that be fun?"

"I'm not joking. If I end up in the middle of a firefight and Desk hangs me out to dry, I'll haunt the shit out of you and your entire fucking family."

"I understand. Now, shall we focus on the problem at hand?"

Taylor gritted his teeth and pushed his suit forward a little faster to take the lead ahead of Bobby and Tanya. He set a steady pace and made sure they headed in the right direction while avoiding canyons or gullies they would have to circle.

"Exactly like old times," he muttered under his breath.

CHAPTER TWENTY-SEVEN

Vickie had been right. It was a long hike for them to reach the location on foot. Taylor had the idea to procure a car or something to perhaps get there faster, but he discarded it quickly. It would take hours to find a vehicle they could use in their suits and get on the road. With everything that entailed, the chances were that word would already have spread to the unintentional kidnappers and they would be on the move by the time the rescuers reached them.

They saved both time and considerable effort by moving in the suits, by his estimation, and hopefully, would manage to reach the location quickly and without being discovered. This was borne out by the fact that they covered the distance at a good speed. He noted that the map Vickie had uploaded to their HUDs was far better than the maps they had made do with in their Zoo trips.

Of course, most of those were inaccurate due to how quickly the landscape changed on a whim.

The hacker had also managed to put the GPS signal

from the container on their HUDs, which meant they didn't need to contact her every time they needed to check the position of the suits and Elisa with them. He assumed their support technician used this time to stay on top of her work, although the reality was that she still had studying to do, and there were also the small details like her need to eat, sleep, and other human necessities.

She couldn't be at their beck and call every hour of every day. The best she could do was make sure there were computer programs that were simple enough for the three of them to use that would help them when she could not.

The jungle animals appeared intimidated by the heavy suits that moved through their territory, which made it easy to ignore them. A few remained visible, mostly simians in the trees that displayed their massive fangs in the hope that it would keep the humans away. They acted like animals generally did—something that seemed a foreign concept to him by now.

They would deal exclusively with them for this trip, though, and Taylor nudged Tanya to keep moving forward and to ignore the other creatures that might try to drive them away. There weren't many that would dare to confront a human in a full mechanized suit in these parts, aside from perhaps the occasional elephant, rhino, or hippo. He had heard stories about hippopotamuses being able to tear through virtually any armor they ran into.

Taylor could only imagine that the Zoo biome simply hadn't had the chance to incorporate the creatures. If it had, there was the possibility of incredibly terrifying monsters. Hippos were the stuff of nightmares all on their own without any alien additions, and he could only imagine the kind of fun the goop would have with one.

He didn't want to imagine it, he decided after a moment and shoved the thought aside.

"Okay, you guys are approaching the location now," Vickie announced over their comms. "If you can see a hill in front of you, Elisa should be on the other side. You might want to prepare for a fight."

"Is there someone waiting for us?" Tanya asked from where she brought up the rear of the team. "Did they catch wind of us arriving?"

"No, but I assume they'll defend the position given who and what they are."

"That's a good assumption," Taylor confirmed and drew them to a halt. Maybe the hacker was a little behind on her tracking, but they were already at the hill and about to crest it. "Stick to the trees and avoid sky-lining yourselves. We need to have a better look at the location before we attack it."

"How will we attack it?" Bobby asked as they separated to inch forward and let the short, gnarly trees cover their approach.

"We won't know until we have a better view of it," he muttered. He was the first one over the hill and hugged the trees as he opened the scanner on his suit to see if there were any defenses or scanners in place that would pick up their approach. It was a new addition, one the US military had begun to add to most of their suits. More than likely, this was in anticipation of being able to use them for something other than hunting rabid monsters in an alien jungle.

Taylor settled his hand on one of the trees to ensure

that he wouldn't move too far away from it before he eased in a little closer and activated the HUD's ability to pick up movement.

He could make out what had been built as a warehouse, although on the smaller side. It was constructed from wood, for the most part, with the roof made of aluminum. While it would be effective against rain, it had to turn the interior into an absolute oven.

A couple of roads led to and from the structure, and there were a couple of clear signs of other warehouses having been set up but then demolished and stripped.

His careful study noted a rail line through the section and what might have once been an airfield back in the day. Most of it was overgrown with weeds, bushes, and even a couple of younger trees that had broken through the concrete. Despite this, it looked like there was enough room for a plane to land, if only the smaller Cessna models.

They hadn't chosen to pull the suits out, which meant they were on foot. The group he could make out were likely the mercenaries, judging by their lack of any kind of uniform. They were all armed, of course, but none of them carried the same weapons as would be issued if they were in any kind of organized, centralized military.

They sat around and a couple of them enjoyed the sunlight, relaxed, and appeared to have no expectation of any kind of attack.

Taylor pulled back. "These guys aren't ready for a strike. If we hit them hard and fast, there won't even be a need for us to kill them."

"Sure, but couldn't we go ahead and do it anyway?" Vickie asked.

"There's enough killing around here without adding to it," he commented. "If we can find a way to get through this without adding to the body count, we'll take it."

Even so, he didn't have high hopes. Pirates like these weren't the type that backed away from a fight, even when it was one they were sure to lose.

If they were smart, they wouldn't have entered this kind of sordid business anyway.

"It looks like you have incoming," Vickie warned him.

Taylor turned and focused on a group of jeeps that moved up one of the roads. They were army jeeps, not meant for combat but which carried enough men to make things a whole new level of dangerous. The vehicles themselves were older models that had not been used by the US military for decades.

"It looks like the buyers are back," he stated quietly and highlighted one of the jeeps that carried a handful of men who weren't as armed as the others, although they wore brown uniforms with medals and ribbons pinned to their chests. Once the vehicles came to a stop outside the warehouse, the pirates gathered in front of the cavalcade. They looked nervous, and with good reason. The newcomers outnumbered their small group of half a dozen. Taylor counted at least twenty-five heavily armed men who climbed out of the jeeps.

Their weapons weren't aimed at the pirates, though, and they were there to secure the perimeter and ensure that the transaction happened without outside interference. This was evidenced by the fact that their weapons all aimed outward and into the jungle around the pirate base of operations.

He noted that a couple of the armed men didn't wear the same uniforms as the rest and instead, were dressed in black fatigues and berets with no markings on them at all. They were clearly not locals either and appeared to either be from Southern Africa or Europe.

"Shit," he muttered and backed slowly away from the top of the hill.

"What's the matter?" Vickie asked.

"These guys aren't military."

Bobby cleared his throat. "The guns and uniforms would beg to differ with you there, Tay-Tay."

"They're paramilitary. That means they're not working officially for any of the local governments but likely working for the Kenyans. They've tried to push into the market coming from the Zoo for a while now."

"How can you tell?" the other man asked.

"Well, the national Kenyan military would never be able to march into Nigeria. They would have to be unaffiliated. Besides, no formal military would take foreign specialists out in uniform and put them side-by-side with their troops in the field. They would be in a position to train but never out in the field. No, these guys are very much the black ops specialists needed for a government to obtain technology that has so far been out of their reach."

"There is a bright side to that," Bobby pointed out.

"What makes you say that?" Taylor countered.

"Well, these guys aren't officially supposed to be here, so if they were to suddenly go missing in the middle of another country, no one would look for them. Ditto our annoying hijackers."

"It's good to see you plan ahead like that," he muttered. "In the meantime, we'll have to find a way to drive through them but I can't see a way through their defenses. They have every approach covered, and you absolutely know those assault rifles hold the kind of armor-piercing ammo that'll power through our suits."

It was a good point, and they knew it, but they had to find a solution fast. The negotiations had already gone through and no one seemed inclined to wait for someone to stumble over their clandestine operation. He pulled back a little more.

The officers discussed something with the leader of the pirates and they laughed. The men talked like they already knew each other well enough that there would be no tense introductions that could end in the kind of violence that would help Taylor and his team.

A couple of the soldiers removed trunks from the jeeps and laid them out for the pirates to inspect. The criminals tried to look calm and collected, but the avarice was clear the moment the contents were displayed. There would be no reason for them to doubt that they would get paid.

The paramilitary group looked like they intended to leave the criminals alive for the moment, which meant only one thing. They wanted to acquire more of the same product from the group, which would entail more raids on the airport. Taylor's scowl deepened. These people planned to rob from his client base regularly, something he simply couldn't stand for.

"Vickie," he said sharply over the comms, "I need you to

send our reporter a message for me. She won't be involved in the fight but I do want her to create a distraction that'll let us get into fighting range without being chewed up by these assault rifles."

"What do you want her to do in there?" the hacker asked as she opened a line with Elisa.

"Only…be seen. Stand up and maybe fire a couple of rounds before she takes cover."

She cut over to communicate with the reporter. It seemed like he might have been involved in the conversation, but maybe there was a problem with bringing two comm lines together, especially if the people they intended to attack monitored the communications in the area.

"Okay," she said before his impatience pushed through. "You guys should be clear to go in a minute or so."

"What's with the delay?" Bobby asked.

"Well, I assumed you guys might want to work up a battle plan or something, and she needs to work up her courage. She's a brave girl, this reporter of ours." Vickie sounded dismissive.

"I think we already knew that," Taylor mumbled. They would need to move fast.

The team had already begun to move toward the doors of the warehouse, and he gestured for his two teammates to follow him as they crested the hill and began to ease down toward the open area where the paramilitary group was still in defensive positions.

The doors opened and sudden movement inside made the group freeze for a moment. The officers retreated quickly and yelled something to the men who guarded them. They turned as one to where someone stood in a full suit of mechanized armor near the door with the weapons drawn.

"I guess we're going!" Taylor shouted.

"What?" Bobby asked.

"We're going now! Now! Now! Move it!"

They had their opening. The paramilitary men whirled and tried to take cover as Elisa fired a couple of shots. Everyone was distracted by what was happening inside the warehouse.

All the three rescuers needed to do was to make good use of it.

CHAPTER TWENTY-EIGHT

E liza decided when it was too late that she needed her fucking head examined. Vickie had contacted her and told her she needed to do something for the team. It seemed simple enough. Her rescuers were already on the way to help her and she had to make a scene. The woman had suggested that all she should do was activate the guns and shoot at something or nothing in particular. She was supposed to be a distraction, that was all.

Her heart had thudded a little while she set the weapons up and readied herself, but she was surprisingly calm until the doors opened. Dozens of men faced her. They all held guns and swung them to aim at her. Those closest to the door tried to back away as quickly as possible.

She was a fucking reporter. While she always knew she would end up in dangerous situations, she'd always thought it would happen when she was doing her job. That kind of danger was simply part of being a reporter, picking clues up, and putting together a story that would win her a Pulitzer or another journalism award.

Never had she imagined that she would be in the middle of a firefight, holding on for dear life and hoping and praying that something would happen to save her from annihilation.

Thankfully, something did. Her fingers twitched and the suit's trigger was pulled. She felt the kick of the massive assault rifle she held thump into her shoulder. The entire suit reacted when she flinched at the sound of the gunfire and the bullets went wide of whatever target she had supposedly aimed at.

The men outside reacted despite this. They yelled in a language she couldn't understand and flung themselves toward whatever cover they could find, sometimes their fellow soldiers. She didn't know what good that would do them but for her, it meant they wouldn't return fire at least.

That changed quickly, however. She tried to gain control of the suit but every movement she made was wildly exaggerated. Her teeth gritted, she took a step back, then forward while the suit tried to keep itself balanced. She wasn't sure what was happening, but they had begun to retaliate and the impacts of the bullets hurled her back again. Almost subconsciously, she held her fingers planted on the triggers and hoped for at least one lucky shot until the assault rifle clicked empty.

The men outside realized what had happened, but instead of storming the building, they rushed to close the doors again and locked her inside.

The doors were wood, which meant that no matter how

thick, they wouldn't keep the bullets she was firing in. Of course, it wouldn't stop theirs from reaching her either.

A moment ticked by, the silence only broken by her suit working to reload her rifle, when she realized what they were doing. She couldn't see them and they couldn't see her, but they were more likely to hit her within while firing blindly than the other way round. They could have stormed the warehouse, but they would risk losing men if they did so. Their action had simply been the most expedient way to reduce their casualties.

She looked at the container, which was still intact. A couple of bullets had hit it but bounced off to leave only minimal dents on the side. In a few seconds, that would be the safest place in the whole warehouse.

Pushing the mech forward was a little difficult. The damned thing felt like it was unsure of what she wanted it to do. Even so, stutter-stepping and almost losing her balance, she managed to reach the door of the container before they opened fire.

Practically a roar of gunfire exploded from outside, and there wasn't much she could do but duck her head, push fully into the container, and yank the doors closed behind her.

Rounds clattered a ceaseless staccato against the steel walls and could be heard sharply over the gunfire. The din was overwhelming, and she realized she was screaming only because she suddenly ran out of breath. In that moment of sheer adrenaline, the suit had acted perfectly. When she didn't think about how to move it, there was no hesitation and no overreaction. The suit simply did its job.

"Vickie!" she shouted into the comms. "What do I do now?"

"You wait," the hacker replied in an unnervingly calm voice. "Your rescue is on the way."

Taylor could see he would be the fastest. Bobby and Tanya didn't ride around in suits as much as he did and certainly not in the suits they currently wore. Even worse, they were out in the jungle. They both chose their routes carefully rather than work through it five or six steps ahead of time.

They all had the same destination but in the same way that he planned five or six steps ahead on his route, he also planned to be in the fight on his own for the first few seconds.

The reporter had certainly played her part. All the men who had dutifully watched the perimeter now faced away to fire on the warehouse—on Elisa, he reminded himself. While she had done what he'd needed her to do, he had hoped she could have done it while still protected inside the structure and simply leave them confused, alarmed, and distracted.

In this case, they certainly were distracted and alarmed but not confused. Not yet, he reminded himself grimly.

"Elisa's inside the container," Vickie announced. "She says it doesn't look like the bullets have punched through yet."

"They will, though. They have armor-piercing rounds." He growled and felt a little out of breath as he rushed toward the combat zone. His team was vastly outnumbered, but the group still attempted to use bullets to demolish the building in front of them. Taylor steeled himself and drew the assault rifle from its holster.

The comfortable weight of knowing there was something in his hand ready to fight brought him down to earth and made it easier to settle into the fighting mode he'd long since learned to channel his instincts into. He was used to it. This was where his mind lived when he was in a state of violence so it could become the cold, reasoning force that broke through when he was in the middle of combat. It wasn't always there but he was always thankful to have it when it was.

He pulled the rifle up as he broke out of the cover of the jungle. It seemed impossible that they couldn't hear him, even over the din they generated. They all fired at the same time, which made it difficult to hear what was happening behind them.

It was no surprise that the first to notice him were the ones in the black uniforms and berets. The former special forces from who the hell knew which countries were the ones who kept track of how many bullets they fired and made sure to keep shooting when the others reloaded. They turned almost before he had broken through the tree line.

One shouted a warning in a language he didn't understand, but that was lost in the wave of gunfire around them. Taylor grasped his weapon, rushed forward, and bulldozed through the group without bothering to shoot at them. They were all so focused on their desire to destroy the mech inside the warehouse that they didn't realize there was one out there with them.

The first man to come in contact with him was crushed underfoot. Taylor charged into him and made sure to step onto the torso and let the weight of the suit he wore do the work for him. The next was caught on the side of the head with a powerful swing from his arm which crushed his skull. It dropped him to the cracked and almost ruined runway before he even had time to pull the trigger.

Another two spun and tried to keep their muzzle discipline in check as they circled to where he continued to move.

Thankfully, he had many more around him who he was willing to shoot at than they did.

The difference between attacking monsters and humans was palpable. It didn't feel like a fair fight when he opened fire. He chose his targets calmly and pulled the trigger. The rifle was set to semi-automatic and he did not intend to waste bullets. The first man's head looked like it had decompressed. The front was left mostly intact, but the back blew out with a hole the size of a tangerine and sprayed blood, brains, and bone on the men who stood behind him.

Taylor pivoted his shooting arm while he kept his suit in motion to make it as difficult a target to attack as he could while he maintained his shooting level. He switched to a three-round burst and opened fire again. This time, two of the larger rounds punched through a man's chest while the third went a little wide and left him mangled as he fell.

The rest of the paramilitary men as well as the pirates finally realized they were being attacked from behind and turned to engage him.

He dove to the side, rolled over his shoulder, and pushed up smoothly in a practiced move, one he had been taught when first training to use the suits. It was a way, his trainers reminded him, to change momentum while still being difficult to target.

A couple of rounds impacted around his torso. A handful of them pinged off the edges of his armor, although his HUD notified him of two breaches. Cover would definitely be necessary.

Quickly, he lowered almost into a crouch and finished in a slide to take him behind one of the jutting pieces of concrete that remained from one of the warehouses that had been demolished. He hunkered there, careful to keep his whole body as well as the armor under cover while he checked his suit.

The concrete was fired at continuously and chunks and pieces of it spewed around him, which made it difficult to see or hear where the attacks were coming from.

He darted out, flicked the rifle into full auto, and laid out a couple of sustained bursts. The paramilitaries scrambled behind cover once more.

None of them had been hit by the time he needed to duck and reload again, but it was enough of a distraction to keep their eyes on him instead of what came in from behind.

Bobby and Tanya broke from the tree line as well and once again, the pirates and paramilitaries weren't aware of them. The mechanic moved with controlled ease and revealed that he knew how to work his mech. He also kept both himself and Tanya in cover as they opened fire and distracted the team once more.

The defenders turned once again toward the two who advanced on them. Very little training had gone into coordinating their attacks, and the special forces men who had survived now worked to pull the officers away toward the jeeps.

Their intention, obviously, was to run away and pretend that none of this had ever happened. Or maybe throw accusations around that would start a conflict in the area. If there was something the locals liked doing when they tried not to think about Zoo monsters, it was to talk about how the tiny-dick-tators started conflicts they wouldn't have to fight in.

Taylor leveled his assault rifle, aimed calmly, and pulled the trigger. He smirked when the bullets punched through the engine blocks of the vehicles and made sure the group would not go anywhere.

Rather than choose to surrender, the officers drew sidearms that were holstered at their sides, yelled something to the men around them, and turned their weapons on him. He assumed they had told their men that surrender was not an option or something.

Bobby and Tanya eliminated the paramilitaries and pirates before they circled behind the group that attempted to shoot Taylor, who dove behind cover once more.

He didn't have to watch to know what happened next. The gunfire didn't last very long, and the heavy steps he could hear were indicative of how the fight had ended.

"It couldn't have happened to nicer guys," he mumbled.

CHAPTER TWENTY-NINE

There was nothing left to do. Elisa was stuck in the damn container, where she covered her head and hoped and prayed that the bullets that impacted the side of it wouldn't punch through.

Vickie hadn't said anything after she'd told her that help was on the way, but for all she knew, Taylor only wanted to recover what was stolen from him. Maybe he didn't care about what happened to her. In fact, given that she was something of a nuisance, maybe he had decided to wait for them to kill her before he walked in and claimed his property after he cleaned her blood off it.

After what seemed like an eternity of terror, the shooting slowed. No, that wasn't quite right. She could still hear it outside but it no longer struck the container. Were they fighting between themselves or had the help that was on its way already arrived?

She remained hunkered as low as she could but slowly gained the confidence to look up. There wasn't much to see, of course. She had wanted to seal herself in but the best she could do was close the doors and hang onto them to make sure no one tried to open them since they could not be locked from inside.

Still, it sounded like the fighting was dying down. The external sensors picked up shouting but that didn't help. It was all in a language she didn't understand. Taylor had mentioned it being Swahili, but one was the same as the other at that moment.

Finally, the gunfire stopped entirely. She didn't know what that meant and waited for someone to burst in and open fire to finish their earlier attempt to eliminate her. Her brief glimpse through the doors had revealed the numbers the pirates had on their side, and there was no way Taylor's little group would be able to defeat them. It wasn't like they were highly trained or anything, right?

Eliza shook her head carefully and made sure not to let the movement be caught by the suit in any way. In the silence, she decided that if they intended to kill her, she would take as many of them with her as she could. It wasn't a matter of standing her ground or even proving a point. If anything, it felt a little petty but justifiable anyway.

Movement outside startled her and she hefted her weapon. If they stood in the doorway when it opened, even she wouldn't be able to miss them.

"Hello in there!" said a voice from outside the container. "This is Taylor McFadden of McFadden's Mechs!"

She winced. That was a terrible, terrible name.

"We're calling out to a feisty Mexi-talian. I'm making sure you're safe in there and don't have your weapon trained on the door. We're about to open it and would appreciate it if you didn't punch us full of holes when we're here to rescue you."

The man made a decent enough point, and Elisa eased away from the doors, released them, and lowered the assault rifle. After a second's thought, she also put the safety on. The trigger was a little too light for her liking and there was always the chance that she would accidentally shoot someone otherwise.

The doors opened slowly and whoever pulled them also used them as cover. He was apparently as careful as she was.

A suit, almost like the one she wore, appeared in the entrance and showed no drawn weapons.

"Elisa?" Taylor asked and stepped inside the container slowly and carefully. "Are you all right in there?"

"Yeah," she replied, a little breathless. "Why didn't Vickie alert me that the fighting was over and you guys were coming in?"

"I'm not sure. She said she was trying to get comms on you but there was no response. Maybe something was clipped and jammed your receiver. Or—and don't be offended by the fact that this is the more likely scenario— you might have accidentally turned your comms off."

She looked down and realized that she had in fact nudged the button that turned the communications off. "Shit."

"Yeah. Do you mind holstering that weapon? Once that's done, we'll get you out of that suit."

Elisa could have come up with an excuse to say no— something along the lines of her not trusting him to not kill her and let everything resolve itself perfectly for him. But getting out of the armor she had been in for too long would be a relief. She did as she was told and he assisted her to remove the suit section by section. The other two members of the team joined him in peeling the bits and pieces off.

Something bunched in her throat and made it difficult to breathe. Tears trickled unbidden from her eyes as they worked to pull her free.

She didn't know why, but all the adrenaline had drained from her system and she felt a little weak. Everything rushed through her mind and her knees buckled.

Taylor caught her before she fell. "There, there, it's not all bad. You're alive and well and you'll have one hell of a story to tell people when you get back home, right?"

The stouter man who inspected her suit after she was pulled out shook his head and made a cutting motion across his neck.

"Oh, right," he corrected quickly. "It'd be best not to tell this particular story."

Elisa nodded slowly and brushed the tears from her cheek as he settled her on her feet. "I know. I…I promised I wouldn't share this story since you guys put so much thought and effort into saving me."

"And you do remember that we're here because of a mess you got yourself into, right?"

She nodded slowly. It wasn't something she particularly liked, but he and his team had put themselves through considerable trouble to get her out of a problem she had created for herself. They weren't wrong about that, at least. She had simply done her job, but it had led her into the kind of rabbit hole not many other reporters escaped from.

Not that she had escaped yet.

"How will we get the container to the airport?" the mechanic asked once the suit she had worn was stashed in its crate.

Taylor pointed behind the container. "There's a truck out back. It's a little rickety but it should get the job done. The real problem will be getting it all into the plane. The jet won't take a container like this but it could take the suits, the guns, and the...extra cargo."

Elisa looked around, not sure what they were talking about, but it seemed no one had any intention to expound on it. The group gathered at the truck when it was moved from the back, and while it was in poor repair, it was still working and there was gas in the tank. The suits they wore were enough to lift the container onto the latches of the vehicle.

She sat in the cab. Interestingly, their female partner was the one who took control of the vehicle, while Taylor and the stout Asian mechanic were in the back, likely making sure that everything was still ready to be delivered. It was a shipment, after all.

It wasn't long before they approached the airfield. They had moved a little faster than the robbers had, likely because Tanya was a better driver and was told not to spare the vehicle. They weren't trying to keep it in good condition, after all.

Taylor wasn't the kind of man who would make her beg for her life, and he had put in considerable effort to make sure she got out of this situation alive. Still, there was something unnerving about sitting in the cab of a dilapidated vehicle. She could still feel her hands shaking gently, even when they came to a stop.

"Don't worry about it," Tanya assured her and turned the vehicle off with a little difficulty. "Adrenaline gets to us all, and it's not like you're used to being in this situation. The first time I was in a life-threatening predicament, all I could think about was how much my hands were shaking afterward. That and how much I needed to go to the bathroom."

Elisa nodded slowly. "It's only… I can't believe it's over. Like something will spring out of nowhere the moment I let my guard down."

The other woman tilted her head and looked pensive. "I suppose that's not the worst mindset to have around you at all times. Especially in our current situation."

The plane appeared to be waiting for them, although a couple of the crew weren't sure what to make of the truck that suddenly appeared with a new passenger and much more cargo.

"Don't worry," Taylor assured them. "Most of this stuff isn't going in for a long haul. A hop and a skip to the French base should work out for us well enough. It would be about an hour and a half of flight time."

"Two hours," Bobby corrected him. "As of a couple of weeks ago, the whole area held by the Zoo is a no-fly zone so we'll have to go around it."

He nodded acknowledgment and turned to the pilot.

The man didn't look entirely pleased by the situation but he shrugged. "I'll file a flight plan while you load up."

The crew began to pull the suits out. These included

those that had been shipped with Elisa and those the team had worn when they had come to rescue her.

The largest surprise, of course, came when Taylor and Bobby boarded once all the suits were loaded. They carried a couple of trunks she vaguely recalled seeing in the hands of the pirates—or maybe their partners?—when they had opened the warehouse.

It didn't take much brainpower to assume it was cash meant to pay for the suits which Taylor, Bobby, and Tanya had commandeered, although she had no idea how he would use it. It wasn't like you could waltz into the States with a shitload of cash and no one would be suspicious.

"Freddie will ask questions," Bobby pointed out as the crew added fuel to the plane to accommodate for the extra weight.

"Yeah, well, the guy was never one to complain about a little extra cash," Taylor replied. "Honestly, I'm equally as happy giving him all this for free. The guy is doing us a huge favor, after all."

Elisa couldn't help the mental state she immediately went into. Years of working as a reporter had a couple of instincts so deeply ingrained in her that it was impossible to resist. Who was this Freddie? She assumed it was someone at the French base outside the Zoo. But what kind of favor had they done for Taylor that allowed him to part with what she assumed was at least a couple of hundred thousand dollars in cash?

Which also begged the question of exactly how much McFadden was worth. It was an interesting question. She'd never been one to consider a sugar daddy but in this case, the former military guy had great looks, a great body, was relatively young, and was loaded.

It was interesting, to say the least.

"So," Tanya ventured once they were asked to board the plane in an orderly fashion, "are you boys excited to head to the Zoo?"

Neither of the two men looked like they were in the mood for jokes. To Elisa, it looked like Taylor was dreading what was to come.

"Yeah," Bobby grumbled as they settled their seats. "It'll be a fucking gas."

The reporter took a mental note. Despite where she had worked for the past few years, she hadn't met anyone coming out of the Zoo in person. Maybe, if she couldn't get in on the mob angle, she could see if either Bobby or Taylor were willing to give her another story to work with instead.

CHAPTER THIRTY

"Tay-Tay!"

Taylor rolled his eyes. It had been a while since he'd seen Freddie, but he hoped that Vickie hadn't spread word of the nickname and how much he disliked it to the rest of their clients.

The man laughed at his discomfort. "You know, I think we found a home run with this nickname."

He smirked. "Given that all you guys had on me before was the fact that I had red hair and you started calling me...what was it again?"

"Giant fucking Leprechaun, if memory serves."

"Right. At least this is a little more creative but you didn't come up with this shit on your own."

"Well, I guess that is why you pay Vickie the big bucks. How is she anyway?"

"Looking forward to everything going back to normal if I know her at all," he muttered. "But enough with the small talk. Do you guys think you want to get this shit unloaded today, or should we wait until tomorrow? Maybe spend the fucking weekend?"

Freddie chuckled. "Come on. It's not like seeing you here where you made such a fucking name for yourself is an everyday occurrence. It's the return of the really fucking big leprechaun. We should head to the bar and have a celebration and a few stories. From the sound of things, I think you might have a couple of good ones that'll keep you from paying for your booze for a while to come."

That was a good point, but the exorbitant costs for the aircraft aside, he also didn't want to be in the area for any longer than was absolutely necessary. These guys had been there long enough that they had embraced the lifestyle. But like him, they would reach a breaking point. It likely wouldn't happen for many of them. They would be killed first. But those who survived would realize that something in them had broken and they wouldn't be of use to anyone out there anymore.

It wasn't something he was proud of. Taylor had once thought of himself as powerful and even indestructible. And then, he wasn't. His confidence was shattered and he wouldn't head into the Zoo any longer.

It was weird that he thought this now. He had resisted the efforts of the psychologists who had told him that something was broken but in the end, they had merely told him something he already knew. He simply hadn't been ready to deal with it yet.

"Is everything okay there?" Freddie asked.

He realized that he had been lost in thought in the middle of a conversation. "Sorry. This place has an effect on me, is all. I kind of expect something to jump out at me and try to chew on my insides."

"Well, I know the feeling," the man replied and patted him on the shoulder. "So, is it okay to ask you what the hell you're doing here at this point? Don't get me wrong, it's good to see you, but I'll go ahead and be honest. Should we expect you to come over to make every delivery?"

He responded with a simple head-shake. "No, but there was a small matter with this shipment and I wanted to make sure it was delivered personally. For one thing, there was the robbery at the airfield we usually use, which Vickie mentioned to you. I thought you should know that we'll send our deliveries through another way from this point forward. It will be a little more expensive but that won't be reflected in our current pricing model."

"Well, that sounded like a crock of shit I don't care about. Is there a second thing?"

"Yes," Taylor replied and nodded at the crates that were being unloaded. "Like I said, there's something special about this particular delivery. Bobby, why don't you go ahead and show him what's so special about it?"

The mechanic smirked and dropped to his haunches beside the first of the crates to be unloaded. They were pulled down with the help of a forklift, one at a time.

Bungees pulled on the back of one of the crates, let it drop, and revealed a false bottom built into the crate. He pulled it out to display a small case where Freddie could see the cash that was being delivered.

"We'll start sending money over in staggered ship-ments," Taylor told him. "And there's a little something extra for you."

Freddie shook his head. "Listen, Taylor, you know—"

"This is something we picked up from the robbers who tried to snatch our shipment," he explained as Tanya brought out the trunks of cash they had picked up from the paramilitaries. "While we recovered your shipment, one of the suits took damage so we'll take it back for another look and repair it. This will probably cover any possible losses you might incur."

The man laughed when he looked at the contents. "Now this is a man who knows how to fucking do business."

Taylor shook his head. "We're still a small operation, and while we're aware that shit like this can happen, we want to make sure you know we appreciate the business."

It was another few seconds before Freddie could show a straight face again. "You know, it's like you're trying to sell me on something. Anyway, the situation is stable. We have a couple of spares we've worked with, so we'll continue with those. I'll probably use some of the cash as a bonus for the boys who have to use the spares, I guess."

The rest of the cash was hauled out of the other crates, leaving Taylor with little to say as he watched the fruits of one of his most dangerous labors turned over to a man he trusted.

Of course, it was only a piece. If Freddie tried to fuck him over on this, they would find another way to get the cash laundered.

But he had no doubts that the man would have his back on this.

As they retrieved the rest of it, he could see the slack-jawed look on Elisa's face. The reporter probably hadn't realized that she had stood on a solid quarter of a million dollars like it was nothing.

"So," she muttered as he approached her. "You did perform that robbery. And you're bringing it out here because..."

Taylor scowled at her as her voice trailed off and she looked at him like she expected him to finish her sentence for her. "Do you really think I'll tell a reporter about the details of a robbery I might or might not be involved in?"

"Come on, Taylor." She laughed. "You know I won't print any of what I heard from this trip anywhere in the world. For one thing, I made a promise that if you helped me, I wouldn't print anything out of respect for you and your team. Of course, had I known you would come in to rescue your ill-gotten gains and I was only a small matter in the larger scheme of things, it might have been different but still, a promise is a promise."

He smirked. "Yeah, I won't lie. I was fully willing to let you hang around here for a few days before getting you a charter home, merely to teach you a lesson about interfering with my business. And yeah, recovering the cash was a big part, but I couldn't help but feel a little responsible for putting you in this mess. I took you off Marino's hands because he intended to kill you and I wouldn't stand for that. Getting you killed by insurgents on the African continent does kind of defeat that purpose."

"I like that," Elisa muttered and shook her head. "And I appreciate it. There aren't many places I knew I wanted to end up in and yet regretted it the moment I touched down than here. I've written about the Zoo for years now, and even though there's still so much mystery and intrigue surrounding it...well, I can't wait to get out of here."

"I'm sure that's what your readers want to hear."

She laughed and nodded at the group of men who stared as the money was transferred to Freddie's people. "I'm fairly sure they're surprised about the big payday you're delivering to these people who are supposed to be your clients."

"These guys work for Marino," Taylor told her. "And they're probably wondering what kind of balls I have to use the man's own plane to deliver money I stole from him."

Her right eyebrow raised. "So, you did steal the money from Mr. Marino. Is there any reason why he won't target you for stealing from him?"

Taylor scowled for a few seconds but couldn't help a small half-smile. "Well, that one's on me. I really should know better than to let myself talk around a reporter."

"Again, simply because my brain works that way doesn't mean I'll print any of this. So, is there a reason why the mob boss of Las Vegas isn't coming after the man who robbed him?"

He shrugged. "Well, let's say you're not the only one who thought Marino robbed his own place. And he wants to keep it that way, which includes leaving his alleged robbers alive for the moment."

She nodded. "I guess that makes sense. It can't last, though."

"Agreed."

They headed to the plane. He felt a little calmer and more in control as he settled into his seat again. He didn't feel the same way he always felt when he boarded planes, though. It felt different.

He did recall feeling the same way when he first flew away from the Zoo. The first time and the last time too. He'd had pills then that helped him sleep all the way through, but even before he took them, there was a sense of relaxation he felt when he turned his back on the Zoo for what he'd thought was the last time.

It wasn't something he would talk about, but even when Bobby and Tanya took the seats across from him and Elisa sat beside him, it felt less annoyingly terrifying than it had earlier in the day.

"Do you need something to help you sleep?" Tanya asked. "I have some Ambien."

"Why would he need Ambien?" Elisa asked.

"Don't," Taylor warned but, as he expected, he was ignored.

"Taylor's afraid of flying," Bobby explained and grinned when his boss flipped him off. "A phobia he always says is under control but every time, I'm afraid he'll tear the arms off every seat he uses. It's not healthy."

"Yeah, having anxiety about hurtling through the fucking air at forty-five thousand feet and six hundred miles an hour is completely unnatural," he protested and shook his head while he tried to force himself to relax in his seat when the plane started to taxi.

"You know, they have many therapy options these days," Elisa pointed out. "Like these new VR therapy booths where they practice a new regimen of what they call exposure therapy. It's great. A friend of mine worked through her fear of heights that way and now, she goes skydiving."

"Yeah," Taylor muttered as his eyes started to drift shut. "One thing I always knew I wanted to do instead of hurtling through the air at impossible speeds was to jump out of the plane instead. Now if you guys want to shut the fuck up, I feel like I haven't slept in a week. Wake me when we touch down."

He could feel the transition, even with his eyes closed, as the added fears and stresses that had nagged at him over the last few days fell away. It wasn't long before the others talking and watching shit on the entertainment system were beyond what he cared to worry about.

They were heading home. While there would be problems there too, at least it wasn't the fucking Zoo.

CHAPTER THIRTY-ONE

The problems did, unfortunately, begin to crowd in as soon as Taylor returned, although most were simple logistics and therefore manageable. Vickie looked like she needed a couple of days off and damned if she hadn't deserved it. He sent her home but she immediately suggested that she stay at the strip mall anyway.

"You won't lock me in the meat freezer again, will you?" Elisa asked once Vickie had climbed into her Tesla and headed home to get some rest and probably more of her clothes. Bobby and Tanya also left to spend time at Bobby's place.

"You won't climb into any of our merchandise and head out to parts unknown again, will you?"

She chuckled and shook her head. "I don't think I'll climb into one of those fucking suits—maybe ever again."

He shrugged. "I don't know, you showed a little skill. Only a little, mind you, because you were almost knocked off your feet when you tried to shoot those bastards. You'd need practice but that's a conversation for another time."

The reporter smiled and shifted anxiously in place. "So…where will you put me?"

"We have a couple of spare rooms. This place…it's a work in progress, so the moment we decide what to do with a section, we work through it. There are rooms that Tanya, Vickie, or Bobby stay in when they need to. Some of the rooms have kitchens, and there's usually food in the break room if you're hungry. Otherwise, we can order something. There's also a gym if you need it."

"Thanks. I don't have any of my clothes, though. Tanya loaned me some of hers but none of them are for exercise."

Taylor had no real response to that. She would be shown to her room and would stay for the weekend, and she and Vickie had already agreed that they would spend time together. The hacker probably wanted to find a way to keep tabs on their reporter without making it too obvious.

He still didn't trust her to not report on everything she had seen and come up with fantastic conclusions based on minimal information, but there were no other options aside from locking her into the meat freezer again. She had already shown that she could break the hell out it, so what was the point?

The woman had settled in and food was on the way before he finally managed to relax. He wasn't sure what he should focus on next, and all he wanted to do was settle in, have something to eat, and let everything return to normal.

It was too much to ask for, he realized when his phone started buzzing in his pocket as he sat in his chair.

"Fucking…goddamn it." He rumbled annoyance and pulled the phone out, expecting it to be one of Desk's unknown numbers. If so, he would be called in for another mission for Niki.

He considered simply not answering it before he noticed it was a number his phone did recognize—one from which someone had called him on more than one occasion.

"Good afternoon, Agent Banks," Taylor muttered once he'd pressed to answer the call.

"Good afternoon, Taylor. I hear you have been a little busy ever since you left Arizona."

"Let me guess, Vickie has given you periodic updates?"

"Nope, she's been a little more difficult than usual. My sister is the one who kept tabs on you and made sure you weren't caught breaking any international laws again."

"Wait, again?"

"Well, I guess we were technically caught the last time, but it ended up with consequences that were a little less... consequential, I guess."

He sighed deeply. "How can I help you, Niki? It's been a long couple of days and I think I should rest."

"I can tell you right now that you should get a shower, trim your beard, and put decent clothes on because you and I need to talk about something face to face, and damned if I'll do it in that hole you call a home."

"Ouch. But sure, I'll meet you. Where and when?"

"Il Fornaio, around eight. Wear something nice."

Taylor reminded himself a little grumpily that he never dressed up for simply anyone. Besides, it had been an odd request, coming as it did from Niki, and after the last couple of days—hell, the last week—he was too tired to even be curious. Dressing up for dinner took more energy than he was willing to put into it, even for her.

Parking presented no problems and he locked the vehicle and walked to the restaurant he had frequented less than he would have liked during the past few weeks. He didn't usually come for dinner either and it gave off a classier vibe than it did during the breakfast hours.

When he couldn't locate her after a few seconds, he decided Niki was a little late since he arrived precisely on time. It wasn't that he was overeager to see her again, of course, and he didn't want to create that impression. Punctuality was simply the name of the game.

He wandered to the bar, where the tender had a glass of beer ready for him almost before he'd asked for it. With an inward sigh, he settled on one of the seats and checked the door periodically.

"So, when I told you to wear something nice, I guess you went for something a little like...cowboy chic, but you forgot to add the chic part."

Surprised, he turned to where Niki stood behind him. It was immediately apparent that she had dressed to display far more style than he did—and way more than he usually saw from the agent. His eyebrows raised at the sight of the slim yet comfortable-looking pale blue dress with a slit up the side of the thigh. Her hair was done in a messy bun atop her head, and she wore a pair of black heels that added about three inches to her height.

She noticed him staring and smirked.

"If you keep your mouth open like that, you're bound to

catch a couple of flies," Niki quipped and tapped the bottom of his chin with her forefinger. It irked him to realize he was a little slack-jawed.

"Well...you certainly came dressed to kill." Taylor noted the obvious and tried not to let his gaze linger where the dress fit snugly enough to be interesting.

"And so did you. A little more literally though—as in fresh off the ranch after slaughtering a couple of cows?"

He glanced at his clothes. A pale red and white flannel shirt had been chosen to compliment jeans and the boots he felt the most comfortable wearing. "Yeah, I guess when you said to wear something nice, I assumed you wanted me to wear something comfortable."

"A casual suit can be comfortable."

Taylor nodded. "Well, obviously, I didn't understand what you meant. So, what? Do you want me to go home and change? That would mean that whatever the hell it is you needed to talk to me about can wait, I suppose."

"It can, but I'm not a stickler for abiding by dress codes anyway. Do you want to take a seat? I already have a table."

He stood from his stool and she stepped beside him and slid her arm through his.

Startled, he fixed her with a wary look. "Well, this is...cozy."

"We have to talk about your taste in women," Niki told him and shook her head in feigned disgust. "Seriously. Jennie told me about the woman you went halfway across the world for and I even have pictures. Tell me, Taylor, why did she look exactly like me?"

"Well...fuck my life. I didn't go halfway across the world to save her. Okay, wait...we did go there to save her, but the reason we put so much effort into it was because there was something hidden in the shipment we needed to get back before it was handed off and lost forever."

"Do I want to know?"

"I'm not sure. Do you want to know that we are smuggling the cash we stole from Marino to the Zoo where it can be laundered for us?"

She scowled at him as they took their seats across from each other. "No."

"Well, then. I guess you don't want to know."

"You still haven't answered my question. Why does she look exactly like me?"

Taylor shrugged. "I'll be honest, I didn't see the resemblance until Vickie pointed it out. Either way, this whole situation was basically forced on me anyway, so it's not like I chose her out of a catalog."

Niki smirked. "Of course you didn't."

"And will you tell me why you called me here or was it simply because you felt jealous that I spent my time with another feisty personality?"

"Don't flatter yourself too much, Taylor. For one thing, our friend Marcello told me that you haven't tried their dinner menu yet, which is almost a capital crime around here."

"And the other thing?"

She tilted her head, an amused smirk on her face. "I guess we can get to that after dinner."

He released a long-suffering sigh and shook his head. "What is it with people who want to take me out to dinner when what they really want is to butter me up for a business agreement or something?"

"Because that's how business is done these days, Taylor. People like to pretend what they're doing is a nice little conversation when really, all they're trying to do is size you up."

"Wait, so you didn't simply ask me out on a date here? Color me disappointed. And I went all out. I brought in my good jeans and my clean flannel shirt. Shame on you for getting a guy all worked up for nothing."

Niki couldn't help a laugh as a waitress brought them a couple of menus. "Yeah, shame on me. I guess I'll have to make it up to you another time."

Taylor narrowed his eyes at her. "You know, you say that and I can't tell if you're joking or not."

The agent smirked at him again. "Come on, Taylor. If we ever went on a date, you would have to dress a little better than that."

"Or we would go somewhere with a more lenient dress code. See, I would look at home at a cowboy bar. Or maybe the kind where they cater to people dressed like this. You know—the old-fashioned places that have a grumpy old man serving people drinks while intimidating those who order things he doesn't know how to make to the point where they leave forever."

"Well, I hate to say it but you do know how to show a girl a good time."

He merely grinned and turned his attention to his menu. "So, do you want to start with an antipasto or should we dive into the main course? You are paying, right? With that fancy new job with the DOD, you can afford to pick up a few more checks."

"Please, the guy who made millions off a casino robbery

is trying to be cheap? I don't buy it. You'll at least pay for what you eat. It's only fair."

"Agreed." He nodded as the waitress came to take their orders. "Anyway, I think I'll have this *Bruschetta al Pomodoro*, followed by their *Filleto di Bue*. I need extra protein to fill this flannel shirt out again. You don't get the full experience when you wear it like a fucking scarecrow."

Niki smiled and rolled her eyes. "I think I'll have the same and whatever red wine the chef recommends."

The waitress collected their menus. "And what will you have to drink, sir?"

Taylor raised the mug of stout he was still nursing. "Keep this baby filled and I'll be a happy camper."

Once the woman was out of earshot, his companion leaned forward. "Well, now that we're done with the small talk, I need to talk to you about the DOD. More specifically, the work you'll be doing for me while I'm with the DOD."

"You wanted a team, as I recall," he responded, immediately focused. "I don't have anyone on the hook yet. I haven't had the time."

"I already sent you the resumes but we can discuss them over dinner."

He looked pensive for a second. "Well, I guess I could spend my time discussing the merits of one hunter or another over a nice beer and good food. Let's do this."

Have you read *The BOHICA Chronicles* from C.J. Fawcett and Jonathan Brazee? A complete series box set is available now from Amazon and through Kindle Unlimited.

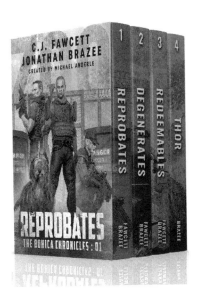

Kicked out of the military for brawling, what can three friends from different countries do to make some needed money?

Grab your copy of the entire BOHICA Chronicles at a discount today!

Reprobates:

With nothing in their future, Former US Marine Charles, ex-SAS Booker, and ex-Australian Army Roo decide to give the Zoo a shot.

Without the contacts, without backing, without knowing what they are getting into, they scramble to get their foot in the door to even make rent in one of the most dangerous areas in the world.

With high rewards comes high risk. Can they learn on the job, where failure means death?

Relying on their training, they will scratch, claw, and take the most dangerous jobs to prove themselves, but will it be enough? Can they fight the establishment and the Zoo at the same time?

And what the heck's up with that puppy they found?

Degenerates:

What happens when you come back from vacation to find out your dog ate the dog-sitter?

And your dog isn't a dog?

The BOHICA Warriors have had some success in the Zoo, but they need to expand and become more professional to make it into the big time.

Each member goes home to recruit more members to join the team.

Definitely bigger, hopefully badder, they return ready to kick some ZOO ass.

With a dead dog-sitter on their hands and more dangerous missions inside the Zoo, the six team members have to bond and learn to work together, even if they are sometimes at odds with each other.

Succeed, and riches will follow.

Fail, and the Zoo will extract its revenge in its own permanent fashion.

Redeemables:

NOTHING KEEPS A MAN AND HIS 'DOG' APART...

But what if the dog is a man-killing beast made up of alien genetics?

Thor is with his own kind as they range the Zoo, but something is missing for him. Charles is with his own kind as they work both inside and outside the walls of the ZOO.

Once connected, the two of them are now split apart by events that overcame each.

Or are they?

Follow the BOHICA Warriors as they continue to make a name for themselves as the most professional of the MERC Zoo teams. So much so that people on the outside have heard of them.

Follow Thor as he asserts himself in his pack.

Around the Zoo, nothing remains static, and some things *might converge yet again if death doesn't get in the way.*

Thor:

The ZOO wants to kill THOR. Humans would want that as well, but they don't know what he is.

What is Charles going to do?

Charles brings Thor to Benin, where he can safely hide out until things calm down. Unfortunately for both of them, that takes them out of the frying pan and into the fire.

The Pendjari National Park isn't the Zoo, but lions, elephants, and rhinos are not pushovers.

When human militias invade the park, Thor and park ranger Achille Amadou are trapped between the proverbial rock and a hard place. How do you protect the park and THOR Achille has to hide just *what* **Thor is...**

Can he hide what Thor is when Thor makes that hard to accomplish?

Will the militias figure out what that creature is that attacks them?

Available now from Amazon and through Kindle Unlimited.

AUTHOR NOTES

APRIL 13, 2020

THANK YOU for reading our story!

We have a few of these planned, but we don't know if we should continue writing and publishing without your input. Options include leaving a review, reaching out on Facebook to let us know and smoke signals.

Frankly, smoke signals might get misconstrued as low hanging clouds so you might want to nix that idea...

OMGoodness!

So, I finished the beats for Cryptid Assassin 07 late Saturday night. I ended up placing an event in 07 that I couldn't fit into the book, so I'm moving it to book 08 (so now, there WILL be a book 08!)

Although the Diary part of this was for last week (I was going to write these author notes over the weekend) I totally forgot. So, I am typing these up minutes before we go live.

You know, like back in the days of Kurtherian Gambit 01-17 or so? No time like moments before pushing the button to be typing up a storm trying to provide a bit of fun in the back ;-)

I hope you enjoyed the switch from FBI to DOD for Niki. Plus the flirting between two people who might or might not be good for each other. During these books I ask myself 'what is it that Niki would want in a guy?' That has been my major question as I ponder if a relationship between the two of them would work.

And whether or not Taylor would be willing to give up the lifestyle to perhaps have to deal with some harsh questions in his own life?

Life is messy. For those who work around ZOO creatures, it's just that much more complicated.

Diary

Unlike some of my collaborators, all of my kids are out of the house. So, in one way it is no different with the Coranavirus situation from a normal day without the children. In another, it is horrible.

They are grown adults, living on their own and I don't know what is going on with them at all.

Are they ok? Should I call? If they aren't ok is it a cold, is it something much worse?

Frankly, I do not have a warm fuzzy knowing exactly where they are, but I also don't struggle with young ones, which is a sword that cuts both ways.

I'm back from a mini-staycation looking at the massive buildings (Las Vegas) out my window that are closed.

I really wish they would let me go in and play, that would be amazing. I'd even write a story about their casino and they would become famous...er.

More famous.

What's not to like about that?

So, you know, anyone from MGM want to let me walk around the Veer (right next door) or MGM, NY NY?

No?

Dang.

Stay safe and healthy out there!

Michael Anderle

One Crazy Set Of Stories (12)

SOLDIERS OF FAME AND FORTUNE

Nobody's Fool (1)

Nobody Lives Forever (2)

Nobody Drinks That Much (3)

Nobody Remembers But Us (4)

Ghost Walking (5)

Ghost Talking (6)

Ghost Brawling (7)

Ghost Stalking (8)

Ghost Resurrection (9)

Ghost Adaptation (10)

Ghost Redemption (11)

Ghost Revolution (12)

THE BOHICA CHRONICLES

Reprobates (1)

Degenerates (2)

Redeemables (3)

Thor (4)

Printed in Poland
by Amazon Fulfillment
Poland Sp. z o.o., Wrocław

58457524R00202